The Devil and the Dark:

Devil to Pay
Dead Reckoning
Enemy Colours

DEAD RECKONING

R.M. OLSON

To Shauntel,
for years of friendship and encouragement, and for going to find street tacos
and margaritas with me.

1

Hollis

It was only the slightest sound, the barest rustle of cloth that woke Hollis.

She wasn't sure, in the dark and the confusion of sleep, how she knew she was in danger. But she knew it instantly and to her bones, and she was rolling out of the way before she'd come to full consciousness.

Someone hissed a quiet curse. Grasping fingers brushed her shoulder, and there was the thin, sickeningly familiar sound of a knife sheering through fabric—the sheets and coverlets of her narrow cot in the officer's rooming house.

She shoved herself up, trying to get her legs under her, trying to orient herself to her surroundings, but an arm shoved her back, the hand catching her tightly around the throat.

"Stay still, damn you," a voice hissed.

It wasn't one she recognized. But she'd lived long enough to hear the deadly intent behind it.

Whoever it was shoved her back against the thin mattress, and she gasped in a sharp breath as the movement tore at the wound across her midsection that she'd gained on the *Agate*, still only half-healed. For a moment she wavered on the edge of blacking out, and the hand on her throat tightened, cutting off her breath. A knee pressed against her chest, heavy enough to pin her down. From the corner of her eyes, now half-way adjusted to the dim mixture of light and shadow from the streetlamps outside pooling under the curtains, she could see the figure raise its hand, and she caught the glint of a blade.

She cursed, bracing herself, and shoved her body to the side. Again, the pain of her two-week-old injury was almost enough to make her lose consciousness, but her attacker's grip loosened just a fraction as they fought to keep their balance. She yanked a hand free, fighting the dizzying waves of pain, and managed to catch her attacker's wrist as they brought the knife down a second time, knocking it to the side.

Again the knife plunged through the coverlet and into the thin mattress beside her, but this time she could feel the sharp edge of it slice through the muscle of her upper arm. Something about the clean, bright pain of it yanked her consciousness back from the edge, and she turned instinctively away just in time to catch the fist that had been aimed for her face in her temple instead.

The blow was hard enough, almost, to stun her, and for a moment she lay there, dazed, as her attacker grabbed her wrist and yanked it brutally behind her back, turning her over and shoving her face-first into the mattress. She managed to gasp in a short, desperate breath before she was pushed into the mattress hard enough that breathing was no longer an option, and then her attacker's knee drove into her spine. She grunted involuntarily, losing the last of the breath she'd been holding as bright spots of pain danced behind her eyelids.

"Bloody Stacks scum," the man hissed, grinding his knee harder into her back and twisting her arm up until she was certain he'd break bone.

Her chest ached, brain woozy from lack of oxygen, the tearing pain in her shoulder and the bright pain of the knife wound and the nauseating, gut-deep agony of the two-week-old injury blending together in icy waves through her body and neon flashes of light and colour behind her eyelids.

She could hear the heavy breathing of the man holding her down, see, in her mind's eye, his arm raising to bring the knife down one final time.

No. Dammit, she hadn't survived the Naval Academy, and then Captain Mad Dog and a black hole and a bay full of ghosts, to die like this.

Her free hand scrabbled under the pillow until her fingers closed around the cool of metal.

She could feel the slight shift of weight above her as the man readied himself for the blow.

She braced herself, clenching her teeth, feeling her whole body tense against the pain that she knew was coming.

And then she twisted, bringing her free arm up and around, fingers clenched tightly around the end of the shiv she'd hidden under her pillow.

The pain of the motion was so intense that it was only from the corner of her mind that she felt the hot spurt of blood around her closed fist as the point of her thin blade drove into flesh, heard the sudden gasp of pain. But the grip on her arm loosened, and she twisted again, pulling herself free as blackness crowded her vision.

The man had stumbled back, clutching his side where her shiv had sunk in up to her fist, and even in the dim light she could see the whites of his eyes, wide with shock, the black of the blood oozing out in a dark stain around the wound.

She staggered to her feet, praying to Our Lady to keep her conscious for just a few more seconds, and lunged for him.

He tried to step back, but he wasn't quick enough. Her shiv caught him in the throat, and he managed a gurgling scream as he dropped to his knees. The motion tore the shiv from her fingers, already slippery with blood, and for a moment she just stood there, staring stupidly at the man in front of her as he grasped at his throat, blood spurting out between his fingers, and then, slowly, tumbled to the ground face-first in front of her.

Her thoughts were coming clear and oddly disconnected.

She really needed to remember to keep a sparker close by. If he turned ghost, that could be a problem. But then, she didn't see the telltale blue haze forming around the body—perhaps this wasn't a sailor at all.

But still. She should remember about the sparker, for next time.

And then she felt her own legs giving out, and the red haze coating her vision clouded to black, and she had the odd sensation of falling and falling, and then there was nothing at all.

When she woke, the room was quiet.

She lay still for a while, her breathing coming short and shallow, pain radiating out from her centre through her limbs and up her spine.

At last, she tried opening her eyes.

Even through the haze of pain, she could tell the shadows had hardly moved.

She hadn't been unconscious for long, then.

The thought made her try to roll over, to see if her attacker was still where she'd left him, and she moved without thinking.

Pain from the old injury jolted through her like a lighting bolt, sharp and bright and blinding, leaving blackness in its wake.

When she woke the second time, she moved more cautiously.

Her arm wasn't broken, probably, and her head ached from the blow, but not badly enough that she was worried about a concussion. But when she tried to roll over, she realized, abruptly and unquestionably, that she wouldn't be doing that without passing out.

She blew out a short, frustrated breath, and tried to force her brain back into focus.

Someone had tried to kill her. She had no idea why, but his intent had been more than clear.

And somehow, she'd killed him instead—at least, if her hazy memories of the blood spurting out around the shiv in his throat were anything to go by.

She needed to get up. She needed to figure out what the hell had happened, and if there was still danger, and then figure out what the hell she was going to do with a dead body in her rented room in the officer's rooming house.

All of which required her to roll over and get her feet under her, which, at the moment, was feeling more and more unattainable.

She hesitated, then at last, she grimaced.

But there was no help for it, at least, none that she could think of right now, with the pain lancing through her like an electric shock each time she so much as blinked her eyes.

Moving cautiously, she brought her hand close to her face, managing to bump the line on her comm against the floor.

"Price?" Her voice came out hoarse and almost inaudible. She tried again. "Mate Price? Are you there?"

"Captain?" They answered almost immediately, their voice

cracked with sleep and sharp with worry. "Is something wrong?"

She drew in a long, slow breath. "I'm sorry to wake you, Price. But could you … could I trouble you …"

She heard Foster's sharp intake of breath. "Captain? God's sake, you sound half dead. What happened? Are you in your room? Hold on, I'll be up there in a minute."

She groaned and let her hand fall as the line clicked off.

There was a soft tap at her door an absurdly short time later— Foster must have run the whole way—and she contemplated, for a moment, the impossibility of getting up to let them in. Then the door swung open, and she had the brief desire to laugh. Of course the door was open, a man with a damned knife had just broken into her room.

The light flicked on, and she heard Foster's soft gasp.

"Mate Price," she tried, and then their footsteps crossed the floor and they were crouching in front of her. The light brown of their face was paler than usual, their expression tight with concern, dark hair mussed and falling around their shoulders, nightshirt tucked into their trousers in a hurried way that was so unlike her normally put-together first mate that it was startling. "Don't try to move," they said shortly. "What happened? Where are you hurt?"

She drew in another shallow breath. "I'm not hurt—"

Foster barked a sharp, incredulous laugh. "You're lying on the floor covered in blood, so you'll forgive my disbelief. What the hell happened?"

She'd never heard Foster this upset.

But then, she supposed, she could hardly blame them, given the circumstances.

She closed her eyes and tried again to breathe. "That man on the floor tried to kill me. He did not succeed, but apparently I'm not quite recovered enough to take part in an unexpected knife fight in the middle of the night in my damn bedroom."

Foster cursed and stood quickly, and she closed her eyes again, listening to their footsteps cross the floor to where the body must be lying.

"Well, recovered or not, it seems you won the fight." Their voice was grim, and when she blinked her eyes open, they were crouched in front of her again. "He's dead." They shook their head. "I'm calling for a medic, hold tight."

She winced, forcing down her instinct to grab their arm to stop them—it would probably only lead to her passing out, honestly. "Wait, Price. You can't …" She drew in a shallow breath, trying to slow the spinning in her head. "Word can't get out."

Foster turned on her. "I'm not watching you die in front of me, Captain!" They sucked in a long breath, and blew it out again. "I'll call someone from the *Verity*, if that makes you feel better. But you're going to need medical care." They raised their hand as Hollis opened her mouth to protest. "Look in a damn mirror if you want. You're not going to be upright in under a week, let alone ready to command your ship, without it."

Hollis blew out a short, frustrated breath, then cursed at the wave of lightheaded pain that the movement brought. "Very well," she said at last. "I don't know who did this, but I doubt it was any of my crew—if they'd wanted to kill me, there was ample opportunity on the voyage."

"And in addition, every member of your crew thinks you're a goddamn hero after what you did on the *Agate*, much as you seem unaware," Foster added wryly, their voice still sharp with concern. "I think we can trust the chief medic."

She nodded and closed her eyes a moment, Foster's sharp

whispered tones over their comm bleeding through her consciousness. When she blinked her eyes open again, they were crouched beside her.

"Officer Smyth is on his way," they said, their voice still clipped with worry.

"Thank you, Price." She braced herself. "If you would be so good as to help me up?"

Foster hesitated, then at last, lips pinched tight together, they maneuvered their arm around her shoulder and eased her upright.

There were a few moments between Foster lifting her to her feet and her finally sinking down on the bed where Hollis was certain she'd black out again, but she clung grimly to consciousness, and at last she was seated on the edge of the cot, the blankets behind her tangled and ripped from the desperate struggle. In the light, she could see more details of the room—the blood spattered across the white sheets and the walls and pooling on the worn rug around her attacker's crumpled body.

He was bearded, tall and heavy, dressed in nondescript sailors clothes—someone she'd never seen before in her life.

"Now—what the hell happened here?" Foster's voice was tight with strain.

She told the story as succinctly as she could.

Foster nodded as she finished, glancing around again almost involuntarily at the bloody scene. "Thank God you survived that," they muttered. They shook their head. "Do you have any guesses as to why?"

Hollis closed her eyes again, pushing back the pain throbbing through her body like a damn heartbeat. "I don't know for certain," she said slowly.

"But you have a theory." Foster's tone was still grim.

She hesitated, then nodded. "As you are well aware, I am currently the only commissioned captain from the Stacks. I served under the Admiral long enough to be damn sure she didn't promote me just because of my personal qualifications. I'm here because she wants to use me as a test case to allow her to appoint more officers from the Stacks."

She opened her eyes to see Foster still watching her, forehead creased in concern.

"Had this man succeeded, and killed me—" she continued.

Foster nodded slowly. "That would send a message to any other potential officer candidates from the Stacks as to what awaited them after promotion," they finished.

Hollis nodded.

"Although I suppose it would send a very similar message even if he didn't succeed," muttered Foster. "Any idea who might have been behind it?"

Hollis shook her head. "It could be one of a thousand people. My appointment was not exactly popular with the Naval High Command, nor with a not insignificant number of captains and admirals and my fellow Academy graduates." She had to pause a moment, waiting for a wave of pain to subside. "I don't know which reason among the many led to someone being sent up to my room with a knife, but believe me, there are no shortage of possibilities."

The wry look on her first mate's face told Hollis that she hadn't said anything Foster didn't already know.

She tried to smile. "As you said, if word gets out, it will likely accomplish my attacker's desired effect regardless of the outcome of this impromptu knife fight," she said. "I believe our best option, at this point, is to keep this quiet from everyone except possibly the Admiral herself."

Foster closed their eyes. "I don't disagree with you, Captain," they said at last. "But you'll need help to deal with this." They paused, then stood. "Will you be alright here for a minute? I'll go rouse Greene out of bed. Officer Smyth will likely need help to get you back to the *Verity*, and when you're taken care of, between Greene and I, we should be able to deal with the body."

Hollis nodded weakly, letting her eyes fall shut as her first mate's footsteps faded down the hallway, the click of the door locking after them loud in the silence.

Archibald Smyth, the *Verity's* chief medical officer, was somewhere in the realm of incandescent with rage when he entered the room behind Foster and saw her. Hollis was watching the world through a hazy corona of pain at this point, and she couldn't tell if the anger in his lined face was for the man who'd tried to knife her, for her for having the audacity to break open her wound yet again, or for the pure irritation of having all his hard work on the ship go for nothing.

Foster must have informed him of the necessity of secrecy, because despite the fury in his expression, he crossed over to her quickly and knelt beside her. "Captain," he said, and when she nodded, he sliced through her nightshirt with his medical blade and inspected the injury, his face grim.

"We'll need to bring her in a stretcher," he said at last, getting to his feet and turning to Foster.

Foster nodded. "I thought we might. Mate Greene will be here in a few minutes."

Archibald tapped his comm. "I'll call Carter and Davis to bring a stretcher from the ship and meet us here."

"I hardly see how we're going to keep this quiet if—" Hollis began.

Archibald turned on her, scowling. "Captain. If you would like me to somehow get you back into a state to be able to captain your damn ship in less than a week from now, I must insist that you let me do my job. Price and I will worry about keeping things quiet."

Hollis slumped back in the bed, too lightheaded to argue farther.

She was vaguely aware of the door opening, Emmett's shocked curse, Foster's low, curt tones in what must have been an explanation. The door opening again, more people entering, carrying a hover-stretcher.

"Captain. Captain, let me help you up …"

She felt herself being lifted and eased back onto the stretcher, then the stretcher was raised, and she saw from the corner of her eye her two mates standing over the bloody body deep in conversation, brows pinched in identical expressions of concern.

Then she closed her eyes and concentrated on staying conscious.

She was aware of vague, disjointed sensations—the jostling of the stretcher, the cool, damp smell of the air around the docks, the click of the sailors' boots off the loading ramp to her ship. And then the familiar smell of the *Verity*, and the much-too-familiar smell of the med bay.

"There you are, Captain," Archibald said, when at last she was on the cot. When she blinked her eyes open, he was standing over her bed, the mad bay lights making a halo of his grey hair, with Foster at his shoulder.

"Captain," her first mate said, "Greene and I took care of the body. You should get some rest. But in the morning, we'll have to discuss what to do next."

Hollis nodded. "Thank you, Price," she said, her voice coming out far weaker than she intended. "You and I and Greene will speak tomorrow."

And the unease that twisted in her stomach was almost as dizzying as the pain.

2

Silas woke to a hangover, and someone pounding at the door.

He groaned and pushed himself up on his elbow, blinking and trying to reorient himself.

"Sil! Captain says get your butt out of bed and get yourself down to Abigail's quick-time. Ain't going to say it again."

"Sil?" came a sleepy voice next to him.

He turned, smiling a little despite the pain aching in his head. "Shh, it's alright, Kate. You stay in bed, I'll get up." He leaned over and kissed the woman next to him, her dark hair spread across the pillow, her eyes still puffy with sleep, then sat up, pulling on his trousers.

"Sil! Damn you, best answer me if you don't want me to ask the tavern keeper for the damn room key."

"Just a second," he mumbled, glancing around for his shirt. He stood, reaching down to snatch it up from the floor and wincing at the way the movement made his head throb, then stumbled for the door.

He pulled it open to reveal Ari, her fist raised to pound again.

She looked much more chipper than she had any right to, if his hazy memories from the tavern the night before were any guide, and as pretty as always—her blonde hair pulled back into a neat sailor's ponytail, the colourful mish-mash of clothing she wore planet-side as disreputable as usual, a grin on her pale, fine-featured face, and her blue eyes bright with amusement.

She took in his appearance, then smirked. He glanced down, and realized his shirt was untucked and unlaced, showing his entire chest, his beard three days old, his hair a tousled mess.

He glared at her, and she snickered. "Don't worry, Level boy, you don't got anything impressive enough to make me look." She peered over his shoulder. "Hey Kate! You two've been keeping busy, haven't you?"

He glanced over his shoulder. Kate had rolled up on one elbow, pulling the sheet up modestly. She grinned back at Ari. "I owe you one for introducing him to me."

Silas shook his head grimly and turned back to Ari. "You're one to talk—I've seen you with Isaac, or whatever his name is. I'm up, alright? Give me five minutes to get myself dressed, and I'll meet you downstairs."

"You'd better," said Ari, still smirking. "Kate, don't let him get distracted, Gracie'll have his hide if he's any later than he already damn well is."

He scowled and closed the door in her face, then leaned back against it and shut his eyes, pressing the heel of his hand to his forehead.

It wasn't like him to wake up hungover three mornings in a row. Back in the Academy, he'd go out to the tavern with friends on occasion, but he seldom drank enough to give himself a headache the next day.

It wasn't like him to wake up in bed next to a woman like Kate, either, who clearly had no intention that their relationship, such as it was, would last longer than their respective shore leaves.

But then … well, back in the Academy, he'd had some damn purpose to his life. He'd known exactly what he wanted, and how to get there. And now?

Well, now he honestly wasn't sure.

He groaned and crossed back over to the bed, dropping down on it heavily to start lacing his shirt.

This was probably not the time to pontificate on moral philosophy. He had other things to worry about. Like, for instance, what the hell Captain Mad Dog wanted with him three days into shore leave.

He wasn't even properly her crew, not anymore. He hadn't told her, for certain, that he was planning to stay on with the *Sweet Jenny*.

Even though he knew well enough that he'd burned through his other options over the last three weeks with a recklessness that he was trying not to think too hard about.

"Everything alright?" Kate asked from behind him.

He shook his head ruefully. "It's fine, Kate. I'm just an idiot."

She hummed in something that could have been amusement or could have been agreement, and he smiled again, a little more genuinely this time.

He finished with his shirt and went to pull on his boots. He hesitated a moment, then lay back onto the bed and rolled over, draping his arm around Kate. She sighed and snuggled into him, and he closed his eyes and stroked a hand through her hair. Then, reluctantly, he kissed her forehead and swung his legs back over the bed. "I'd best get going. Wouldn't put it past Ari to be waiting downstairs with a buck knife to skin me alive if I'm a minute later than I promised."

Kate laughed. "Go on, then," she said, her voice still rough with sleep. "I'll see you this evening?"

He grimaced. "I guess that depends on what the hell Mad Dog wants with me." He finished pulling on his boots and stood, blinking hard to push back the headache. "Thanks, Kate," he said, his voice going a little softer.

She smiled up at him, and he tried to fix the sight in his memory as he turned for the door.

Maybe it wasn't like him to wake up in bed next to a woman like Kate, but he wasn't sure he could bring himself to regret it.

Ari was waiting for him downstairs. The tavern was crowded even this early in the morning, an unmistakable tension heavy in the air.

She shoved a mug at him, and he frowned.

"It's coffee, Level boy," she said, rolling her eyes. "And here's some headache tablets, you look like you need them."

He swallowed them and the coffee, grimacing, and Ari waited until he was done. Then she took the mug from his hands, placed it on the table, and gestured with a quick jerk of her head. "Come on. Captain's back at Abigail's, and she ain't going to be happy to be kept waiting."

"What the hell does the captain want?" he grumbled as they stepped out the door and into the busy streets of the pirate city. "I thought we were on shore leave."

There was a thick tension in the streets of the pirate settlement as well, a fraught, frantic edge to the noise and bustle, a humming unease that crawled under his skin and settled in his bones.

Ari shook her head. "No idea, to be honest." She sounded sincere enough, although he could never quite tell with Ari. "Just told me she wanted the whole damn crew, and you specifically, so I spent my whole morning rounding everyone up." She grinned a little and glanced up at him. "Least I knew where to find you. You and Kate are getting along well, looks like?"

He gave her a rueful smile. "As long as shore-leave lasts, I suppose. She doesn't want anything longer-term than that."

Ari slowed a little and gave him a sympathetic glance. "Not what you're used to back in the navy, then?"

He shook his head shortly. "It has nothing to do with the navy. I just … I prefer relationships that have a chance of actually lasting."

She watched him for a moment. At last she shook her head. "Listen, Sil, you can't blame Kate. Not like the Level around here. Back in the navy, on your three-hundred-and-fifty crew ships, fighting pirate skirmishes and going through the regulated naval jump-ports, there's a damn good chance you come back alive. Ain't like that around here. Far as Kate's concerned, you might have walked out the door this morning and never come back—get cut down trying to take a merchant ship, shot down by the navy. Life ain't a sure thing on Blackrock. You enjoy what you can while you can, and you sure as hell don't gamble on anything else."

He sighed. "I know. I don't blame her. I just …"

Ari gave a small, humourless chuckle. "You just wish it was a bit more like the navy. The one that you left because they'd have hanged you for treason."

He shook his head and didn't answer.

The streets of Blackrock were the same perpetual semi-twilight as always, lamps and torches burning in niches in the walls, the whining, clanking grumble of the fans set in the ceilings of the caves to move the air to keep it from becoming too stale, the ever-present moisture dripping from the ceiling and glistening on the walls and making trails of algae and mildew along the edges of the rough boardwalk. The buildings were packed in close together, rooming houses and taverns and whorehouses mingled in with small shops selling food and alcohol and ships parts and black-market tech and luxuries.

It wasn't the port district on the Level, where Sil had grown up, but there was usually something about it that felt more familiar and homelike than any other part of Blackrock.

But the crowded bustle of the streets now wasn't what it had been when he'd come back on the *Sweet Jenny*. There was an air of repressed panic to the press of people now, a frantic undertone that he recognized all too well.

The navy was planning an attack on Blackrock. He didn't know details, and he didn't know where the rumour had started, but it had spread through the settlement like cholera.

It hadn't caused outright panic—naval attacks on Blackrock had happened more than once in the past. But if you didn't have a ship that was space-worthy, or were between crews, it was much more likely to be a death sentence than if you could simply get aboard your ship and take off until the whole thing blew over. He'd heard, vaguely, that people were evacuating to the deeper caves in the rock, bringing food and supplies to last them until the attack was over, but not everyone could do that. If you owned an inn or a tavern or a shop, your entire livelihood was here close to the surface, and it would be a calculation of risk—the possibility of an instant death when the navy attacked against the possibility of a slow death later, if everything you'd spent your life building was destroyed— starvation, perhaps, or a far-too-potent combination of alcohol and despair, or a quicker death when you were caught stealing to stay alive.

He shook his head, pushing back the creeping unease, and followed Ari back to Abigail's tavern, through the main room and up the small set of back stairs that led to the room that served as Gracie's de facto office.

Ari tapped at the door, and sang out, "Captain! Brought Sil back with me."

"Come in." Gracie's familiar voice, low and raspy, floated out under the door, and Ari shoved it open and gestured Silas ahead of her with a jerk of her head.

Silas stepped cautiously in past her, blinking as his eyes readjusted to the dim room and fighting to keep from wrinkling his nose at the heavy stench of Gracie's cigar smoke that thickened the air and permeated the walls.

It was crowded with more people than he'd been expecting, and he glanced them over quickly. He recognized Jumper, the *Sweet Jenny's* weapons master, and Toothpick, the first mate, Jumper's pale face and downcast eyes and obvious discomfort with the crowd a contrast to Toothpick's dark skin and calm, steady presence. Vee, the *Sweet Jenny's* medic and cook, stood in the corner, a forbidding look in her stern green eyes. She was shorter than most in the room, but he noticed people had stepped back to give her space. He didn't see Freddie's hover-chair, or Temple's grey hair and slight build—the *Sweet Jenny's* mechanic and pilot must be back on the ship, which didn't bode well for their extended shore leave.

The others in the room he didn't recognize at all—a scattered handful of dour-looking individuals, who'd all turned to scowl at him with various degrees of hostility as he entered.

"Sil," said Gracie, smiling as he stepped through the door.

She was seated in front of a battered table, her chair pushed back, an ancient oilskin coat draped across the back of it. A foul-smelling cigar glowed between her fingers, and charts and papers were spread across the table in front of her. There was a thoughtful look on her weathered face, and that, combined with the crow's feet around her eyes and the strands of grey in her black hair, had been enough, once, to lull him into underestimating her.

He knew better, now. He could see, now, the hardness under her thoughtful expression, the sharp, calculating intelligence in her eyes. The obvious deference from every other person in the room.

She gestured him to an empty seat, and he took it cautiously. Ari shot him a look over her shoulder as she stepped inside that could have been sympathetic, and jumped up to sit on the edge of the table near Gracie.

Gracie was still watching Silas, her gaze as sharp and perceptive as ever. "Glad you could join us, lad," she said mildly, but he could hear the hint of amusement in her tone.

He went over his preparations quickly in his memory, but he was fairly certain that there was nothing about his appearance that would indicate that half an hour ago he'd woken, hungover, in someone else's bed.

He nodded, keeping his expression neutral with an effort.

"I guess you've heard about your navy's plan to attack Blackrock," she continued, voice still mild.

He nodded again. It would have been hard not to have heard, honestly.

Gracie leaned forward, resting her elbows on her knees. "Thing is, Sil, the captains here and I, we just got word back from a ship flying not too far off the Level, tech-shielded to pick up information. Didn't tell us much we didn't already know, but there's something in there I'm having a hard time figuring out. I thought maybe, since you were on the Level so recent, you might know something about it."

There was something in her tone that sent a shiver up his back.

There had always been a tension to Gracie, a restless energy under her veneer of calm. But there seemed to be a sharper edge to it now than there had before, and he wasn't entirely sure why.

Did she think he'd betrayed her, somehow? That despite everything that had happened on the *Sweet Jenny*, he'd been a plant of the Admiral the whole time?

The thought came with a sharp jolt of anger.

He'd betrayed everything he'd grown up believing to keep a bloody pirate crew alive. And he'd turned his back on his entire moral code when he'd saved Gracie's life back on the *Agate*.

He'd made that choice himself, sold himself out, and he knew damn well it wasn't her fault, but he couldn't entirely help resenting her for it.

But when he glanced at her again, her face didn't bear the trace of suspicion that he'd expected.

He frowned.

This was something else, then.

Gracie was still watching him, and he could see by the faint amusement pulling at her lips that she'd tracked his thoughts across his face. She pulled up a note over her comm, and, with a flick of her wrist, sent it to hover over his own wrist comm. "Information came to us a little too easily for my liking, but there was something in it that I found interesting. Take a look at that, lad. Any of it look familiar?"

He frowned down at the information she'd sent him, scanning over it. Then he looked up sharply. "This is from the documents I gave you."

She smiled a little. "No, Sil. It's not. I looked those documents over, like you asked, and that's why I recognized this. But it didn't come from anything you gave me. This came from broadcasts from the Level."

He stared at her for a moment, then turned back to the note.

Now that she'd told him, he could see the technology it described wasn't identical to the specs in the classified documents he'd stolen.

Gracie was still watching him. "I'd hoped you'd be able to tell us something about it," she said quietly. "Maybe the navy'd started using this before you left?"

He shook his head absently, still pouring over the information on the note that hovered over his wrist comm. "No," he said. "I haven't seen navigational tech like this before. It wasn't something we used when I was still shipping before the mast, and it wasn't something we were trained on in the Academy."

From the corner of his eye he could see the small frown on Gracie's face, feel the attention of the other pirate captains, all focused on him.

But there was something else, too—a thrumming, reckless excitement that had lit itself in the base of his brain, a grim smile tugging at the corners of his mouth that he had to fight hard to push back.

Because for the first time since he'd returned to Blackrock on the *Sweet Jenny*—this was something he could hold on to.

He'd sworn he would take down every person on the Level who'd been involved in the Starfire naval disaster—who'd killed his parents. Who'd shifted the blame to innocents, who'd seen Gracie's parents hanged for treason, driven Gracie out of the Academy and into Blackrock. Who'd created the ruthless pirate captain Mad Dog. He'd sworn to do it, knowing it would mean finally and utterly turning his back on everything in his old life that had meant anything to him.

And three days later, he still hadn't come to Gracie to discuss their agreement. To talk with her about the contents of the stolen documents, to convince her to help him. He'd made excuses to himself, that Gracie was busy, and Kate was beautiful, and he'd spent his evenings drinking with Kate and Ari, and woken three mornings in a row with a hangover, and had been very careful that he'd never had a moment where he was alone and sober enough to think about what he had to do next.

But now that he was here, looking at the note Gracie had handed him, the sharpness of the captain's eyes on his back, he could feel the dangerous mixture of fury and excitement relight in his chest.

He'd lost his family, his career, his friends. He'd discovered that everything he'd grown up believing was true and just and right, had been willing to give his life for, was a lie. And he'd been running from that realization since he'd arrived back on Blackrock, because without those things to hold onto, what else did he have?

But he'd been wrong. He still had something.

He still had this.

He couldn't change what had happened. But he could make the people who'd done it pay. He could make sure they never had a chance to do to anyone else what they'd done to his parents.

What they'd done to him.

He looked up, ignoring the other captains, and found Gracie's gaze. "Captain," he said in a low voice. "I don't know this technology. But I spent a damn lot of time in the Academy library, and I know how to get into the classified documents archive. If knowing what they're doing with this tech will help—I think I could get you the information you need."

Gracie raised her eyebrows at him.

For just a moment, he felt a small, residual lurch of guilt.

His entire life he'd believed his duty was to the navy. His duty was to the aunt and uncle who'd raised him, to his superior officers, to his family and the Level—his duty was to uphold his parents' legacy.

But it had been a lie. Everything he'd been taught about his parents' deaths was a lie.

"You think you can do that, lad?" she asked at last. "Because I'm thinking I'd like to know more about this new tech, compare these specs to the tech they used before, in the Starfire disaster. If I brought you back to the Level, you think you could get me that information? Need information from the Level anyways—the size of the fleet they're sending out to Blackrock, what weapons they're carrying. I was going to ask one of these other fine captains to go, but if you can get me what you say you can, might be worth taking the *Sweet Jenny*." She caught his eye. "But I won't send you without your say-so."

He hesitated only a moment. Then he gave a short nod.

"Mad Dog," one of the other captains growled, their voice thick with disgust. "You're going to trust this pup with our lives? Look at him, he's Level through and through."

Gracie turned on the speaker, her expression still mild. "You're questioning my judgement, Holdfast?" She asked. "You're questioning the *Sweet Jenny's* crew?"

"Don't think you'd have to wonder why," the speaker grumbled, but Silas noted that the hostility in their voice was a little more muted now. "He's flown on one job with you, Gracie."

"And have I ever given you reason to doubt my judgement?" Her voice was calm, but something about the inherent threat under it made the hair rise on the back of Silas's neck.

The rest of the room, too, stilled as the other captains turned to watch the confrontation.

"Not saying I'm challenging you, Gracie," said the speaker at last, turning away. "If you trust the lad, that's good enough for me, I suppose."

"Good," said Gracie, leaning back in her seat.

The tension in the room eased.

She turned back to Silas. "Thank you, Sil. You'll do this, then?"

He should, probably, have asked for time to think it over. He should probably have at least hesitated.

But honestly, there was a thrill of excitement pumping through his veins that would never have let him say no, even if he'd wanted to.

"If you get me to the Level, Captain, I'll get you the information you need."

She nodded. "I suspect it'll be easier if you have someone along to help."

He frowned. "Probably."

"Good. I'll get you to the Level, lad, and Ari'll go with you. Now, why don't you and Ari get yourselves cleaned up and ready to go? We'll leave at six bells."

Silas closed his eyes a moment.

He was grinning, though. He couldn't seem to help himself.

He'd expected to feel torn about this. He'd expected to have to force himself to agree. Instead, he found himself restlessly impatient to get started.

He stood abruptly. "Aye, Captain," he said. "Six bells. I'll be ready."

3

Silas made his way out the door and down the back steps into the main room of Abigail's tavern. The place was as dark and unwelcoming as it had been when he'd arrived in Blackrock weeks earlier. But it felt familiar now, in a way he hadn't expected.

Abigail glanced up when he stepped inside and nodded to him, and he nodded back and wove through the crowded bar towards the exit.

"Careful out there, lad," Abigail called. "Streets are a little excitable these days."

He dipped his head in acknowledgement and pushed through the doors and back out into the streets.

Now that he was awake, and the remnants of his hangover had settled into a dull ache in the back of his head, he could see more clearly how much the pirate settlement had been affected by the news of the attack.

He should have been paying more attention, honestly. But he'd been trying very hard the past three days not to think about anything, and he seemed to have succeeded far too well.

He shook his head and pushed his way into the crowd, heading back the way he'd come.

He'd left most of his kit in Kate's rented room, everything he hadn't left on board the *Sweet Jenny*. And in truth, those were the only things he had to his name.

He'd only made it a few hundred meters before someone shoved into his shoulder, hard enough to make him stagger.

He turned in irritation, and saw a man standing in front of him, eyebrows lowered, a grim look on his face.

"Watch where you're going, lad," the man growled.

Silas bit back a sharp retort and sighed. "I'm sorry," he said curtly. "Now, if you'd please let me pass?"

The man grinned, and grabbed him by the arm. "Level boy, are you?" he said, and there was something in his tone that sent off danger bells in Silas's brain.

And he wasn't sure what the hell it said about him that it sent a thrill through him of something much closer to anticipation than fear.

"I am," he said, keeping his tone neutral even as his hand closed around the projectile pistol in his pocket. Everyone in Blackrock was armed. No one would expect less, which meant this man was either too drunk to think straight—unlikely, considering the steadiness of his posture—or he had friends with him. "Do you have a problem with that?"

"Maybe I do," said the man, still grinning.

Silas ducked as the man swung, yanking his arm out of the man's grasp with a quick twist of his body, and came around with his pistol raised, his back against the corner of the alley next to him. "Stand down," he began.

From the corner of his eye he caught a flicker of motion, and before he could react, something hit him across the temple, hard enough to send him staggering. Before he recovered his balance, the man had grabbed him, hauling him backwards into the dark of the alley.

He caught a fist in his stomach, and doubled over, wheezing and trying to regain his bearings.

There was another figure beside the man, a woman from the looks of it, with a metal billy-club in her hands—probably the one who'd hit him just now. And behind her, at least three others.

He cursed, trying to straighten, and the man hit him again. He hunched on instinct, and managed to take the blow to his shoulder rather than the side of his head, then he shoved himself off the wall, tucking his chin, and slammed his forehead into the bridge of the man's nose.

The force of the blow was enough to make him see stars, but his attacker staggered backwards, hands over his face as blood spurted out between his fingers. Silas ducked, grabbing for the pistol that had been knocked from his hands in the fight. Before he could reach it, a boot came down on his fingers, and he caught another boot in his chest, knocking him sprawling. Whoever it was kicked him again, and he grunted, the breath knocked out of him.

He curled up on instinct, trying to protect his stomach. Above him, someone laughed, then he took a kick to his spine that sent a bright shock of pain up his back and set off starbursts behind his eyelids.

But his scrabbling fingers had finally found what he'd been looking for—the butt of his pistol.

He rolled onto his back, biting back a curse at the jolt of pain, and fired up at the woman standing over him, her boot drawn back for another kick.

She gave a short, gurgling shout and staggered backwards, eyes wide and blood spreading across her chest, and Silas shoved himself to his feet and shot twice more.

Even through the blood and the haze of pain, his muscle-memory sent the shots true. One of his attackers collapsed against the wall of the alley, wheezing, and the other grunted as the shot went through his shoulder.

"Stand the hell down," Silas panted. His muscles were trembling, every movement sending a shock of pain up his spine, but his gun-hand was steady. "Stand down before I shoot the rest of you."

One of his attackers made an abortive move towards her belt. He cracked off a warning shot over her shoulder, and she froze.

His mind was doing the calculations in the back of his head, leaving the rest of him free to react.

Four shots. His pistol could hold eight, and he kept it fully loaded. That meant four more shots before he'd have to reload, and he counted at least five figures in the alley—at least, five he could see.

He cursed under his breath, taking stock of his options.

If he knew what the hell this was about, it might have helped. But he had no damn idea who these people were, or why they were after his blood.

Out of the corner of his eye he caught a hint of movement, someone trying to get around him, and he swung his pistol over to cover them. "Stand still, damn you," he hissed. "Tell me what the hell this is, and maybe you all walk out of this alive."

The man who was slumped against the wall let out a long, rattling breath, his body going still, and suddenly every eye in the alley, Silas's included, swung towards the dead man as if pulled by a magnet.

A blue haze was forming over the man's body.

The man who'd first grabbed Silas yanked out a sparker, alarm clear on his face even through the blood streaming from his nose and mouth, and turned to the new threat.

A ghost was much easier to deal with if you could stop it before it had completely formed.

Then the woman holding the billy-club hissed something, pointing, her eyes wide with horror.

From the looks on the others' faces, Silas knew, without turning, what he'd see—a ghost, in the shape of the woman he'd shot in the chest, likely already fully formed.

His attackers shared a look. The man shoved his sparker back in his pocket and jerked his head, and as quickly as they'd come, the group of them melted back down the alley.

Silas gritted his teeth.

The blue haze over the dead man was slowly taking shape, but if he moved to disperse it, he'd be asking for the ghost behind him to spring.

If he didn't, though …

He closed the fingers of his free hand around the sparker at his belt, and, moving as carefully as he could, pulled it out and ignited it.

There was the faintest whisper of air behind him, bringing with it the freezing cold that roiled off ghosts, the fear that surrounded them like a fog. He threw himself to the ground on instinct, every bruised muscle in his body screaming in protest.

He felt the cold of it as it flowed over his head, and it turned in a fluid, horrifying motion as he scrambled to his feet, pressing his back against the wall of the alley.

Sweat beaded on his forehead, whether from pain or fear he wasn't entirely sure, but his muscles were steady, his mind as clear and sharp as it always was when he was in danger for his life.

He'd be torn to pieces in a moment—maybe he could stop one

ghost, but he stood no chance against two—but dammit, he'd missed this. He'd missed feeling alive, and he hadn't realized how dead his life had become, back in the Academy, until moments like this.

He held up his sparker defiantly, and despite the fact he was going to die, he couldn't quite keep the grin from his face.

The ghost drifted towards him, the black hole of its mouth stretching impossibly wide, fingers lengthened to claws of icy darkness. He crouched on the balls of his feet, ready to lunge at the thing.

Then, just as the ghost sprang, a hand closed around his arm, and he was yanked out of the way and pulled around the corner of the alley.

He cursed. The hand let go of his arm and shoved him, hard, down the street, and a voice he recognized hissed, "Go on, Level boy, unless you want the both of us to get eaten."

He caught his feet under him and started after Ari, who was already half-way down the street.

"There's two ghosts back there," he panted as they ran. "Shouldn't we—"

She gave him an exasperated glance before slowing. "Blackrock is crawling with ghosts, if you hadn't already noticed," she said. "No one expects any different, and we lure them into an empty airlock and vent them every couple of months anyways. 'Sides, it's only one ghost. I caught the other before it could finish forming."

He shook his head, then winced, stumbling a little at the sharp rush of pain. Ari caught his arm in time to keep him from falling, but the motion pulled on the bruises in his gut and across his spine and he hissed a quick curse.

"Sil? You alright?" she asked, her tone more worried than he would have expected.

He managed a small grin, turning to her and wiping the blood from his face with the sleeve of his battered jacket. "I'll live." He paused. "What the hell happened back there?"

Ari's expression was grim. "Don't know. Was hoping you'd be able to tell me. Not many around here who'd risk messing with one of Mad Dog's crew, and word's got around that you ship with the Captain." She paused. "You didn't recognize any of them?"

Silas shook his head, keeping the movement cautiously gentle this time. "I didn't. And they didn't say anything, either, except to accuse me of being from the Level." He snorted a short, bitter laugh and shook his head. "Although I'm not sure that's as apparent now as it was when you met me."

Ari grinned, but the worry didn't leave her eyes. "Believe me, Level boy, it's still pretty damn obvious." She glanced over her shoulder. "Come on, can you walk? Let's get you back to Kate's before someone else tries to jump you, get you cleaned up."

She slipped an arm around his waist to steady him. He gritted his teeth and faced forward and resolutely ignored the warmth and shape of her body against his, and how the worry on her face— worry for him—made something inside him twist.

She'd made her boundaries about relationships with crewmates clear, and respecting them was the least he could do. Even if he hadn't been certain she could cut him wide open with her buck knife if he didn't.

Now that the adrenaline of the fight had faded, every damn muscle in Silas's body ached. By the time they reached the tavern where Kate had rented a room he was staggering, and only Ari's arm around his waist kept him from weaving like a drunk. She dragged him inside, said something curt to the innkeeper over her shoulder, and pulled him up the stairs to Kate's room. "Kate's out, but she won't mind," she said, rummaging in her pocket and pulling out a key. He frowned at her as she fitted it into the lock.

"Wait, you had a key to Kate's room this whole time?"

She rolled her eyes at him. "'Course I did. But I sure as hell wasn't going to use it and risk catching the two of you in the act. Got enough things to have nightmares about."

He glowered at her, and she snickered, pushing the door open and pulling him through. "Sit," she said, shoving him onto the bed. She glanced around quickly, then wet a rag in the small sink and shoved it at him. "Clean yourself up, I'll go down and get some bandages and ask Rill to put new sheets on the bed when you're done, get rid of the bloodstains."

By the time Ari returned, Silas had mopped up most of the blood and taken stock of his injuries. Blood was dripping into his eyes from a shallow gash on his forehead, and he was probably not going to be able to walk without wincing for a few days, between the boot to his spine and the kicks to his stomach. But nothing seemed broken, and bruises he could deal with.

Ari sealed a bandage across his forehead and handed him something to wrap his split knuckles, and he nodded in gratitude. She made him tell the story again, and when he finished, she shook her head. "Ain't all that rare to be rolled for credit chits here on Blackrock, but it don't happen much to Gracie's crew—them as know her generally wouldn't risk it. And I don't think you've been here long enough to offend anyone bad enough that they'd chance taking on Mad Dog. Possible they didn't realize you were Gracie's, but still ..." she trailed off, still frowning. "You're sure you didn't recognize any of them?"

"No," he said shortly. "But the only pirates I'd recognize on sight in this place is someone from the crew."

"Or Kate," Ari said with a smirk.

He rolled his eyes and turned to gather his things.

Ari waited as he packed, making little effort to hide her impatience, and at last he turned to her with a scowl, ready to snap out some suggestion that she go downstairs and get drunk or something so he could finish packing in peace.

Then he noticed her expression, and frowned. "Ari?"

There was an odd look on her face, something that he didn't remember seeing there before. It was so foreign on Ari that it took him a moment to recognize it.

Fear.

"You alright?" he asked.

She blew out a short breath and tried to smile. "'Course I'm alright."

He raised a skeptical eyebrow.

She sighed. "Just not looking forward to going back to the Level, is all. Don't have the best memories from back then."

He could see the small tells now that he hadn't noticed before— the way her hands were clenched, the tightness in her shoulders.

He closed his eyes. "I'm ... sorry," he said at last. "I was the one who suggested it."

She gave a soft, bitter laugh. "Not like I haven't done worse in my life, if Gracie asked it."

He opened his eyes, and she shook her head at him. "You packed yet? Figure I could have gotten the *Sweet Jenny* ready to sail on my own in the time it's taken you."

He sighed ruefully and threw the last of his spare shirts into the battered knapsack. "I am now." He paused. "Are you ... listen, I can tell the captain—"

She cut him off with a sharp shake of her head. "Captain's got a mind of her damn own, she'll do as she sees fit. I've trusted her the last ten years, figure I can keep doing it now. Anyways, probably better to spend our time worrying about why the hell someone thought they could get away with jumping one of Mad Dog's crew in an alley."

He nodded without speaking, and shouldered his backpack, fighting back a wince at the motion.

She was right. Whatever had happened in that alley, not to mention the fact that the navy was sending ships to Blackrock in under a week, should be plenty to worry them.

But he couldn't help casting another glance at Ari from the corner of his eye as they started back down the stairs, she, for once, going slow enough that he could keep up, bruises and all.

And he couldn't help the tight knot in his stomach, something between fear and worry and anticipation at the thought of what they were about to do.

4

Chief Medical Officer Archibald Smyth scowled at Hollis with unmitigated concern. "Captain," he said at last. "If you're determined to go, I can't forbid it. But I'm going to state, before God and everyone present, that if you get yourself knifed again, even all the best medical tech on the *Verity* won't get you back on your feet in time to sail out with the rest of the fleet. I've pulled you back from the brink twice now. I can't guarantee a third time."

Hollis bit her tongue to hold back an irritated retort. Archibald didn't deserve her ire.

Apparently, she hadn't done anything irreparable to herself during her impromptu midnight knife-fight. Besides the few cuts her attacker had managed to land, most of it had been bruising and tears to her two-week-old injury that, although certainly not harmless, would respond well to the standard navy medical tech.

But she'd been flat on her back for two days now. Archibald hadn't even allowed her to sit up when the Admiral had appeared via holo-image to discuss the assassination attempt with her, much to her

36

humiliation. And now that she was cleared, however reluctantly, to move around again, the thought of lying helpless for one more second was making her teeth ache.

"My presence at the briefing is required," she said instead, her tone just a little short. "But I'll be careful. I appreciate your efforts on my behalf."

Archibald snorted, muttering something about at least this time she'd deigned to listen to him when he told her to lie still, unlike the last time she'd been injured, and turned to Foster.

Foster was their usual put-together self again—curly hair pulled neatly back into a sailor's ponytail, uniform immaculate on their lean frame, every bit the model ship's officer.

"Mate Price. I'm going to tell you, too, in case our captain forgets —if she gets injured again, she won't be captaining a ship the day after tomorrow. It's simply not possible. So please, watch out for her."

Foster nodded. Their face was cut with concern, their jaw clenched, but they, at least, hadn't protested when Hollis had insisted that she appear for the captains' briefing from the Admiralty.

Foster likely knew as well as she did how many questions her absence would raise.

"I've brought your dress uniform, Captain," they said brusquely, turning to her. "I took the liberty of having it cleaned while you were resting."

Hollis closed her eyes and tried not to swear.

She'd lived on the Level long enough to know that an offer to repay a gesture like that would be considered rude. But the thought of her first mate casually paying for Hollis's uniform to be cleaned and pressed, when Hollis had stayed up nights starching and washing her own dress uniforms all through her years at the Academy because she couldn't afford the credit chits it would take to get them cleaned without skipping dinners for a week, made her faintly sick to her stomach.

"Captain?" Foster sounded concerned.

She opened her eyes and tried to smile. "Thank you, Mate Price. I appreciate the thoughtfulness."

She sent up a quick prayer of gratitude to Our Lady of Mercy that she was able to dress herself without assistance, if a little stiffly. She knew perfectly well that Foster was waiting outside the door in case she called, but she could at least ignore that fact.

At last, she straightened her dress coat, grimacing at the way the movement tugged on her still-painful injuries, checked the shine on her boots, and stepped carefully out the door.

As she'd guessed, Foster was waiting just outside, their posture perfectly correct, their gaze focused politely on the middle distance. She wasn't sure whether the sight made her irritated or absurdly grateful.

"Come, Mate Price," she said stiffly. "We shouldn't keep the Admiralty waiting."

Foster nodded, and followed at her elbow as she turned and made her way off the *Verity* and onto the dock.

There was a transport waiting for her, a private one, but at least this time she could pay for it with her own credit chits, now that her pay had come in from the last voyage.

She sat without speaking. Foster took their seat across from her, and she stared blindly out the clear transport windows as the transport bumped along the cobblestone streets towards the Admiralty buildings

She wished she knew what the hell Foster did to project that air of bland, polite unconcern. Her own palms were damp with sweat, and she was clenching her jaw so hard it hurt.

But if she looked closer, she could see that Foster's hand never strayed far from the pistol they'd shoved into their belt under their coat, and their dress sword had been replaced with the serviceable cutlass they used on shipboard.

Perhaps they weren't as entirely unconcerned as they looked, either.

"Captain," Foster said quietly at last, their voice pitched just high enough to be audible over the noise of the transport. "Greene and I have been looking into the identity of the man who tried to kill you."

She turned to them. "Yes?"

Foster hesitated. "There was … nothing."

Hollis frowned. "What do you mean, nothing?"

"I mean, there were no records whatsoever. No fingerprint records, no prison records, no ID records."

Hollis shook her head. "I somehow doubt the man was a paragon of law-abiding virtue, considering the familiarity he had with a knife."

"I know." Foster's voice was grim. "He should have had a record. That means money, or influence, or both."

Hollis nodded slowly.

She'd guessed whoever had sent the would-be murderer would be someone with some degree of influence—killing off a captain in the Level Navy, even a new captain such as herself, was an audacious move, and chances were, anyone who considered her a threat would be someone well above her in terms of power. This could be, as she'd originally assumed, as simple as someone who was irritated by a woman from the Stacks receiving a high-ranking promotion. But the inherent politics of the matter suggested more than that.

The fact that she had, for the moment, the support of Admiral Usher meant she was more important than her rank, which further complicated matters. Admiral Usher had put her reputation on the line to get Hollis her posting, she knew that well enough, and there was at least an even chance that whoever had come after her had the Admiral as their ultimate target. But she didn't know enough about Level politics to know who that might be, and why. She'd mostly paid attention to the local shipboard and Academy politics during the course of her career, as those were the ones that ruled her life and determined her survival. And she'd felt her lack of greater political knowledge keenly these last few days, as she stared up at the med bay's dimly lit ceiling in the long, sleepless hours.

Foster was watching her with that uncomfortably perceptive expression, and she sighed. Much as she hated to admit her own ignorance, if she knew her first mate at all, they were as well-informed on Level politics as they seemed to be on every other matter.

"Do you have any ideas of who might have done it, then?" she asked.

Foster sighed ruefully. "I've been looking into that as well. I have a feeling this is political. The timing, too—it seems odd, don't you think? Taking you down would weaken the Admiral's position, but the *Verity's* next assignment is to go with the fleet to Blackrock."

Hollis raised her eyebrows, and Foster huffed a laugh. "Surely you've been in the navy long enough to know that keeping secrets from the sailors is like trying to hold a drop of dye in a pot without colouring the water. Every sailor below decks has a mouthful of gossip about the mission." They shook their head. "So why now? Why try to hamper the navy's ability to hamstring the pirates? Because whatever their personal feelings towards you, every person with knowledge of the navy would know having their captain murdered in her bed just before a mission would harm a crew's morale and performance, no matter who replaced her. And as it stands, there are more ships in need of captains than competent captains to command them."

"They could have wanted to kill me while I was still in disgrace with the Admiralty," said Hollis, still frowning.

"Possibly." Foster leaned forward. "But there's something going on politically that I haven't been able to put my finger on, and I'm afraid we've somehow gotten caught up in the middle of it. Anyone with the power to wipe someone's records before sending them after you isn't someone who'll try once and give up."

Hollis closed her eyes a moment. "I'm aware of that," she said at last, quietly. "I'm taking all possible precautions that won't hand them their ultimate objective on a credit chit—whether that's frightening off future Stacks officer candidates, or seeing me replaced on my own ship, or damaging the Admiral's reputation."

"Or getting yourself killed." Foster's voice was wry.

"I have no intention of getting myself killed," Hollis said brusquely. "We're going to sit through the briefing and keep a low profile, then get back to the *Verity*." But she found her hand straying to the pocket where she'd tucked her own projectile pistol.

The street outside the Admiralty courtyard was crowded with private transports, and, to her surprise, with people on foot. When she listened, she could hear shouting voices.

She glanced at her first mate questioningly.

Foster gave a quick shake of their head. "From what I've heard, this has been going on around the Admiralty offices for the last few weeks. Anti-war protesters, they call themselves, but from what I hear they're more anti-navy than anti-war."

Hollis frowned, watching out the transport window as their driver wove through the protesting people.

There weren't many, but more than she would have expected.

"They weren't protesting when we left to go after the *Agate*, were they?" she asked under her breath.

Foster gave a small shrug. "If they were, it wasn't as publicly as they are now."

Hollis nodded, but she found her breath was tight in her chest.

When their transport drew to a halt, Hollis pushed herself gingerly to her feet. Foster had taken up a position at the transport entrance that served to hide her momentary unsteadiness before she caught her balance.

She cast them a quick, grateful glance, and saw the flicker of a smile in return. Then the two of them stepped down from the transport and into the courtyard.

One or two heads turned to look at the two of them as they dismounted, Hollis holding her breath to keep from a sharp gasp of pain as her foot hit the cobblestones. She could see the disdain in their expressions, but she ignored it.

Disdain she could handle. She was watching for something else— an expression of shock at seeing her there, perhaps, or the kind of glare that she'd seen often enough to know that the person giving it wanted her dead.

The reception hall at the Admiralty office was crowded with at least thirty captains and officers—mostly older than her by decades, although she caught sight of one or two faces she recognized from the Academy.

"In the back, I think, Captain," Foster said in a low voice.

She nodded, and made her slow way across the marble floor until at last she sank into a chair with its back to a corner wall. Foster took their seat next to her, their posture stiff, their lips pressed into a thin line, and she realized how they'd stiffened, just a little, at every insulting glance and intentional snub.

She smiled wryly.

Foster, as a sailor from one of the resource planets, an officer who'd never been recommended to the Academy, would know as well as she did the weight of those glances.

She shook her head and turned her attention to the room.

None of the captains or officers gathered here surprised her, from what little she knew of the mission—a fleet of seventeen ships, the briefing had said, a quick strike on Blackrock and then a retreat. She frowned, trying to parse out anything unusual in the gathering, but this sort of politics was far from her area of expertise.

"Well, if it isn't Foster Price."

Hollis looked up quickly to see a figure she recognized instantly—Irene Grady. The woman had been in the Academy a year ahead of Hollis. She was, if Hollis remembered correctly, from a very wealthy family.

There was no mistaking the scorn in her tone.

"Officer Grady." Foster's voice was measured, but Hollis could hear the strain under it.

The woman pulled up a seat and dropped into it, still smiling that wolf's smile. "Price. It's been a while, hasn't it?"

Foster nodded, their expression polite, but their jaw was clenched.

Irene's smile broadened. "Still in the navy, are you? I have to admit, I'm a little disappointed. You struck me as someone who knew their place." She paused delicately. "Heard from your family recently?"

Foster's lips had gone white.

Hollis knew that expression. She'd worn it herself, far too many times—the expression of someone who would swallow insult after insult, because they had to. Because they didn't have a choice, because if they stood up for themself they'd find that every person they'd thought was an ally would have disappeared, and they'd be standing alone.

"Come now, Price. Answer to your superiors—aren't you trained to do that?"

Hollis stood so quickly that she had to grab for the back of her chair. "Did you have something you wished to say to my first mate, Officer?" she said, ice cracking from her tone.

The woman turned to her with a look of surprise that turned rapidly to disdain. "Hollis? Hollis Ives?"

Hollis smiled, a thin smile. "Captain Ives, as a matter of fact. Perhaps you hadn't heard. Price is my first mate. I assume you've met?" She glanced at Foster.

"We served together a few years ago," they murmured.

Hollis turned grimly back to Irene. "I would expect, since, from all accounts, you graduated the Academy, you know how to address a superior officer. As Price is a first mate, and you were assigned to a second mate's position out of the Academy, if I remember correctly, perhaps you'd be wise to put that knowledge to use." She made her tone as cutting as possible.

Irene was still blinking at her in shock. Then the woman gave a slow smile. "Hollis Ives. So the stories they tell about you are true— so concerned about your honour that you jump into a fight with no regard for consequences. They say you challenged Lucian Ainsley to a duel in the Academy, and almost lost your place for it." she laughed, a bright, brittle laugh. "You're in luck, it seems. Ainsley is first mate on a ship of the fleet, the *Consolation*. I don't believe he's here tonight, but I'm certain the two of you will run into each other at some point—it's always good, in the middle of a battle, to have friends one can count on, I find. Especially if you're a new captain with an untested crew."

Hollis smiled coolly, despite her racing heart.

She knew the rumours—that she was a hothead, that she was obsessed with her honour. The reality of it was much simpler—she knew what it took to survive, when there was no one who'd ever take your side or have your back, and the world was a pack of hungry ghosts arrayed against you. That duel had been as thought-through as every desperate calculation she'd made in the course of her career, and she'd weighed every risk.

The fact that she'd likely, at some point, have to serve in the same fleet as the man had been part of the calculations. But it sent a small chill through her regardless.

"If you'll excuse me, Officer Grady," she said in her blandest tone, "I was in the middle of a conversation with Price—Mate Price to you, I believe." She sat again deliberately, hiding her wince at the motion, and turned to Foster. "I am sorry for the interruption, Price. You were speaking of the arrangements you and Greene had made?"

"Yes, Captain." Foster's voice was tinged with shock. "As I was saying …"

The chair Irene had been sitting on scraped loudly on the floor as the woman pushed it back.

Hollis ignored her.

Once she was gone, Foster leaned in. "Captain," they hissed under their breath. "Do you know who that is?"

Hollis nodded grimly.

Foster shook their head. "That was hardly keeping a low profile. She's second mate, yes, but she's second mate on the damn flagship of the fleet, the *Resolve*. You've just put yourself on the radar of the Commodore, if you weren't firmly there already. Her family has the clout to ruin your reputation. Why did you—"

Hollis cut them off with a curt gesture. "She had no right speaking to you like that. I'm your damn captain, Price, and I won't stand by as someone insults you. You're a better officer than she'll ever be, Academy or no."

Foster stared at her for a long moment. Then, at last, they leaned carefully back in their seat again. "Thank you, Captain," they said quietly.

Hollis snorted. "I hardly see how that merits thanks."

Foster gave her a small, wry smile and turned back to watching the room, but Hollis noticed how their gaze flicked back to her every so often.

Finally, there was the rustle and quiet hum of people taking their seats, and Hollis glanced up to see that Commodore Webb had stepped forward to the podium to address them.

"Captains," he said when the noise had died. "I asked you together because I need you to understand the importance of what we're doing. We are launching a full-on attack on Blackrock. This will not be a mere skirmish. The Admiralty planned this mission such that the pirate stronghold will be weakening for decades hereafter."

Hollis raised her eyebrows, watching him.

He'd said "the Admiralty," not "the Admiral." That, in and of itself, was unexpected. While it was technically correct for any decision coming out of the Naval High Command, Hollis had served in the navy long enough to know damn well what that meant. Admiral Usher hadn't been the one behind this plan. Admiral Usher, who'd spent her entire tenure as Admiral of the Fleet cracking down on the pirates with an iron fist, hadn't signed on to it. The Admiral had a reputation for ruthlessness when it came to pirates. But she was measured, cautious, canny. She never did anything without a reason. If she'd not put her stamp of approval behind this mission, she'd had a reason for that, too.

What that meant, and especially what that meant in relation to Hollis's attempted murder, if anything, Hollis wasn't certain. But it would damn well give her something to think over later.

"The pirates have been growing increasingly bold. Our merchant ships are being terrorized, our resource planet settlements extorted. We must put an end to this. And you will ensure that we do." The commodore paused, looking out over them. "This will be a straightforward mission. You will all receive your mission orders when your ship seals, as is the custom, but we do not foresee any significant pushback from the pirates. Even should word of the mission reach them ahead of time, there's nothing they'll be able to do against a force of this size. And in addition, we have new navigational technology that will allow us to work much more effectively as a body. This means we can jump in fleet formation, instead of small groups, which denies the pirates their favoured tactic, splitting us off to attack our ships separately. Against our full fleet, the pirates will be all but helpless, even should they attempt to fight back." He smiled. "Do your duty, Captains. That is all we ask of you. Now I shall turn the time over to Captain Hartman, who will brief you on the parameters of the mission."

There was a murmur of voices around Hollis as the commodore stepped away from the podium and Hartman came forward in his place.

There was something tight and nervous in Hollis's stomach, and when she turned to glance at her first mate, she could see it in Foster's face, too.

Webb hadn't mentioned the *Sweet Jenny*, or Captain Mad Dog. But

Hollis could remember all too well the woman's laconic tones over the *Verity's* ship comms, the horrifying moment when Hollis had realized the pirate was about to drag the entire ship and every soul aboard into a black hole.

The same pirate who, if rumour was correct, was the de-facto leader of Blackrock.

And Hollis was suddenly very, very certain this mission would not be as simple as Commodore Webb would have them believe.

5

Judith

Admiral of the Fleet Judith Usher tried to keep the irritation from her tone as she turned and surveyed the rows of politicians in their fine seats. "Honourable members of Parliament. I do understand wishing for peace. However, as this briefing makes very clear, that is no longer an option. We are in desperate need of more ships, and more captains to command them, unless we wish to be caught completely unprepared."

There was the rustle of papers and the flicker of holonotes from the cushioned seats around her.

"Admiral Usher." Parliamentarian Louisa Montgomery's tone was dry. "With respect, your navy has a history of stirring up its own trouble when there's not enough for your liking at home. Was the Basalt War not less than a century ago?"

Judith sighed. She'd known, somehow, that Montgomery would be the one to bring that up. "As you can see from the briefings in front of you, the Rosette System is preparing for war. Intelligence operatives died for that information, and I would hope that we would give more meaning to their deaths than debating the issue ad infinitum."

Montgomery cleared her throat. "And what about the reports we're receiving from the Blackrock mission? Perhaps that is the issue we should be focusing on at the moment." She turned her imperious stare on Judith. "I understand, Admiral Usher, that you chose not to personally involve yourself with that mission. Perhaps you would be so kind as to explain why?"

Judith bit back the first response that came to her tongue.

Damn these bloody politicians and their bloody self-interested political games.

"As you no doubt read in my earlier parliamentary briefing documents, I did not believe that an expedition to Blackrock was necessary or advisable at this time." She turned, so she was facing the entire parliament. "At this juncture, it is critical that we conserve our forces. My honourable friends in parliament voted to go forward with this mission; far be it from me to stand in the way of political mandates. However, I believed that Commodore Webb was up to the task of carrying out the raid, while my attention was better focused on things such as this upcoming threat of war."

"Are you certain, Admiral, that you're not growing soft on piracy?" Montgomery's tone was laced with irony.

Gracie's face, haunting behind her eyelids—her small, mocking smile, the aching, heart-wrenching familiarity of her every gesture, her every movement. Small things Judith had memorized—the way she cocked her head, the way her smile turned up a little more on one side than the other, the impatient way she brushed back her hair, once jet black, now streaked with grey. The way she'd watch you, as if she was weighing you in her gaze. The way her breath had brushed against Judith's ear, warm and thick with cigar smoke, as she'd whispered her threats and endearments. The way Judith's heart had pounded in her chest, rough and unsteady, fear and guilt and desire mingled until she wasn't sure she could tell them apart. The feel of Gracie's hands, rough and calloused against her skin.

Judith turned to the woman and arched her eyebrow. "I believe that my record speaks for itself on that point. If you'd prefer I prioritize going after a few petty pirates over the prospect of a full-scale war, please do send me a duly-authorized order."

The briefing was exactly as long and contentious as Judith had expected it to be. Even if she hadn't been working herself to exhaustion these past few months, she would have found it hard to keep her temper with the politicians who seemed so wilfully blind at their own danger. But, she supposed, when you were able to outsource your System's protection, as well as the blame for any failures, onto another body, it made sense that you might feel unjustifiably comfortable nitpicking Admiralty briefings rather than focusing on the threat itself.

She'd barely made it back to her office and settled into her seat with a groan of relief when there was a tap on her door.

She sighed. "Come in," she said resignedly.

Vice-Admiral Edwin Wright pushed the door open and stepped into the office, hat under his arm. "Admiral, I'm sorry, but we just received a new batch of briefings. I thought you should see them right away." He pulled out a chair and dropped his bag onto it, then extracted a sheaf of papers and a box of data chips and placed them carefully onto her desk.

She frowned and moved the box to one side, glancing over the top document in the stack.

Then she swore, and flipped quickly through the pages.

"The data chips are more of the same," said Edwin grimly, when at last she looked up.

"Have these been brought before Parliament?" she snapped. "They weren't in my briefing this morning, and I'd like to know why."

He shook his head and dropped into another seat. "I'm afraid not. There are at least three admirals who are blocking the motion to bring it before the political body. They cite security concerns, but I'm afraid it's more than that."

Judith swore again, glaring at the pile of documents on her desk.

Damn the entire Admiralty to hell. The petty backstabbing and infighting was bad enough when it was just pirates they had to defend themselves against.

With war on the horizon, it was all but suicidal.

"Call a general meeting," she said at last, looking up. "Tomorrow morning, at six bells. Inform every member of the Admiralty that I have personally requested their presence, and if they do not appear, I shall have them censured for insubordination."

Edwin raised his eyebrows. "They won't like that."

Judith bit back the retort that had leapt to her tongue. He was hardly the one she needed to shout at, at the moment. Although it was possible that was coming.

"I suspect they won't. But from what I can see of these documents, I'm weighing the Admiralty's displeasure at getting up early against the security of the entire goddamn Level." She slapped her open hand down on the stack of documents, making the box beside them jump. "If they'd like to keep this from Parliament, they will damn well explain their reasoning, in person, in front of every damned member of the Admiralty, myself included."

Edwin glanced at her, and wisely refrained from whatever he'd been about to say. Instead, he bowed his head respectfully. "Aye,

Admiral," he said. "I'll notify them at once."

"See that you do." She made no effort to soften her tone.

He nodded again, pushed back his chair, and ducked out the door, closing it carefully behind him.

When he was gone, Judith let out a long breath and turned her attention back to the documents, worry tightening her stomach.

Even a cursory glance told her this had already gone much farther than she'd imagined.

A long list of ships and captains, weapons manufacture records and shipping manifests, told a story that was impossible to mistake, even for self-interested politicians—it was enough to shock her, and she'd been paying attention. And now the damnable fools in the Admiralty, who were letting their ears be bent by the protesters and provocateurs who were peddling naked anti-naval sentiment covered with the bare fig leaf of pacifism, were trying to keep her from putting this in front of the politicians who needed desperately to see it.

The Rosette System was preparing for war. It had been an open secret for almost two years now, and inevitable for years before that. There had been sabre-rattling over ownership of the lithium mines on the planets near their shared border for decades, but the threats had grown much more overt over the last few months. This mission to send a fleet of good ships and captains to Blackrock was nothing more than another distraction—something to keep the war- and glory-obsessed members of the navy happy without committing the sailors and resources to prepare for the war that, Judith knew well enough, was drawing inexorably closer.

She could understand caution—she'd served in the navy long enough to know there were plenty of overeager officers who believed a war would increase their prospects of advancement. But this was willful blindness. These same people had spent the last months hamstringing her every effort to procure resources she desperately needed for the navy.

And after the attack on Hollis Ives … she was starting to wonder if there was something intentional about it. If there was, perhaps, someone in the navy who was being bribed or blackmailed to slow their preparations.

But she had no proof, and without it, the best she could do was what she was doing already.

She shook her head and turned back to the documents.

Her name held enough weight behind it, she knew, that she could likely push the Admiralty meeting tomorrow in her direction, and it was possible she could call for an emergency briefing in Parliament and get these documents in front of them within the week. But she'd have to be meticulous in her preparations.

And she knew damn well that her focus was split. It had been for days now.

She couldn't afford this.

She'd had to repay Gracie's favour—leaving Hollis Ives and her ship and crew alive back in the Adrian Sector. That was the unspoken arrangement they'd worked out over the years. Gracie would have expected some favour in return, and Judith knew well enough the brutal and bloody reprisal she could have taken had Judith not reciprocated. The information about the attack on Blackrock had been what she'd chosen to give—helpful enough to Gracie, hopefully, to serve as payment, and not harmful enough to the navy to outweigh the advantage Judith gained by having her Stacks captain back, honour intact, alive and only a little scathed.

But she hadn't realized the full cost. She hadn't realized what seeing Grace Madox again, after almost five years, would do to her

—how it would burn through her focus like fire through paper, how it would make her question every decision, every motivation.

Grace, lying beside her in the darkness, decades ago when they were both young and life hadn't yet destroyed them. Her arm was wrapped loosely around Judith's waist, the warmth of her body a drowsy comfort against Judith's bare skin, the hard muscle and whipcord strength of her softened by the curves of her hips and breasts. "I'd burn the world for you, Jenny," she'd murmured, her voice slurred with sleepy contentment. "There's nothing I wouldn't do. I'd burn the world and walk through the flames if you asked me."

And Judith had known, even then, that her lover was telling the truth—even sleepy and satiated, there was an intensity to Grace that she could feel in her bones, thrumming through her body and singing in her tendons.

Grace Madox would shape the world to her wishes, because she could. Because she was brilliant and driven and audacious, the navy's golden child. Grace simply couldn't imagine the world not re-forming itself to what she wanted it to be, and she had the sharp intelligence and the ruthless determination to make it so.

Everything she'd told the politicians about her reasons not to take personal ownership of the expedition to Blackrock had been true.

But she wasn't sure, in the inner part of her that would never bend to the lies she'd learned to tell, over and over throughout her years in politics, that politics and reason had been why she'd refused to sign off on the action against Blackrock. She wasn't sure if she was, somewhere deep inside her, trying to save Gracie by refraining —or if she'd been tempted to sign off on it in the first place to get her revenge on the woman she'd once loved. To finally quit herself of Gracie's soft, mocking voice in her ear, Gracie's image in her dreams, the memories of Gracie's hands on her skin. And she couldn't afford this. She couldn't afford to be unsure.

She'd given her life for this position. And she'd done it because she believed the navy, flawed as it was, was necessary, believed that the people living on the Level and in the Stacks and on the far-flung resource planets deserved protection—deserved to be able to live their lives in peace. And most of the time, she could play the game against the pirates, against internal agitators and external enemies, with cool strategy, and without thinking too hard about the lives her decisions would cost, because in order to serve the greater good she had to make sacrifices.

She'd almost forgotten how Gracie could cut that away from her —the way she had when they were lovers, the way she had those endless years after the trials when Judith had woken with tears streaming down her cheeks, sobbing into her pillow.

She hadn't known. That, at least, was the truth—she hadn't known Gracie was innocent. Every word of her testimony had been the truth.

But that hadn't kept the guilt from rising around her like a flame, banked in the morning by the inevitable weary string of duties and responsibilities that kept her from going mad, but flaring back to life every night, when she was alone in her cabin and the darkness crept in around her like the ghost of her beloved—vicious and bloodthirsty and ready to shred flesh from bone.

And there had been nights—more nights than she could count— that she'd wished, desperately, that it had been Gracie's ghost come to take its revenge. That if tearing flesh from bone would exorcise the hissing demons of guilt in her mind, she'd welcome it.

And in the mornings, when she'd woken from the nightmares, there were more times than she cared to remember that the realization that she'd lived through another night was, rather than a relief, a bone-deep despair.

She shook her head.

She'd be rational about this, because the survival of the Level

depended on it. She *was* being rational about it, she was certain of it.
Almost certain.

6

Silas

Silas clenched his jaw so tightly it hurt, his palms damp with sweat as he watched the pressure gages on the *Sweet Jenny*. It was a two-day standard run to the Level from Blackrock—or to the Stacks, he reminded himself. But the *Sweet Jenny* ran quickly, and Gracie knew a shortcut jump-rout that would get them there in just over twenty-four hours.

And twenty-four hours wasn't nearly long enough, he'd realized, for him to wrap his head around what he was about to do.

An alert beeped. He cursed under his breath and glanced down at the sensors in front of him, feathering one up just a little, pulling one down.

He needed to keep his mind on his work. He'd thought he'd managed to train this out of himself over his long years in the navy. He thought he'd been able to figure out how to keep his mind on one thing at a time, even if the effort of it was like a hot poker being stabbed through his brain.

A few weeks on the *Sweet Jenny*, a few weeks without the iron-clad discipline he'd forced on himself his whole life, and it seemed all his effort had been for nothing.

He hardly had to pay attention, though, that was the worst of it. His hands knew the controls by rote, and he knew instinctually exactly where each gage had to sit to give the *Sweet Jenny* the perfect amount of pressure for a smooth landing.

Dammit, he needed something to take his mind off what he and Ari were going to do.

"Strap in for landing," Ari sang out over the comm, and there were murmurs of ascent from the other members of the crew.

Sil was already strapped in, but he reached back absently to check the fastening.

Secure. He'd known it would be, he'd checked it before he strapped in.

The bruises along his back and gut had stiffened, and he could feel them every time he breathed in too deeply or bent over, but even that wasn't quite enough to stop the way his brain was spinning.

There was the sudden jerk of deceleration, and he lifted his sleeve to wipe the sweat from out of his eyes.

The pressure room was the hottest part of the ship. He knew it full well, since he'd spent much of his early time as cabin-boy in the pressure room.

And now here he was again.

But then, someone had to do it, and he was the newest member of the crew by several years.

He felt a small chill at how easily the thought had come.

He wasn't really a member of the crew yet, was he? He'd never officially confirmed with Gracie that he was signing back on to the *Sweet Jenny*—he was here because he'd agreed to steal documents from the Level, and she'd agreed to bring him here to do it. But there was something uncomfortable in the back of his brain that reminded him that he didn't really have an argument against it any longer.

He closed his eyes as the ship shuddered, the soft *hiss* of the landing sequence followed by a gentle settling as it set down on a docking pad.

By God, he wished he could go back to being the person he had been. He wished he could un-know everything he'd learned since he'd first stumbled across those accursed documents. He wished things were as simple now as they had been only a few months before, when he'd known, with a child's certainty, what was right and what was wrong.

But nothing was that simple anymore, and he had no illusions it ever would be again.

"Sil? You ready? Ari's asking."

He glanced up. Freddie's broad face peered through the hatch at him, the bulk of her hover chair mostly concealed behind the door.

He managed a small smile. "Yeah. Tell Ari I'll be up in a sec, let me set the gages and unstrap."

She nodded and disappeared, and he turned back to his tasks, trying resolutely to force his brain back into some semblance of discipline.

When he emerged from the pressure room, Ari was waiting for him. "Captain's getting things set up, said stay on board until she calls for us," she said shortly.

Silas nodded. The tension in his muscles radiated up the back of his neck and set his head aching.

Ari, perched on the deck railing beside him, didn't look any less tense.

"So. Isaac seems nice," he said at last, for something to break the silence.

She turned to him with a jaunty smile that didn't quite reach her eyes. "Yeah, he is. But he only goes for women, so don't be getting any ideas."

He guffawed. "Ah, I see. You're only introducing me to your straight lovers, because you know how temptingly handsome I am."

She rolled her eyes at him, but the reluctant smile on her face was a little more genuine than it had been. "Speaking of Blackrock—Abigail sent word that they caught one of the people as came after you. From the Level, they said."

Silas raised his eyebrows. "From the Level?"

"You got enemies there?"

He snorted bitterly. "I imagine everyone who knew me is currently my enemy. But I didn't tell anyone where I was going. I can't think of a good reason they'd have been able to track me down, or if they did, why they'd have jumped me in an alley rather than try to bring me back to stand trial."

Ari raised her eyebrows. "That's the question, then, ain't it?"

There was a soft sound from her wrist comm, and she glanced down at it, her entire body stiffening. "That's the Captain. She's waiting for us outside," she said shortly. "The others'll stay on the ship, but you and me'd best get moving. No point in getting eaten by a damn ghost while we're stopped by."

Silas raised his eyebrows, but followed Ari down the ramp.

He glanced around surreptitiously as he stepped out into the dock. It was a dry dock, secured from ghosts and surprisingly well-maintained. Although, he realized with a twinge of discomfort, the surprising part of it may have been only a product of his own biases —a dry dock would have to be well-maintained if there was any chance of it functioning well enough to keep out ghosts. But he'd grown up hearing stories of the squalor and poverty of the Stacks, and the realization that they had dry-docks as functional as the ones on the Level—probably more functional, honestly, if the stories he heard about ghosts in the Stacks were true—was odd, and slightly disconcerting.

Gracie was standing on the other side of the dry-dock, deep in conversation with a man who looked to be in his early forties. She looked up at their footsteps and beckoned them over, and, after a moment of hesitation, Silas came.

"Sil, this is Recoil. He's the current leader of the Ghost Army," the pirate captain said casually, gesturing at the man in front of her.

Silas had to bite back an exclamation.

Everyone had heard of the Ghost Army, the terrorist organization —or political faction, depending on your perspective—from the Stacks that had been harrying the Level for decades. If what Gracie had said was true, he was standing in front of the one man who was more wanted on the Level than anyone except, perhaps, Gracie herself.

He stared at the man for a moment.

Recoil was undeniably handsome, with dark blond hair, dark blue eyes, and a dark scruff of a beard, and there was a hardness to his expression that spoke of someone who would do what needed doing and damn the consequences. There was a scar across his cheek, standing out against his pale skin, and another, long faded, circling his wrist.

He looked the part of a leader of the Ghost Army.

He looked like someone who'd watch the Level burn, and laugh.

"And you know Ari, of course," said Gracie, turning back to the rebel leader. "Sil and Ari're going up to the Level to run a favour for me. Thought you might be willing to help them up there."

Recoil raised an eyebrow. "Thought that, did you, Gracie?" There was the hint of an old antagonism in his voice, but just barely. Whatever rivalry he and Gracie had had in the past, it was clearly old news.

Gracie laughed. "Don't worry, there's something in it for you. Picked up some weapons recently. Put them out on the pirate market, but I'm willing to let you take a look."

Recoil tipped his head to the side, considering. "Fair enough," he said at last. "Let me see what you're offering, give me the same price as you put out to the pirates, and I'll get these two up to the Level without anyone knowing."

"And back down when they're done," said Gracie mildly. "Not much use to me otherwise."

Recoil gave a snort of humourless laughter. "Our Lady pay you back, Gracie. You'd bargain your soul away if you thought it'd serve you."

Gracie smiled, seemingly unfazed by the implied insult. "Don't like the bargain, Recoil, just say so."

He shook his head. "No. Bargain's fair enough, I suppose." He turned, letting his eyes run over Silas and Ari.

Silas had to hold back a shiver. There was something compelling in the man's gaze, something that made you not want to look away, but there was something else there, too—a cold, casual, predatory air, as if he were sizing up a potential meal.

"Need clothes for them if they don't want to be arrested the moment they set foot up there," he added.

Gracie nodded. "Show me the outfits, I'll pay you a fair price for them. Trust you enough to know you won't cheat me, any more'n I'd cheat you."

At last, reluctantly, Recoil smiled a little. "Wouldn't dare, Mad

Dog, any more'n you'd dare cheat me."

She smiled back. "And that's why we do business together so well."

"Come on, then, I'll show you what I have," Recoil said, turning. "You can pick what you want for those two. Should have something that'll fit them. Got enough of my people have to get up to the Level undetected, we've got a bit of a stash."

Gracie gestured with her head, and Silas and Ari fell in with her as she walked after Recoil.

"Speaking of that, I didn't see your second, Shine," she said as they walked. "Hope the boy's alright."

Recoil grunted sourly. "Boy's fine enough, from the sounds of it. Have him out on a mission." There was an edge to his voice that told Silas that whatever this mission entailed, Recoil was far from happy about it.

They stepped out of the sealed portion of the dry-dock, and paused as Recoil held up a hand. "Wait here," he said shortly. "Best check for ghosts before you step outside, 'less you fancy yourself a hand with a sparker." He pulled open the door and glanced out cautiously, then stepped outside. At last, he turned back and beckoned them to follow. "No ghosts in sight, anyway, which is as much as you can ask for in the Stacks."

There was no disguising the bitterness in his tone.

Ari glanced over at him as he stepped outside after Gracie. "First time in the Stacks, Level boy?" she asked in a whisper.

He nodded. She raised her eyebrows. "I remember my first time here. Ain't the Level, that's for sure, and don't fool yourself into forgetting it, or you'll wind up slit open in an alley with ghosts feeding off your blood."

He nodded again, and turned his attention to the streets around them.

It was midday, according to his timepiece, but the light was hazy and filtered, leaving the Stacks in the perpetual fog of twilight, or an exceptionally misty day on the Level. The buildings around him were built up in high, towering stacks, some of which looked sturdy enough, others which looked on the verge of collapse, wires running overhead in wild, chaotic abandon. Neon lights lit the edges of the buildings, illuminating signs and advertising places to eat and places to buy the types of things he'd only thought existed in Blackrock. The constant buzzing hum of them set his teeth on edge, and they flickered drunkenly, made dimmer by the dim sunlight. The streets themselves were a mishmash of cobblestones and black asphalt, with the occasional hearty weed poking through a crack or winding up the side of a building—not much grew down here, he knew from his history studies, due to a mixture of the bad air and the dim sunlight. The air itself tasted stale, like during drills on shipboard, when you locked the air-proof ghost-doors in the crew's quarters and hunkered down for hours, sometimes, the air around you stinking of fear and sweat and heavy breathing.

He shivered, and pulled his officer's coat closer around him.

Recoil glanced back at him with a humourless smile. "Cool in the mornings, yeah. By afternoon, though, boy, you'll be sweating through that fine white shirt of yours. Gas traps the heat down here, no way around it. Most folks don't go out much in the afternoons. But then, most don't dare go out in the evenings, either. Ghosts are harder to avoid in the dark."

They made it three streets down before Recoil held up a hand, bringing them to a stop. He didn't speak, but the tension in his posture told Silas exactly what this was.

He drew in a steadying breath, his hand reaching for his sparker. Around him, no one moved, and he could hear the soft hiss of their breaths.

At last, Recoil relaxed. "It's past us," he said quietly over his shoulder. "But no guarantee it won't come back. Best get inside quick."

The safehouse wasn't much farther—they made it inside without incident, and Silas and Ari stood in front of a jumble of assorted clothes in a dimly lit open warehouse.

Ari bent down, grimacing, and rummaged through the clothing. At last she came up with a dress in a rich blue, with lace ruffles down the sides and lace up the bodice. "Need a hat to go with this," she said. "And stockings and boots if I'm gonna fit in."

She sounded thoroughly disgusted.

Silas shook his head and turned to examine the stacks of clothing as Recoil led Ari over to a closet of boots and hats.

The clothing here was surprisingly good quality, some of it, and he found himself wondering where it had come from.

He shook his head resolutely.

Best not to know, probably.

He was tempted to grab a naval uniform, but that would probably be unwise, considering the reasons he was down here in the first place. At last, he chose a men's walking suit, with grey pinstripe trousers, a cream shirt under a light gold-silk waistcoat, and a frock coat of a powder-blue that would complement Ari's dress—an ensemble that would set him firmly in the upper middle-class without drawing too much attention.

He glanced down at his boots in regret.

They were far too obviously naval. He'd have to leave them behind, and use walking boots instead.

When he'd finished his selections, he stepped into the necessary to change. The cut and fabric of the clothing felt uncomfortable after years of breeches and a loose shirt on shipboard, and a naval dress uniform on land. It was too lightweight, and at the same time too constricting, and there was no good place to tuck a pistol or a sparker. The boots, too, pinched uncomfortably, nothing like the naval boots that were practically formed to his feet by years of wear, the soft soles of them giving his feet grip on the ratlines or the unsteady deck of a ship in the midst of battle.

Recoil had thoughtfully provided a razor, and Silas shaved quickly, then wet his hands and ran his fingers through his hair. He straightened, grimacing, and looked at his reflection in the mirror.

The picture of a Level middle-class shore-bound gentleman.

He sighed, trying to ignore the pang of disgust at the thought.

He hadn't realized, until he was in the process of losing it, how much of his identity had been tied to the navy—his rank, the clothing he wore, the way he spoke and carried his weapons.

Now that it was gone, he wasn't sure how much of himself was left.

He took a deep breath and stepped out into the main room of the warehouse.

Gracie and Recoil both glanced up at his entrance, the dull click of his walking shoes off the hard floor nothing like the crisp sound of the heels of officer's dress-boots. Gracie looked him up and down, raising her eyebrows a little. "Well, lad. Don't look naval at all any more, do you?"

Recoil snorted. "Boy was raised to be a Level middle-class gentleman, from the looks of it."

Silas bit back the retort that wanted to form on his lips. What Recoil thought of him hardly mattered.

"Will I pass?" he asked instead, keeping his voice mild.

Recoil studied him for a long moment, then gave a terse nod.

"You'll pass just fine, boy." His tone was disdainful.

A moment later, Ari emerged from a small room to the other side.

She glanced over at him with a glare that dared him to say anything, and he choked down the comment that had risen to his tongue.

He hardly recognized her. Her blonde hair was piled on her head in thick curls, one or two escaping artfully to frame her face, a soft, broad-brimmed hat perched on top and pinned in place at a coquettish angle. The dress brought out the blue of her eyes and hung in flattering folds down her frame, and the high ankle boots accentuated the look. The lace ribbons of the hat were tied loosely under her chin, her ship-calloused hands covered in elbow-high white kid gloves with pearl buttons up the sides.

She was beautiful. But it wasn't that that made Silas stare—she'd been beautiful in her ragged pirate's kit. It was the undefinable air of sophistication about her. She was born to be a Level woman of society, he could see it in every movement, every glance, even the way she held her head.

There was something discomfiting about it, and he couldn't put his finger on exactly what.

Then he realized what it was—the stiffness in her posture. The small lines of strain around her eyes.

He'd seen Ari angry, and happy, and frightened, and determined. But she'd always been Ari. Now she looked like someone trying to press herself into a role that would suffocate her.

He gave a rueful sigh, and smiled at her.

The same as he was, then.

"You look lovely, Ari," he said, holding out his arm.

She hesitated a moment, then took it. "You look well yourself, Silas," she said, her tone crisp and cultured. "However, I think it best that you address me as Arabella for the foreseeable future." Something about the precision of her words—the tone he'd heard so often growing up and learned to mimic himself as he grew older, of someone unable to let their guard down for even one moment— made his stomach twist a little.

"Of course," he said smoothly, bowing his head. "Now." He turned to Recoil. "If you would?"

Recoil gave him another humourless grin. "I'll send someone to get you on your way." He paused, then pulled two small chips out of his pocket. "Put these into your comms. It'll let you send through word to me, and I'll send someone to pick you up when you're ready. And you'd damn better be subtle about it—you bring the peacekeepers on your trail and my people'll leave you up there to rot. Ain't putting anyone here in danger for you if you ain't smart enough to save your own damn skin."

Silas tipped his head in acknowledgement. "Of course. I'd hardly expect more."

Recoil's eyes narrowed. "Best not, Level boy," he said, the acid in his words sharp enough to burn. "Now, get out of here, the two of you."

Silas gave the man a bland smile, ignoring the spark of fury at his tone, and turned towards the door, Ari beside him, her fingertips resting on his arm.

"Ari, Sil, get me what I need and then come back down here. Don't matter what else you find, no cause to do anything else. Don't want to lose crew over this."

He glanced up. Gracie was leaning up against the door, half-hidden in shadow, the glowing tip of her cigar the only thing giving her away.

"'Course, Captain," said Ari jauntily, lapsing back into pirate cant.

"Nothing up there worth being a hero over, no?"

Gracie smiled, the expression barely visible in the shadows except for the faint light reflecting off the white of her teeth. "Good. Off you go, then."

There was someone waiting for them when they stepped outside the safehouse, a middle-aged woman with a gaunt face and a wary look. She didn't speak, just gestured them after her with a jerk of her head. She led them on a winding path, cutting between buildings and through alleys. Silas found he was gripping his sparker tight enough that his knuckles were white, and wishing, irrationally, for a weapon better than the tiny needler pistol he'd managed to shove in his waistcoat pocket. But whether it was because she knew the place, or because everyone here knew she was one of Recoil's, no one living bothered them, and they managed to slip past the ghosts of the dead, lurking in the shadows like hungry wolves, without notice.

She came to a halt at the end of a dead-end alley. It led into the base of a long, narrow shaft, with a rickety wooden platform set with chains on both sides set within.

"Get in there, I'll start the machinery to pull you up," she said, the first words she'd spoken to them since they'd arrived.

Silas glanced at Ari.

Her jaw was clenched, and he could feel her tension through the tips of her fingers on his arm.

He had a feeling it had nothing to do with the rickety lift, and everything to do with what waited for them on the other side.

He took a deep breath and stepped onto the platform. Ari stepped on beside him, visibly bracing herself, and he turned and nodded to the woman.

She flipped a switch at the base of the shaft, and there was a rumble of machinery grinding to life. The platform began to rise in a series of jerks and starts that almost threw Silas off his balance, and he had to grab at the chain to keep from falling.

"This'll drop you at a half-way point," the woman called over the noise. "There's a ladder from there that'll take you the rest of the way. Don't get your fine clothes dirty, Recoil'll want them back."

He ignored her, staring up at the blackness overhead.

When he'd left the Academy, he hadn't expected to ever return, much as the thought had ached in his chest.

And he was suddenly very, very certain that he would have preferred it if his original expectation had been proved correct.

7

Gracie

Gracie watched Ari and Sil as they stepped out of the warehouse, and the door swung shut behind them.

"Well, Gracie?" Recoil's voice was at her elbow, but she didn't deign to turn.

She'd known the man for long enough to know that, for all his posturing, he wouldn't pose a threat to her or hers. They were too useful to each other for him to risk their alliance over petty grievances.

But she also knew him well enough to know he'd never entirely stop trying to intimidate her.

She blew out a long stream of smoke and watched it dissipate in the air, then, at last, turned to the Ghost Army leader.

He'd aged in the two years since last she'd been here.

She'd done business with his predecessor as well, Apple. They'd been a solid leader of the Ghost Army, but mostly content with things staying as they were, as long as conditions weren't getting worse. Recoil was different. In the decade or so since he'd taken over, after Apple'd been killed by the Peacekeepers—tortured to death, Gracie knew well enough, although the official reports would certainly say otherwise—the Ghost Army had been ramping up its attacks on the Level with a frightening intensity.

It was a calculated risk. It could either win the Stacks more autonomy, or send the Peacekeepers cracking down with a viciousness that was unprecedented in Stacks memory. But when Gracie remembered Apple—their mischievous grin, their easy banter, the weariness that had grown more and more pronounced on their face as the years passed—when she thought of the way they'd certainly died, it lit a hot flame of rage in her chest. She could hardly blame Recoil.

She'd lost too many friends to the Level. They all had.

The information they'd picked up from the Level about the attack had come suspiciously easy. But most of it had been what Gracie had already known—what Judith had come to tell her, in exchange for her sparing the *Verity* and Captain Ives. Whoever was behind the leak, it was unlikely to have been the Admiral. But she'd seen something in that information, something she may be able to use, if Sil could get her what he'd said he could.

"You did what you promised," she said, keeping her tone mild as she surveyed him. "You have my thanks. Come back to the dry dock with me, I'll get Jumper to pull up the weapons specs for you to look through."

He nodded shortly, and turned to the door.

She followed him outside and down the streets, where hooded figures walked cautiously, like ghosts themselves.

The air of the Stacks was a familiar stink. It'd been the first place she'd run when she'd escaped from prison—terrified and injured and angry, so angry she'd thought it would consume her in a white-hot ball of flame and leave nothing behind.

It wasn't the pictures burned into her mind of her parents being marched to the gallows that had seared through her veins like molten steel. It was Jenny's face, pale and set, as she'd taken her place on the witness stand.

The cool of the courtroom air, the way the shackles had hung on Gracie's wrists and ankles, cold and heavy.

There was disdain and fear in the looks of the faces around her, but she was too numb to notice, too numb to care, her stomach a tight knot of despair and nausea.

She'd heard about her parents' trials, what the verdict had been. One day, it would sink in—one day she'd realize they were dead, murdered by the very people they'd given their lives to serve.

The allegations weren't true. They couldn't be, she wouldn't believe they were true.

"The court calls Officer Judith Usher, from the Naval Academy."

Gracie's heart jumped at the name, a painful mixture of dread and hope.

It should have been just hope. There was no reason for the small seed of dread in her stomach. This was Jenny—the woman she loved.

But there had been something in her lover's face when she'd come for the short visit she'd been allowed after Gracie had been arrested, something distant and unfamiliar in her expression that had sparked a cold unease in Gracie's chest.

Her heart stuttered as Jenny entered the room—the familiar silhouette of her body, the aching familiarity in the way she walked, the way she moved.

But she didn't turn to look at Gracie, just took her place on the stand.

And somehow it was that moment—the moment when Jenny turned her face to the judge, without a glance towards her lover in chains—that Gracie had known.

The breathtaking horror of it, washing over her in a cresting wave, was worse than anything that had happened before or since—the ground crumbling and dissolving under her feet, falling with no chance to stop. The knowledge that there was no coming back from this—not for her, and not for Jenny.

Everything up to that moment, she'd believed she could survive, figure out. That it had been a misunderstanding, that it was something she could fight and win, even when they'd read her the charges, even when they'd dragged her away to a cold, miserable prison cell.

But she knew, deep down, that she wouldn't survive this.

Perhaps Judith hadn't realized what the outcome of her testimony would be. Perhaps she'd honestly believed the lies they'd spread about Grace. But Gracie would have gone to damnation for her, back then.

And now, by Our Lady, she'd go to damnation to bring her down.

She should never have agreed to read through Silas's documents. She'd known that if she reopened those wounds, they wouldn't easily close again. But there was no going back.

"Surprised to see you here, Gracie," said Recoil as they walked. "Thought you'd be back in Blackrock, planning a defence."

She smiled a little. "Oh, figure I didn't leave them as stayed on Blackrock completely defenceless. Some of the captains and I talked it over, made a plan. With the information Sil's bringing back on the fleet, they'll do well enough, I think, until I can get back there. And if Sil can get me what he says he can, figure it'll be worth the wait."

Recoil glanced at her, then turned back. "You taking that boy on your crew?" The disdain was clear in his tone.

"He's a good enough lad," she said mildly.

"That's not why you're taking him on, though, is it? Known you for long enough, Gracie Madox."

She smiled. "He is a good lad. But you're right, ain't the only reason." She paused. "Lad's parents died in the Starfire naval disaster twenty-five years ago. Ain't the only one it happened to, but he's smart, and from what I was able to learn about him, the other officer candidates admire him. Was on track to be a captain, from what I hear, three-hundred-and-fifty-crewed ship, most likely. Good lad for the navy to put on a pedestal, but they'd hardly have to. Lad makes friends easily enough as it is. And I'd say a fair number of the current captain candidates'd be on that list."

For a few moments, they walked in silence. At last, Recoil said, "You're going to use him to take down the damn navy." There was something like admiration in his voice.

She smiled again, just a little. "Might be a bit of a stretch. But I figure he can make a lot of them rethink their loyalties, if it comes to it."

"You ain't sending him up there just to get information, then." Recoil's tone had taken on a calculating air, as if he were trying to figure out her angle.

She tipped her head to one side. "It's a reason. Need that information for what's waiting for the navy back on Blackrock. And maybe more'n that, too, if my guess is right. But it ain't the only reason, no."

"What you expecting him to find up there, Mad Dog?" he asked. "You think he'll run into old friends?"

She glanced over at Recoil. "Not sure, and at the moment, don't really care. What I need is, I need that lad on my side, body'n soul. Sil's still naval, much as he thinks he's turned pirate. Right now, he wants to take down them as made the lies, clean up the navy. Thinks it's that simple. Thinks that's as deep as the rot goes. I need more'n that. I need him to hate the Level much's we both do. And I figure, what better way to get him there than let him figure out, for his ownself, what sort of things they value? You think all he's going to find in those vaults is the information I'm looking for? I sent him up there for information on the fleet, yes. But I also sent him after the records from the disaster. Figure he'll find out everything about it that he ever wanted to know."

Recoil shook his head without speaking. But she saw the look on his face.

Recoil wanted the Level taken down as much as she did. And any blow to the navy was a blow to the Level.

"You see why I need you to get them back safe for me," she said.

He nodded slowly. "Guess I do," he said. "And if you can do what you're telling me, figure I'll do everything I can to make sure of it."

She could hear the ice-cold anger under his words.

It matched her own.

"Ari'll keep the lad safe," she said as they stepped into the dry-dock. "Figure the documents'll do the rest."

"You're not worried about Ari?" he asked.

Gracie smiled a little. "Lass knows how to take care of herself. And Sil'll have her back if it comes to it." And for a moment, she was almost surprised at the ease with which the words had come.

She did trust Sil, in that, at least. He'd have Ari's back. He was loyal, and brave enough when it came to it, and he had skill.

He'd make a good crew.

And he'd make a very good weapon to turn on the Level, when she was done with him.

8

Hollis

The *Verity* was the organized chaos of a ship preparing for departure. Hollis stood on the captain's deck, watching the scene below her. Her hand rested on the rail in a way that probably looked casual, since no one below would be able to see the way her knuckles had whitened with the strain of holding herself up.

"Captain." Emmett appeared at her elbow, his posture respectful. The lines of worry on his pale face had grown more pronounced over the last few days, Hollis was certain. She could hardly blame him. She wondered if the strain was already starting to tell on her own face.

"What is it, Mate Greene?" she asked, turning to him.

There was concern in his expression, and she saw his gaze go to where her hand clutched the rail, but he only said, "We've got almost the full complement of sailors on board. The petty officers are rounding up the stragglers. Mate Price has asked Officer Cooper to take a final inventory of our supplies, and I have the crew preparing the pressure gages. Is there anything else you'd like me to do?"

Hollis shook her head. "Thank you. That will be sufficient. Please inform the petty officers that they may take reasonable steps to discipline the stragglers. If there is any outrageous behaviour, I shall take charge of the discipline myself, but barring that I trust their judgement."

Emmett nodded. "Aye, Captain." He hesitated a moment. "Captain. Commodore Webb is on the docks. He's taking a final inspection of the ships, and he asked to speak with you personally."

Hollis gritted her teeth and tried to keep from swearing.

She was entirely certain she would be able to captain her ship, injury notwithstanding.

She was not entirely certain she could believably fake non-injury.

"Please inform the commodore that I shall join him shortly."

She could see the worry in Emmett's eyes, but he ducked his head respectfully. "Aye, Captain. I'll inform him."

Hollis had barely made it across the captain's deck before Foster materialized beside her. "Captain," they said. "I was hoping you would look over the provision list with me as you walk." They held out their arm, expression carefully neutral, and after a moment's hesitation, Hollis took it, wavering between gratitude and irritation.

The bare fact was, she wasn't entirely sure she'd make it down to the gangplank without having to pause and support herself against a wall. Which would look less than impressive to a commodore who may or may not be looking for an excuse to get her taken off the mission and replaced "temporarily" by a more suitable captain—a temporary replacement which, she was quite certain, would prove to be very permanent indeed. Now she could lean surreptitiously on her first mate's arm while appearing to peruse the documents they were showing her. It was a neat trick, and more clever than she would have thought up herself.

But the fact that either Emmett had informed them, or Foster had known without being informed, that Hollis needed the assistance, irked her more than it reasonably should have.

She knew damn well that Foster was probably analyzing every one of her thoughts through the minute expressions on her face—they were far too perceptive for Hollis's entire comfort—but at this point, she hardly cared. The important thing was, she could talk to the commodore without danger of falling on her face, and she could be grateful for that, at the least.

She sighed. "Well," she said in a low tone, "How are we doing as far as preparations for launch?"

"We're mostly there, Captain," said Foster. "Greene's done inventory, and we should have everything onboard in the next couple hours. The petty officers have been informed that they're to have their divisions sober and ready to sail by seven bells in the forenoon."

"Good," said Hollis. "Our ammunition is laid in, and the naval mechanics have checked over the guns? I'd like our own ships' technicians to re-check everything as well, from the guns and FTL drive to the supplies, considering the circumstances."

"Already done, Captain," said Foster. "I had the same thought. I had our people checking everything as it came on board, and inspecting the work done by anyone Greene or I do not know personally. I had personally-selected members of the crew go over our supplies manifest as well." Foster's voice was impressively bland, and if they were watching her with concern out of the corners of their eyes, it was subtle enough that Hollis could pretend not to notice. "I've cross-checked it with the supplies manifests on the other ships, and I'm comfortable that we're well-prepared."

Hollis raised her eyebrows. She'd shipped with Foster on exactly one voyage, but she could see how they'd risen to a first mate's position, despite their lack of Academy training.

"Very good, Mate Price." She attempted to match her first mate's bland tone. She was leaning on them more heavily than she'd expected to have to, but she could hardly use the lifts while there was a chance the commodore's officers were watching, and the steep stairs were playing havoc on her newly reopened injury. "And is there anything I need to know as far as the weaponry or tech?"

Foster shook their head. "I don't think so. The *Verity's* nav systems were reconfigured to the specifications of the newest standard model, but I inspected the changes, and they're in line with the other ships. I don't believe we'll have any trouble interfacing."

She heard the words they weren't saying—it wasn't intentional sabotage, at least, and unless the navy had intended that all the ships of the line be sabotaged, there was no particular danger to the new technology.

"Very good, Mate Price. Anything else I should be aware of?"

Foster hesitated a moment. There was the smallest stiffening of their posture, something so minute that Hollis might not have noticed it had she not been leaning most of her weight on their arm.

"Mate Price?" she asked again after a moment, trying not to let the concern show in her own voice.

"I … think perhaps there is more we could discuss after your conversation with the commodore," Foster said after a moment, their tone smooth. "It appears he's sent someone to meet us."

Hollis looked up, and not for the first time thanked Our Lady of Mercy that Foster had the sense to be discreet. Two petty officers, dressed in uniforms that were starched stiffly enough that it was apparent they hadn't been worn on shipboard before, stood waiting for her.

"Thank you for your advice, Captain," Foster said, turning to nod respectfully at Hollis in a gesture that hid any momentary unsteadiness on Hollis's part as she straightened. "I shall leave you to your conversation."

"Thank you, Price," said Hollis brusquely. "Please meet me in my cabin afterwards to discuss the matter."

"Aye, Captain." Foster nodded again, then turned and strode away, their posture straight, their steps perfectly measured.

Hollis watched after them for a moment, not entirely sure whether she wanted to sigh or laugh.

One of the commodore's petty officers cleared their throat, and Hollis turned, lifting her eyebrows imperiously. "Please, Midship Officer. Lead the way."

She managed to keep her posture entirely straight, and if her steps were slower than usual, she could at least play it off as a simple matter of a shorter stride. To her everlasting relief, when she reached the commodore, he was leaning against the railing, which gave her an excuse to join him.

"Captain … Hollis Ives, isn't it?" he asked, turning to her as she approached.

"Yes, Commodore," she said, keeping her tone neutral.

He studied her critically for a few moments. "Well," he said, his voice jovial. "I'd hardly know you were from the Stacks. Goes to show what good discipline can do."

"Of course, Commodore." She managed, barely, to keep her words civil.

"Hollis. That's not a Stacks name though, is it? Must have changed it. Good job, I say. Don't want people getting the wrong idea."

Hollis was clenching her teeth hard enough to give herself a headache. She wasn't sure any answer she'd give wouldn't lead to her immediate demotion.

She hadn't thought of her Stacks name—the name she'd gone by as a child, before she'd run away to join a merchant ship, taken the name Hollis Ives because it would make her life a thousand times easier, because even though they'd know she was from the Stacks, they wouldn't have to think of it every time they spoke to or about her—in years. She'd always hated it, hated that she was from the Stacks, hated that her name hadn't been Hollis Ives from the time she was born. And she'd served in the navy, and then in the Academy, for long enough to know damn well how to handle being baited. But for some reason, the tone in the commodore's voice set her teeth on edge.

He was watching her, a small smile on his face that told her he knew exactly what was going through her head. He paused delicately. "I hope you are feeling alright, after ..." He let the sentence hang.

For an instant, a wave of cold terror drowned the fury. He couldn't possibly know about what had happened, the only way he could know is if someone had given her away—

"We were all very impressed by the tales your officers told about your bravery on the *Agate*," he continued, and Hollis felt herself sag in relief.

"Thank you," she managed.

He was still studying her, and now she caught the hint of a frown between his eyebrows. "I had heard rumours that you'd had a ... setback in your recovery, that's why I wanted to see you," he continued at last. "As you know, such rumours are of utmost concern to the Naval High Command—we take the health and well-being of our captains seriously. I've just come from talking with your chief medical officer."

Hollis managed to keep the polite, vaguely questioning look on her face, but she could feel the cold sweat beading on her forehead. "I trust his report was satisfactory?"

The man shook his head. "His report was glowing—you had followed every one of his instructions on the flight back to the Level after your most recent skirmish, and there had been nothing whatsoever to concern him since that time. He assured me he had no concerns as to your health or fitness to serve."

Again, Hollis had to fight to keep her expression neutral.

Archibald had lied to a superior officer for her.

She hadn't expected him to go running to the commodore the moment he saw her injured, but … he'd lied for her, to the commodore's face. He'd been laying it on a bit thick, perhaps, when he mentioned how she'd followed his every instruction—her clearest memories of the flight back to the Level after the *Verity's* engagement with the *Sweet Jenny* was Archibald visibly holding himself back from cursing at her every time he came in and saw she'd broken her wound open again—but he hadn't given her away. Nor, it appeared, had her crew. And … the way Foster had held out their arm for her, assistance disguised as politeness, how they'd moved to hide her stagger as she let go of their arm.

For a moment, she had to blink at the almost dizzying sensation of the world she knew settling into a new and unfamiliar pattern.

Her crew—her mates, her chief medical officer, the petty officers the commodore had certainly spoken to before she had arrived— were loyal to her. Not to the navy, or a higher-up officer, but to her. Captain Hollis Ives, from the Stacks.

"I was glad to hear that, of course," the commodore continued. "But since I was out inspecting the ships anyways, I thought I'd speak to you myself. You know how rumour spreads."

"Of course," Hollis said. "I am well aware that more than a few rumours have been spread about me in my time. I must say, rumours about my health have generally not been among them, so I suppose we must be grateful for the change, at least." She let a hint of dryness creep into her voice.

"I do hope you're not implicating the navy in spreading these alleged rumours about you." The commodore's voice had dropped any semblance of friendliness.

Hollis turned and gave him the full benefit of her raised eyebrows. "I hardly see, Commodore, how they can be allegations when your presence here confirms their existence. I sincerely appreciate your concern for my well-being, but I do hope the assurances of my chief medical officer, not to mention my own presence here, have reassured you. And now, if there is nothing else you need from me, I am currently in the process of overseeing the final preparations of my crew as we prepare for departure. So if I may?"

There was a look on the commodore's face that told Hollis he would very much have liked an excuse to keep her ship shore bound —or if not her ship, at least its captain. But he merely gave a brusque nod. "Of course, Captain Ives. Best of luck with your preparations." He turned to go, and Hollis watched him stride off. She didn't dare turn back to her own ship until she was certain he was gone.

Then she swallowed her pride, and tapped her comm. "Mate Price," she said stiffly.

"Captain. Give me a moment, I'm almost there," said Foster.

She closed her eyes and grimaced, leaning up against the railing.

She'd follow every damn instruction Archibald gave her from this moment forward if it meant never again having to bear the embarrassment of calling her first mate for assistance in walking up to the damn captain's deck.

Foster appeared quickly enough that it was blatantly apparent they'd been waiting for her summons. "Thank God you called me, rather than trying to get back up to the captain's deck alone and passing out along the way," they said quietly as she took their proffered arm, their tone impressively dry. "That would have been a little difficult to explain away. Not to mention Officer Smyth would have skinned me alive, and probably you, too. He told me he wasn't damn well going to the trouble of lying to a commodore if you were going to throw all his hard work back in his face."

Hollis managed a small smile, and for some reason found herself swallowing down a thickness in her throat. "Well," she said, when she could trust herself to speak. "You may tell him I am grateful for the consideration." She paused, frowning at her first mate. "Do you have any idea who was spreading rumours?"

Foster shook their head, their frown matching hers. "I don't, Captain. But Officer Smyth said the commodore seemed quite surprised to hear you were fully recovered."

Hollis closed her eyes a moment, fighting the tightness in her stomach. "You don't think—" she broke off the sentence.

Foster shook their head again, slowly. "Do I think the commodore was behind the attack? It's possible, of course. But I can't think of a reason he'd be willing to take that sort of risk. No offence meant, Captain, but you're not the most important playing piece on the board at the moment, not with the campaign against Blackrock ramping up. And he'd be risking his entire career if it came out. I think it more likely that someone passed a hint on to him of what happened, and he came to see if the rumours were true."

"And do you think it was someone from our crew?" Hollis asked.

Foster gave a short laugh. "I'd be willing to put my reputation on the line for any of the crew who know the whole story of what happened. And the rest don't know enough to spread rumours. No, I suspect the person behind the rumours was the person behind the attack."

"And we still don't know who that is," Hollis murmured.

Foster stopped, and Hollis stopped with them. Their face was grave. "I didn't want to alarm you, Captain, but I did want you to know—we have new sailors on board, to replace the ones we lost on our last voyage. And when I tried to go through their service records, I was told the information was unavailable. That's unusual, and when I asked around, it seems that it's only been blocked for our ship. None of the others. And I couldn't find any hint of who'd given the order to classify the information." They shook their head. "I don't know what's behind it. There aren't enough new sailors to force a mutiny, at least, not unless they manage to turn far more of our sailors than I think would be possible. But I somehow doubt that whoever was trying to kill you has entirely given up. I recommend we set up a security detail to watch you." They held up their hand, forestalling her protest before it had time to form. "We don't have to make it obvious. But whatever the hell you were going to say about morale, it'll be worse if you're killed by one of your own sailors while captaining your ship."

Hollis bit the inside of her cheek to hold back a curse, and nodded curtly. "Thank you for the warning, Price," she said at last. "I shall take your recommendations into account. Please give me a list of those who you feel would be suitable for this duty."

Foster glanced at her from the corner of their eye, and the startled expression that flickered across their face at her acquiescence was almost enough to make up for the bitter taste of the words.

She managed a small smile. "Mate Price. Your insight has proved invaluable more than once. I would hardly be a competent captain if I disregarded it at this juncture."

Again, that quick look of shock flitted over Foster's expression, and Hollis was left wondering, just for a moment, if Foster, who'd never studied at the Academy themself, had had to work just as hard for respect as she had, and found the receiving of it just as disorienting.

The two of them had almost reached the captain's deck, but Hollis turned at a corridor. "I think it best that I go over our mission instructions one last time. If you and Mate Greene would finish overseeing the crew, then meet me in my cabin?"

"Aye, Captain," said Foster. They walked with her down the short corridor, until the two of them reached the door to the captain's cabin.

"Thank you," she said, nodding stiffly.

Foster nodded back, the gesture respectful, but she caught the hint of a smile on their face. "Of course, Captain." Then they turned away and were gone as quietly as they'd come.

Hollis leaned up against the door to her cabin, bracing herself, and trying to bring her thoughts back into some semblance of order.

She was accustomed to watching her every step. The fact of the attack in her bedroom, and then the commodore's impromptu visit, made it very clear that her vigilance was entirely necessary.

But she was entirely unaccustomed to having people on whom she could rely to watch her back for her, and the feeling was odd in its entire unexpectedness.

9

Silas

When at last Silas and Ari clambered out of the dusty entrance that opened into the drab interior of an abandoned building, Silas had to hold his breath to keep from sneezing at the dust.

"Hold still," Ari instructed, and brushed him down quickly. He returned the favour.

"Are you ready?" he whispered.

She nodded. She was still wearing that frozen expression.

"Alright," he said, holding out his arm. "Shall we, Arabella my dear?"

She cracked a quick smile at that, and for just a moment he saw the Ari he knew in the expression. "Very well, Silas," she said, resting the tips of her gloved fingers on his arm.

He grinned at her in return, then the two of them stepped through the broken-down door and into a grimy back alley.

Silas glanced quickly around at the filthy cobblestones and dirty back entrances to buildings, some of the doorways boarded over, others thick with dust and cobwebs, then crossed to the alley entrance and peered out.

They were on the upper east side of the city, around the meatpacker district. Not the most genteel part of town, but it would only take a few minutes on public transport to get somewhere more central.

He glanced at Ari one last time, his heart beating fast and strange in his chest. Then he stepped out of the alley and into the bustle of the crowded streets, Ari beside him.

He could tell immediately why the Ghost Army used this entrance. It came out on the edges of the open-air meat market, and the place was swarming with people—servants of the richer households, here to shop for their employers, dockworkers and labourers, and, of course, the merchants themselves. The entire sector stank of the thick, sickly-sweet smell of fresh blood and offal, meat warmed by the sun, and the stomach-turning scent of the alleys and gutters, where the waste from the day before hadn't been entirely washed away. Flies buzzed incessantly, the vendors shouted, and the clank and groan of transport vehicles through the streets only added to the noise.

He could see, here and there, other people in fine dress, the crests of the fine houses on servants' uniforms.

"Well," he said in a low voice, "I suppose we should find ourselves a transport that will take us in the direction of the Academy."

Ari glanced around and managed a grin. "What, you don't want to buy a pig's head as a gift first?" She turned to one of the stalls, where the shopkeeper was watching her with narrowed eyes. She tipped her head at Silas and gave the man a conspiratorial grin. "I'm taking my cousin out to see the town for the first time," she said in a loud mock-whisper. "My aunt thinks he's too naive to go around unattended, so I'm on nursemaid duty."

Silas shot her an outraged glance as she tugged him along. "Come now, cousin," she said. "I know it's all very interesting, but we can't keep your mother waiting."

He turned to glare at her when they were out of sight. Her eyes were dancing, and she shot him an unrepentant smirk.

A public transport was making its slow way down the street, and Silas stepped forward to flag it down, after a last dirty look at Ari. It slowed at the corner, and he stepped quickly forward, beating Ari inside. "Passage for two to the naval quarter," he said, pulling up two credit chits on his comm and sending them over to the transport driver with a quick flick of his fingers. "I've got to get my sister home. She feels unwell at the sight of blood. A bit of a fainting flower, to be honest, but she wouldn't listen when I warned her not to come along with me."

An older woman from the centre of the transport chuckled. "Ah, these sheltered young ones. Can't say as I haven't seen it before. Like their breakfast meat well enough, but less excited to see where it comes from."

Silas avoided Ari's gaze, which he knew must be molten, and shook his head in a convincing display of sincerity. "It is hard when they're this young and innocent," he said sagely. "But Mama was adamant that Arabella have the experience, at least."

The woman tutted, shaking her head, and Silas turned, taking Ari's arm solicitously. "Come, sister," he said, drawing her towards the back of the transport. "Sit down, and I'll fetch you your smelling salts."

"I wonder how squeamish you'll be when you're staring down at a pile of your own guts," Ari muttered.

"Now, now, sister dear," he whispered back, hiding his grin. "You wouldn't want people to think you had the capacity for violence."

Ari snorted, but he could see the reluctant amusement tugging at the corners of her mouth.

To Silas's unending delight, the older woman came over and offered Ari her smelling salts and a fan, and Ari was forced to lean back against the arm of the chair, under the woman's helpful instruction, with smelling salts under her nose and Silas fanning her face solicitously.

She bore it with good enough grace, but every time the woman wasn't looking she mouthed increasingly dire threats at Silas, which had him on the verge of breaking his cover by guffawing too loudly to have any possibility of excusing it.

It took almost two hours to reach the naval quarter, and when the transport finally shuddered to a halt at their stop, Silas stood, thanking the old woman profusely. At the woman's insistence, he slipped an arm around Ari's waist to prevent her from falling into a faint, and drew her out the transport door.

When the transport had pulled out of sight, they looked at each other for a long moment. Then Silas was bracing himself with his hands on his knees, Ari leaned back against a wall, her head tipped back, hands clutching her stomach, both of them howling with laughter.

At last Ari wiped her eyes on the back of her gloved hands, still hiccuping a little, and straightened. "Damn you, Sil," she managed. "Let's get out of here before we attract too much attention."

Silas straightened as well, trying desperately to bring himself back under control. People were already looking at the two of them askance as they walked by.

He took a deep breath. "You're right. You're right. Shall we go, then?"

Ari nodded, glancing around. "Yeah," she said. She paused.

"We're going to find a way into the Academy, I guess?" He could hear the tension returning to her voice, see the slight stiffening in her posture.

"No," he said shortly. "It's difficult to get into the classified documents archives from the Academy library—it took me long enough last time, and they'll have changed the security by now, so we'd have to start over from scratch. Besides, there are too many people there who'd recognize me. I doubt the navy will have put out wanted posters, with how much they hate embarrassment—they'd never admit to letting an officer-candidate run off with classified documents, not publicly. But you can't stop rumours among the students. I've no doubt half the Academy either knows what I did, or has some guess." He shook his head. "There's another entrance to the classified documents archives, through the Admiralty offices. And it should be easy enough to get Gracie her information from there, on the fleet they're sending to Blackrock. With how fast gossip spreads in the navy, everyone who has anything to do with the Admiralty will know all the details."

Ari raised her eyebrows. "Really? Didn't think they'd tell that sort of thing to civilians. Or let civilians into the classified document archives, for that matter."

He cracked a grin at her, despite the tension seeping through his muscles. "They don't," he said. "I thought I could distract whoever was on duty, and hopefully get some information out of them. And in the meantime, you could steal the key to the archives."

Now Ari's grin matched his own. "Well, why didn't you say so in the first place, Level boy?" she drawled.

Silas glanced quickly around them, then pulled down on his frock coat to straighten it, and, with a conscious effort to affect the air of a mid-level government man, started off towards the imposing government buildings at a brisk pace.

Ari's hand rested lightly on his arm as she followed. When he cut his eyes in her direction, her face wore the frigidly polite expression of a high-society woman, and he had to bite back a grin.

As they got closer to the Admiralty buildings they had to slow their pace, weaving through crowds that seemed unnaturally thick. There was shouting ahead of them, and he could make out the sound of someone speaking through an amplifier over cheers and heckling from the crowd, but it took him a moment to pinpoint the speaker—a man standing on the top of the steps, shouting through an amplifier at the crowd below.

Silas paused for a moment, curiosity tugging at him.

"We cannot let those who hunger for war sacrifice our own sons and daughters," the man on the steps was shouting. "How can we expect our neighbours and trading partners not to react when our navy is growing consistently larger, and when we promote officers from the Stacks and resource planets—that is proof, for anyone who is looking, that we are building, not a civilized navy as in the past, but a military that will be as vicious and brutal as the Stacks themselves. That, my friends, is a navy formed with one purpose only, and that purpose is war. They say we have intelligence that our neighbours are arming themselves. I say, we're provoking this by our own navy's warmongering."

The crowd was rapidly growing. Hecklers shouted from the back, scuffles breaking out here and there, and at least two dozen peacekeepers were standing around the edges of the crowd. But with any luck, the commotion would help with his and Ari's ultimate objective.

He glanced at Ari, raised an eyebrow, and tipped his head towards the entrance to the archives.

He'd been right—with the chaos at the entrance, the guards at the door nearest the archives barely gave the two of them a second glance as Silas mumbled something apologetic and stepped through the doorway. One of them nodded at him distractedly, the other was watching the scene outside.

Silas hesitated for just a moment. "You know what's causing all that racket out there?" He tried to keep his voice as imperious as possible.

The guard glanced up and shrugged. "Same bit of stir about the war, isn't it?" she said.

Silas nodded.

The fact that the woman hadn't bothered to elaborate meant this was common knowledge, and the fact Silas hadn't heard of it meant it was something that had started in the past few weeks.

He stored it away in the back of his mind for future consideration as he stepped past her through the doorway and into the staircase leading down to the archives.

At the top of the stairs, he paused. The old, damp-stone smell of it brought back a rush of memories so strong he almost had to brace himself. He took a deep breath, and, ignoring Ari's worried glance, led the way resolutely down the stairs.

At the bottom of the steps, the wide-open landing branched off, with corridors to either side. There was another guard posted at the elegant set of doors directly in front of them, who looked up as they stepped into the room.

He didn't look much older than Silas, and Silas caught the way his eyebrows rose just a little as he took Silas in, his back straightening, a small grin flickering on his lips.

Silas grinned to himself. He'd been in the navy long enough to recognize that kind of look.

He smiled easily, leaning up against the wall as Ari ducked down the nearest corridor. "Well. When they said there was a guard down here, I wasn't expecting the navy's finest."

"What are you doing here, then?" The guard's words were sharp enough, but there was a teasing cast to his expression.

Silas winked. "Well," he drawled, "I was looking for a set of documents, but now I'm wondering if I might be able to find better things to do with my evening than studying."

The guard's grin widened. "A scholar, are you?" he asked. "Always good to see a studious man."

Silas let his eyes drag up and down the guard's body, lingering a little longer than could possibly be construed as platonic. "Oh, I'm very good at studying."

The guard laughed and shook his head. "I can see that. I can also see that you're an incorrigible flirt. I'm afraid I'm going to have to disappoint you, though—no matter how handsome or studious you are, no one gets in without a letter of recommendation signed by someone in the Admiralty."

"Signed by someone in the Admiralty?" Silas raised his eyebrows. "That seems a bit excessive."

The guard shook his head again, ruefully. "You'd think. But apparently there were classified documents stolen out of the archives not a month previous."

Silas schooled his expression, trying to look interested rather than guilty. "How did someone steal classified documents? I thought they were all tracked."

The guard gave an eloquent shrug. "If we knew, I wouldn't be here detaining handsome strangers in the corridor."

"Oh, I have a feeling you're the type to detain handsome strangers in the corridor regardless." Silas raised his eyebrows suggestively, and the man laughed.

"Not all handsome strangers. Although I think I'd make an exception in your case." His grin faded. "But whatever it was, they're taking it seriously. The security here is no joke at the moment. Not just the letters of recommendation—the letter has to specify which documents you're allowed to take out, and they've set an alarm to alert the Academy guards whenever someone leaves the classified section with documents, letter or no. Only way to shut it off is to show a guard your letter and have them do a cross-check." He shook his head, a note of grimness creeping into his voice. "Pity the poor bastard that stole those documents when they catch them. The powers that be aren't pleased about it, that's for damn sure."

Silas breathed a quick sigh of relief. At least he'd been right about the navy—they hadn't, it appeared, made his name public. But he understood the man's grimness well enough. He'd known exactly what he was risking when he'd decided to steal those documents.

What he and Ari were risking now.

But he'd promised Gracie he'd get the documents, and he wasn't coming back without them.

He glanced sideways at the man's face, and decided the gamble was worth it. He turned away with a reluctant sigh. "Well, I suppose if I can't get in without a letter, I should be on my way."

The guard rose to the bait, his grin returning. "And here I thought you were studious. You're not going to convince me if you give up so soon. What are you studying, then?"

Silas paused, then turned back with a slow grin of his own. "I guess I could spare the time to explain, since you're so interested. But you'll have to trade me some naval gossip. I've heard about you military men and your exciting lives."

The guard was both good looking, and exceedingly interested—if not in the topics of study, at least in Silas. And it had been some time since Silas had allowed himself to be an incorrigible flirt.

He didn't need much information on the fleet—with the number and class of ships and the name of the commodore leading the fleet, he'd be able to figure out the rest of what Gracie had asked for. And now that the fleet was safely away, he guessed it was no longer much of a secret.

It was enough, at least, that he was able to push back the tendrils of guilt that were trying to wind their way around his stomach—he wouldn't be getting the guard in trouble for releasing classified information, at least.

When at last he heard Ari's delicate throat-clearing behind him, he almost jumped.

"There you are, brother dear." Her tone was perfect—the high-society ring to it, the implicit assumption that no matter who Silas was talking to, it must be someone below his rank. "Come, mother's waiting. She sent me to look for you."

Silas sighed, and gave the guard a rueful glance. "And, I suppose all good things come to an end."

The guard grinned. "Well, if you should ever be in need of further studies, or more naval gossip—" he raised his eyebrows suggestively and Silas chuckled, then Ari grabbed him by the arm and dragged him off.

When they were out of hearing, she turned to him, shaking her head. "God, Sil, I thought Kate was a flirt! You put her to shame. Maybe the two of you deserve each other more than I thought."

Silas gave her a smug look. "I did my job very well thank you," he said archly. "Can you say the same?"

Ari's grin widened the little. "Figure I can, lover boy," she drawled, tapping her comm. A keycode appeared over it. "And I got a scan of the layout of the archives, too. Figure I could've done more with how distracted you had that guard."

Silas laughed, but there was something tight in the pit of his stomach, and he wasn't sure if it was fear, or excitement. "Well," he said quietly. "I suppose we'd best get the hell out of here and find a place to lay low until dark."

Silas had lived on the Level for long enough to know that the best place not to be noticed, whether you were a beggar or a gentleman, was down around the docks. The quickest path there took them past the Academy, and after a moment's hesitation, he turned down one of the familiar streets. He could feel his body tensing at every step.

The streets around the Academy were busy this time of evening, crowded with pedestrians and transports, public and private, at least half of which had the naval crest displayed prominently on their sides.

Silas gritted his teeth.

A month ago, on an evening like this, it would have been him out on the streets with his friends, perhaps headed out to a tavern to celebrate the completion of an exam, gathering scandalized glances from the higher society at their antics.

A young officer candidate stepped out of one of the transports of the Academy gate, paying the driver with the quick twist of her wrist. Something about the sharp cut of her uniform, the crisp precision of her movements, made Silas's chest squeeze.

He shoved the feeling away and forced himself not to watch after her as she stepped through the Academy gates, not to wonder if he'd recognize her.

It wouldn't matter if he did. He'd closed the door on that world forever.

He wasn't sure if the sickness curdling in his stomach and creeping through his veins was from fear of being caught, or exhilaration at the risk, or something that he might, in other circumstances, have called homesickness.

He shook his head. It was absurd, feeling homesick for a place like this.

And he couldn't tell, honestly, if his disgust was because the Academy didn't deserve his loyalty, or because he, apparently, had never deserved its trust to begin with.

Ari glanced over at him. "I know I probably should say I'm sorry you lost all this," she whispered. There was an edge of bitterness to her voice. "But I'm not. Because if I figured you were the type of person who belonged up here—really belonged—I'd slit your damn throat so fast you'd be dead before you figured out what'd happened."

He frowned at her, realizing, suddenly, she was as tense as he was. She scowled.

"Let's just get this done and get the hell out of here," he muttered.

It wasn't until they were well past the Academy and onto a narrow back street, and he heard the unmistakable click of a pistol being cocked, that he realized he'd been hearing footsteps behind them for some time now.

He cursed, grabbing Ari and shoving her against the wall of a building as a shot whizzed past his head. He fumbled for the pistol he'd tucked into his outer pocket, but Ari was quicker.

"Duck," she hissed, and he obeyed on instinct. The sound of her needler pistol going off beside his head was enough to set his ears ringing.

She cursed. "Missed," she snapped, grabbing his arm. "Come on!"

He pulled them down an alley, turning between buildings into the maze of back-streets, but he could hear the footsteps ringing off the cobblestones behind them.

His heart pounded, his muscles tight with adrenalin, but something about the whole situation was making it difficult for him to keep down a grin.

Being shot at wasn't ideal, perhaps. But it was a hell of a lot better than having to think about the Academy, and everything he'd left behind.

As they turned down the entrance to a broader street, he slowed, gasping for breath, and Ari slowed with him. He shot her an apologetic glance, then slipped his arm around her waist and ducked into a tavern, pulling her in after him.

The patrons looked up in surprise at the newcomers, but Silas ignored them and stepped quickly over to the bar. He caught the bartender's eye, and when the man came over, whispered, "My lady-friend and I got into a spot of trouble back there. I wondered if you could let the two of us out your back way." He tapped his comm, and a credit chit sprang up over it. "We'd be grateful."

His arm was still around Ari's waist, his hand resting on her hip, her body leaned in to his so he could feel the rise and fall of her breath, and something about the warmth of her beside him and the adrenaline pounding through his veins were combining in a potent cocktail that he was having to work hard to ignore.

The bartender's eyes went between Silas and Ari and the door, but at last, grudgingly, he nodded and beckoned them around the bar.

He led them through a back room, crowded with boxes and thick with the smell of liquor, then through a small door that opened onto an alley. "Know your way from here, I guess?" he asked gruffly.

Silas nodded, and tapped the credit chit over to him with a wink.

"Not the first time I've had a spot of trouble. Much obliged."

The man gave a terse nod in return and disappeared back inside.

A quick glance around told Silas that they'd lost whoever was after them for the moment.

He shook his head and blew out a long breath, then realized he still had his arm around Ari.

He let go abruptly, dropping his hand to his side and turning away before she could catch his eye. He could feel her gaze on him, but he steadfastly refused to look at her.

"Come on," he said, jerking his head towards the docks. "I know a tavern where we can lay low, and they won't ask questions."

They started off, and he took care to keep enough distance between them that his shoulder wouldn't brush against hers.

If she noticed, she didn't comment.

"So. What the hell was that about?" she whispered as they got closer to the docks.

He shook his head, still not quite ready to meet her eye. "No idea."

"You think maybe you were wrong about wanted posters up for you?"

He hesitated, then shook his head again. "No. I know how the navy works. If they'd put up posters for me, it'd be peacekeepers after my head, not someone following us down the alley with a pistol."

"Those people as jumped you back on Blackrock were Levellers," she said, her tone uneasy.

He closed his eyes. "I know. But I don't know how anyone would know we're up here." He paused. "Maybe it was nothing, just a petty thief."

She raised her eyebrows at him. "You seen many petty thieves in this district try to shoot someone in the head from a distance?"

He didn't answer.

She was right—the whole situation was far too convenient to be coincidence. But he honestly had no idea who the hell it could be. There were a hundred reasons someone could want him and Ari dead—a pirate feud, someone on the Level angry with his defection, hell, someone after their purses—and not a one of them entirely fit.

And in the end, it hardly mattered. Whoever it was, whoever was trying to stop them, he'd get the documents and get them to Gracie. He'd promised, and he'd do it if it killed him.

"Let's just get somewhere we can wait it out," he said quietly. "We'll head back to the Admiralty buildings once it's dark."

10

The night smells of the Level were as comforting and familiar to Silas as the smell of his own home—more so, really. He'd probably, honestly, spent more of his childhood wandering the streets around the docks, as close as they'd let civilians get, at any rate, than he had in his home. The mist from the perpetually damp cobblestone streets, the sulphuric wisps of gas from the gas planet below them wafting up from the edge of the Level, the scent of ozone and oil and hot metal from the ships at the docks, only a few minute's walk away, was as homey as the smell of his aunt's cook preparing dinner.

He closed his eyes for a moment as he walked, trying not to think of the life he'd left behind.

His stomach was twisted with a mixture of regret and nostalgia and anger, a thick knot of emotion he had neither the time nor the desire to deal with at the moment.

But the smell of the docks and the Level streets around the Academy sent more than waves of nostalgia through him. They still lit that same spark of heady excitement in his chest that they'd done when, as a child, he would climb up onto the roofs of the warehouses surrounding the port and watch the naval ships dock and depart, and dream about the day he'd sail on one of them himself.

Ari had changed from her dress into the dark, shapeless outfit of trousers and a tunic that she'd tucked into her oversized handbag, a scarf wrapped around her head, but she carried the dress under her arm. Silas's clothes, in the dark of the evening, were shades of grey that should blend him into the shadows well enough, and besides, it would probably be a good idea to have at least one of them dressed in a manner that would give them plausible deniability.

To be safe, he'd gargled with some of the rum Ari had stashed in her bag, and slapped enough of it onto his cheeks that, if needs be, he could pose as some drunken young fop staggering home from the taverns.

His ears were straining for any sound, any hint of a disturbance, and he could tell by the tension in Ari's posture that she was doing the same.

He'd been telling her the truth—whoever had come after them last night, it was almost certainly not someone sent by the navy. But whoever it had been, and whatever their reason, he and Ari clearly weren't meant to live through it.

It wasn't a far walk to the Admiralty buildings, and the streets were mostly deserted this late at night. The shops and markets and taverns in the centre of the city would still be doing a bustling business, he knew well enough, as would their rather seedier counterparts down by the docks, but the streets surrounding the government buildings themselves were quiet, with nothing but the occasional peacekeeper walking by to disturb the stillness. The streetlamps illuminated the cobblestones and the old stone buildings, but it wasn't difficult to keep to the shadows.

"You're not bad at this, Level boy," Ari whispered as they crept along.

He turned to her with a tight grin. "Don't tell me you think the Academy students go quietly to their beds every night after their studies."

She rolled her eyes, but she was grinning too. "When we get there, you get up to the second story and get in through a window," she whispered. "I can override the alarm with the key I nicked from your swain back there at the archive entrance, but I can't shut it off, so I'll hold the override while you get in. Then you can come downstairs and unlock the door from the inside to let me in."

Silas nodded. The thrill of excitement in his chest was enough, almost, to block out the sickness in his stomach.

This, he could do. Dammit, this was the sort of thing he'd been born to do.

"Once we're inside the archives, you stand watch at the doors," he said. "I know what I'm looking for, and I think I know where to find it. I don't think we'll get out without setting off an alarm, so we'll just have to be quick on our feet."

She nodded, and they walked on in silence.

It was only the scuff of a shoe on cobblestone that alerted him.

But this time, he'd been listening for it.

"Go!" he snapped, shoving Ari ahead of him, then they were both running. He could hear the soft hiss of an energy pistol—not as effective as a projectile pistol at long range, but much quieter—and he ducked on instinct, dragging Ari down a nearby alley. "Follow me," he hissed, and she fell in behind him.

"How the hell'd they find us?" she panted as they ran.

"I don't know. They could have guessed we'd be back, and been watching for us outside the Admiralty offices."

They could worry about the implications of that later. In the meantime, the important thing was getting away.

He led them at a full-out run back towards the ports, and then through the warren of streets and alleys that made up the port district.

It wasn't until he could no longer hear footsteps behind them that he slowed. Ari slowed as well, gasping for breath. "Dammit, Sil, didn't ask you for a full tour of the Level, pretty sure," she grumbled.

He gave her a tight grin. "Better that than a tour of the morgue. Come on, I think we've lost them."

"Don't like not knowing who's after us." Her voice was still uneasy.

He grimaced. "Nor do I. But I don't think they're going to stand still and let us ask them about it, so let's get this done and get the hell away."

It took enough backtracking that Ari was swearing under her breath before they were done, and Silas found himself checking over his shoulder for their pursuer every few steps, but they reached the government building without further incident. They waited until the guard on night duty had passed the entrance, then they darted across the open courtyard and ducked into the shadows in the small entranceway.

Ari pulled up something to hover over her comm. "As long as I'm holding this to the alarm system, it'll override it," she whispered. "Once you're in, get down here and get the door open. As long as it's closed again within about five seconds of my taking off the override, we should be in safe. But hurry up. Don't want to give whoever the hell that was time to find our trail."

Silas glanced up, taking stock, and rubbed his hands absently on the smooth fabric of his trousers.

The walls here were old, but well maintained, and the cracks and crevices in them were hardly enough to make a handhold. But he'd grown up clinging to the ratlines as his ship shook with a pirate broadside.

He grinned to himself and stepped to the place that looked to have the easiest way up to a window. "Ready?" he whispered.

Ari nodded. Her pale skin, visible beneath her scarf, stood out in the darkness, her blue eyes black in the shadows.

Silas reached up, exploring the wall for a moment with his fingers, then wedged the tip of his shoe into a mortar joint in the stone and his fingers into a divot in one of the stones just above head-height, and began to pull himself up.

Clambering up a rock wall was different than climbing the rigging, and his fingers began to cramp long before he reached his objective, his Level walking boots not nearly as suited for the work as his comfortable sailor's boots. Even so, it was only minutes before he'd pulled himself up onto one of the window ledges.

He shifted his weight until he could reach into his pocket, and pulled out his buck-knife and a small torch. He flicked the torch on and held it between his teeth as he studied the window lock.

The newer government buildings had much higher security, but the Admiralty had never particularly enjoyed modernization. The alarms on the outside of the building and the force-fields over the doors and windows, the ones Ari was currently overriding with her key, were thought to be enough, without the cost of changing out the entirety of the windows and doors.

He grinned to himself and inserted the tip of his buck-knife between the base of the window and the windowsill. It was only a few moments of careful twisting before he managed to pop the lock free. He flicked off the torch quickly—no point in drawing more attention than he needed to, and the next night-guard would be coming in the next few seconds—pulled the window open, and wriggled through.

It was a high window, and he had to hold himself up on the sill with the fingertips of one hand while he pulled the window shut and relocked it awkwardly with the other. Then he let himself drop to the floor a metre or so below him.

He glanced around quickly as he brushed himself off.

He was in a large hallway lined with doors that must belong to the government bureaucrats in the Admiralty offices. He closed his eyes for a moment, picturing the map he'd memorized from Ari's comm.

The stairs should be down at the end of the hallway, and from there it was a straight shot to the door where Ari was waiting.

He started off briskly, doing his best to keep his footsteps from echoing in the empty corridor.

He'd almost reached the end of the hallway when a door across from him opened. In the sudden flood of light, he saw a woman frowning out from the opening, blinking against the darkness. "Who the hell—" she began. Then she wrinkled her nose. "Whoever you are, I can smell the rum from here."

He closed his eyes for a moment, thanking his lucky stars that he'd thought to wear a disguise.

"What're you doing still here?" he slurred, blinking at her and weaving a little on his feet. "Thought everyone but me'd … 'd left a while back."

She scowled at him. "Who are you?"

He scowled back. "'M new here. Today. Just … just started with the accounting depart … dep … with the accountants."

She rolled her eyes in disgust. "From the looks of it, you're trying to make sure it's your last day as well."

He made a valiant attempt to straighten. "Jus … jus celebrating the new job, 's all. No need to be like that."

She pinched the bridge of her nose. "What's your name, then?"

Silas gave her a drunken approximation of a crafty look. "Not going to tell you that. I know what you're planning to … to do with it."

She sighed again, shaking her head. "I'll find out easily enough. Now, go home before I call the peacekeepers to drag you there."

"'M on my way home right now," he managed, with offended dignity.

The woman slammed her door shut, and Silas sagged with relief, biting back his laughter.

He staggered noisily down the rest of the hallway for the look of the thing and hit the button for the lift, then, with a final glance around, straightened and sprinted on silent feet for the stairwell. He was through the door and halfway down the stairs by the time he heard the soft voice indicating the lift had arrived.

Ari was waiting for him outside, and as he pulled the outer door open, she tapped the key off her comm and slipped inside, shoving the door closed after her. The lock reengaged, and there was the faint hum of the security system and the force-fields reactivating.

"Let's get going," Silas whispered. "Someone saw me upstairs. I don't think she was suspicious, but I had to act incredibly drunk, and she was less than impressed. There's always a chance she'll call the peacekeepers, and I'd rather not be here when they come."

"As drunk as you were the night before I had to come rouse you out of Kate's bed to fetch you for Gracie?" Ari whispered as they ran silently down the corridors. He turned to glare at her reflexively, and she snickered.

When they reached the entrance to the archives and peered around the corner, the door was unguarded. Ari held up the key and the alarm override, and the door unlocked.

Once they were inside, she swung the door shut and pulled out her pistol, holding it casually pointed towards the door. "Figure you've got until opening time before either we get caught, we kill someone, or both," she whispered.

Silas nodded, his grin fading, and turned towards the shelves of stacked data chips in the archives.

It was here that he'd found that small case of chips that had changed the entire trajectory of his life. And now, a month later, he was back to repay that betrayal with a betrayal of his own.

He took a deep breath, bracing himself, and stepped into the shadows between the tall shelves.

The path between the dusty shelves had been imprinted into his brain, and it only took him a few moments to locate the place where the information on the Starfire disaster was stored. Where he'd find the specs of the old technology that Gracie had asked for, the technology that was so similar to the new tech on the naval ships. If he remembered correctly from the documents he'd stolen, all the evidence from the disaster that had been viewed by the military court behind closed doors was contained here, and the technological specs were certainly among them.

But he knew, already, that wasn't all he'd find in these documents.

He ran his fingers along the cases of data chips. His breath was coming harsh and unsteady, his hands trembling just a little as he flicked his torch on.

It didn't take long to find what he was looking for—there was an entire shelf dedicated to the disaster. He settled himself down on the floor, resting his back against the shelves, slipped one of the chips into his comm, pulled up the documents, and began to read through the headings.

"Sil?"

He glanced up with a start, and it took him a moment to realize Ari's voice was coming through his comm.

He fumbled for the button to answer her. "What is it?" His voice sounded strange.

"Sil? What happened? You alright?" Ari's tone was sharp with concern.

He swallowed down the thick knot in his throat and closed his eyes, trying to slow his pounding heart.

He'd only skimmed the document headings, just enough to be sure they contained the information Gracie had asked for. But he'd been right. The documents contained much, much more than that. He'd seen enough to know that what he held in his hands, right now, held not only the details of the failed technology—it spelled out in excruciating detail everything that had led to his parents' death. Everything that had set his life on the trajectory it was on.

And even his brief glance over the documents told him this would be something that would make him sick.

"You sound awful, dammit! You hurt? Something happen?"

He managed a wan smile. "I'm not hurt. I found the documents Gracie needs, I think."

"Good." Ari didn't sound noticeably less worried. "Then get your sorry carcass back here. I can hear noises upstairs, and I'm guessing we have a few minutes at most before we run out of options."

"Yeah," he said. His voice was distant. "Yes, I'll meet you there in a moment."

"You'd better do," she muttered under her breath.

Silas stood, emptying the rest of the chips from the case into his hand. He found the tracker hidden among them and pulled it out, replacing it in the case that would have its own inbuilt tracker—in that, at least, he'd learned his lesson from last time—and slipped the case neatly back into the shelf. Then he turned and strode back through the shelves of data chips, tucking the stolen chips into his pocket as he went.

Ari was waiting at the door, her pale face even paler than usual, her eyes wide and dark with worry. "The hell's wrong with you, Sil?" she hissed as he approached. "Thought someone'd slit your damn throat, the way you sounded back there."

He somehow pasted a smile on his face, although it felt more like a grimace. "I'm fine. Let's get out of here, we can talk then." Now that he was by the door, he could hear what Ari had heard— footsteps, the muffled sound of voices. Nothing that sounded like an alarm, but the moment someone stepped inside the archives and found them there, that would change.

He glanced around for a moment in indecision, then shook his head. "Come on," he said, turning back the way he'd come. "We'll have a better chance to get out through the Academy. The doors between the classified archives and the Academy library will be locked, but we should be able to open them from the inside, and the rest of the library stays open all night."

She raised her eyebrows and looked him up and down meaningfully. He sighed. "It's not unheard-of for bureaucrats from the Admiralty to use the Academy library. As long as you change clothes and I don't run into anyone who recognizes me, we'll be fine."

She hesitated.

Outside, there was the sound of footsteps on the flagstones.

"Come on!" he hissed. "That's got to be the guard. Once he gets here, we've run out of options."

At last she nodded, and he turned and led them quickly through the maze of shelves.

When he reached the door that led to the Academy library, he halted, glancing at Ari.

"I'll get changed," she said tersely. "And best hope you're right about the library being empty."

He nodded, and she ducked behind a row of shelves.

She emerged a few minutes later. Her hair wasn't in the neat ringlets of the day before, but she'd piled it into an artfully messy stack on top of her head, held in place with a hairpin. "Help me with the buttons," she hissed, turning, and he obliged, doing them up quickly by feel without letting his eyes stray to her bare back.

She'd probably have laughed at him, but he'd learned, over his years in the navy, how to be in close contact with someone you would, if you let yourself, have feelings for, and he knew damn well what made it easier and what made it harder.

"There," he said, and she turned.

"How do I look?"

He studied her critically. "You look perfect, honestly. How ..." He gestured to her hair.

She let out a short breath. "I used to study women's fashion, back when ..." she trailed off. "Practiced in the mirror sometimes, when no one else was home." She gave him a tight grin. "Then I joined up with Gracie, and turns out hairstyles like this one aren't much use when you're stabbing someone through the guts with your cutlass. Figured I may as well make some use of it."

He could see the way her eyes had tightened, the small lines of strain at the corners of her mouth, the way her shoulders hunched, just a little.

He nodded curtly and turned away.

Damn the Level and everyone on it.

It was easier to be angry on Ari's behalf than to think about what was sitting in his pockets right now, weighing his whole body down like lead.

She gave him a brusque nod, and he stepped forward, putting his hand on the handle. "Once we step through the door, I'm guessing we'll have maybe five minutes at the outside before the Academy guard gets here," he whispered.

Ari gave a short nod.

He pushed the door open and stepped out into the Academy library, Ari behind him.

The door to the archives opened onto one of the smaller, seldom-used lobbies in the massive library, and to Silas's immense relief, it was empty.

"Come on," he whispered, and he and Ari started for the stairs at a pace just slow enough to still be called a walk.

If he remembered correctly from his days here, this was almost the perfect hour, if someone in the library wanted privacy—the night-owls had already gone to bed, and the early-birds wouldn't yet have made their way down from the barracks.

He led the way swiftly up the long, elegant staircase and through the library proper, shoving back the guilt and the yearning both. How much of his childhood had he spent dreaming of studying in these halls? He wouldn't have been able to put a number on it, no matter how long he had to think about it. It was as long as he could remember.

As they walked past the lines of study carrels, he found his footsteps slowing almost involuntarily.

The carrel three from the end had been his, where he'd spent hours, days, sometimes, pouring over maps and charts and history texts.

"Come on!" Ari hissed, grabbing his arm and dragging him

forward. "You can mope over your damn memories when we're back on the *Sweet Jenny*."

He let her pull him away, and forced himself not to look back over his shoulder.

The Academy courtyard, too, was mostly empty when they stepped cautiously out through the library doors. The familiar lamp posts set along the cobblestone paths were just beginning to wink out in the fading grey of the morning, the grass sharp with dew. A few students were out, heading to early morning classes or coming home after a night of carousing, their figures half-hidden in the morning mist.

From behind him, Silas could hear the footsteps and muffled calls of the Academy guard, heading towards the library, but he and Ari didn't seem to have been noticed yet.

They'd made it half-way across the courtyard when a figure loomed up out of the mist a few steps away, and Silas had to pull back sharply to keep from bumping into them. The figure murmured a quick apology, glancing up, and then stopped dead.

Silas stopped as well, staring.

"Silas?" the man said at last. He sounded stunned.

Although, Silas reflected almost hysterically, he couldn't possibly feel more stunned than Silas did.

"I thought you were … they said …"

Silas closed his eyes a moment, trying to force his mind back into a functional state. "Lawrence." His voice came out hoarse. "I'm … sorry. I can't … I have to …"

Lawrence was still staring at him.

From the corner of his eye, he saw Ari gently sliding a knife loose. He reached out and grabbed her arm without turning. "Arabella," he said. "This is Lawrence. My … friend."

Lawrence swallowed visibly. "Silas," he said again. Then he seemed to make up his mind. He glanced around quickly, and pulled Silas off the path. "You've got to get out of here," he hissed. "They're going to hang you if they catch you, if they don't just shoot you on sight! What the hell were you thinking, coming back here?" He was dragging them out of sight around the corner of one of the buildings. Once they were out of sight, he paused, glancing around quickly. "Go out the back gate," he whispered. "The guard there doesn't pay as much attention, usually." He turned back to Silas, his gaze flicking over him, taking him in. His green eyes were wide in his pale face, the old scar across his cheek as prominent as Silas remembered. The damp from the fog and mist had beaded on his skin, droplets forming on his dark eyelashes and glinting in his brown hair.

At last his eyes caught Silas's. "Are you … is everything—"

Silas shook his head. "The less you know, the better," he whispered, voice short. "And … thank you." His voice choked a little on the words.

Lawrence nodded, his expression tight. He hesitated a moment, then grabbed Silas's arm in a tight, familiar grip. "Be careful," he said. Then he turned and was gone, and Silas let out a quick breath, sagging back against the wall.

When he glanced up, Ari was watching him. Her posture was tense, and her needler pistol was just visible in her hand—one of the smaller weapons favoured by fashionable ladies of the Level if they were worried about their safety, or by pickpockets and thieves if they needed something small enough to stay concealed.

"Come on," he said, jerking his head towards the back entrance. "Let's get out of here while we still can."

They made it through the gate without incident. Lawrence had been right—the guard looked Ari over in a bored fashion as she stepped up to him, and his gaze barely flicked over to Silas before he nodded them through.

From inside the Academy, Silas heard shouts, the sudden clang of an alarm—but they were already out in the streets and walking quickly towards the nearest transport station.

"Friend, was he?" said Ari. Her tone was jesting, but Silas could hear in it that she was attempting to lighten the mood.

He sighed. "It's … complicated."

Ari's grin widened. "Guess I should tell Kate that she has competition."

Silas shook his head grimly. "You can tell Kate whatever you damn well want to. She's not going to be there when I get back, she told me as much, and I'm certainly not going to see Lawrence again unless it's at the wrong end of a pistol or a cutlass. Alright? Now let's go before they get our description out, and every peacekeeper on the Level is after us." His tone was shorter than he'd meant it to be, but he couldn't help it. The shock of seeing Lawrence again had cut through his defences like hot water through ice, and he still felt half-way in shock from it.

It was still early morning, but by now the sun was peeking over the edge of the horizon, light spilling out like the sky had been slit neatly with a cutlass to let it through. The streets weren't yet busy, but already servants from the wealthier households were out, probably headed to market to pick up the day's supplies. He and Ari ducked around them, blending into the trickle of people headed to the transport station.

Then Ari stopped dead, her hand tightening on his arm.

He glanced over at her quickly. Her already pale face had gone even whiter, and she was staring straight ahead.

He followed her gaze.

There was a group of three women walking together, clearly serving staff, and it took him a moment to see what Ari had seen.

They were wearing the Davenport crest on their cloaks.

The crest of Ari's family, the family she'd run from the moment she'd found a way to escape.

He closed his free hand around her fingers, tight on his arm. "Just keep your head down," he whispered. "I'll keep us away from them. They probably won't recognize you."

She nodded and dropped her head, and he led them forward, weaving through the scattered clusters of people to keep himself between Ari and the small group of servants.

Ari was gripping his arm so tightly he thought he might have bruises.

"Arabella," he whispered as they stepped onto the transport and he paid the fare. "It's alright, they're gone."

She glanced up reflexively, and he was almost shocked by the drawn look on her face.

He gestured her into one of the seats, bending over her solicitously so that anyone watching would see nothing more than a doting gentleman helping his lover, and slid into the seat beside her.

She stared out the window, and didn't even look up at him.

"Ari?" he said after a moment. "They didn't see you, I'm certain of it."

At last she did turn to him, her smile bitter. "Wouldn't much have mattered if they had. Wouldn't have recognized me. None of them would. I could probably walk right through their damn gate and they wouldn't recognize me. Wouldn't care to, either."

He closed his eyes for a moment. "Ari, I'm ... sorry."

She swore, her jaw clenched. "They're not worth being sorry over.

Damn their eyes, every one of them." She met his gaze again, and he could see the anger and the hurt warring in her face. "Every damn time I pray to Our Lady of the Ghosts, I'm only asking for one thing—I want them to die. I want them to suffer, I want every bite of food in their mouth to turn to ash and every touch of sun on their skin to burn, and every brush of their fine clothes against their body to feel like sandpaper."

He tightened his hand over hers, and didn't speak, and after a moment, she looked away. "Sorry," she muttered.

He managed a small smile. "You have nothing to apologize for." He paused. "I don't know if it makes you feel better, but if we do run into your parents, I'll happily hold your things while you punch them in the face."

She gave a small, humourless chuckle and turned back to the window. "Don't much matter, anyways. Don't plan on ever coming back here again, not if I can help it. First time back since I ran off, and far as I'm concerned, it was one time too many."

He nodded. "I can't blame you," he said, half under his breath.

The winding guilt that had tightened around his stomach on seeing Lawrence was still there, coiling through his insides. Lawrence had helped them escape. He should have turned them in, both of them knew it, but he'd helped them instead. He'd put his own damn life in danger, even though he'd owed Silas absolutely nothing.

Silas let out a short breath. "At any rate, it doesn't look like whoever was after us last night has picked up our trail again yet," he whispered. "I'll put word through to Recoil so he can have someone waiting to let us back down before they do."

Ari nodded, still staring out the window, and Silas slid the chip Recoil had given him into his comm and tapped through the message.

By the time they'd alighted from the transport and made their way back to the alley where they'd arrived, a woman was waiting for them. She gestured them to follow, and soon they were climbing back down the rusty ladder that led down to the rickety lift.

Ari didn't speak during their trip back down, and Silas didn't press her. When they reached the dirty streets of the Stacks, their guide led them quickly through the streets, the ubiquitous buzz of neon lights and creeping fingers of foul-smelling fog that wound around their legs, the stale air of the place, enough that Silas would have known where he was even if he'd been blindfolded.

They had to stop twice as ghosts drifted past. Once, one of them turned in their direction, the burning black pits of its eyes searching them out, and he closed his fingers around the sparker in his pocket. Then they were back at the dry-docks at last. He could feel his entire body relax as he stepped onto the *Sweet Jenny's* gangplank, and it was only then he realized how tense he'd been.

Gracie was waiting for them inside, talking to Recoil in a low voice. When she saw them, she smiled. "Got what you went for?" She asked.

Silas nodded, his stomach tightening uneasily at the reminder. "I have the chips. I didn't have time to look through them, but ..."

She raised her eyebrows, still with that hint of a smile playing on the corners of her lips. "Well, let's get ourselves back into space then, lad. And then why don't you do just that?"

11

Hollis

It was, generally speaking, a two-day flight to Blackrock, using the naval FTL lanes. But generally speaking, they were two or three ships of the line traveling through the jump lanes at one time.

This time, they were a fleet of seventeen fully crewed ships. Which meant that there was no way to take them all through the jump-lanes at once without breaking formation, which meant they were making a series of smaller jumps outside of the jump lanes to keep the fleet intact at all times.

The maneuver wouldn't have been possible without the new nav tech, and Hollis was impressed despite herself at the precision of the jumps. In addition, she had full confidence in her navigator's ability. That wasn't what was setting her teeth on edge.

It was the fact that the maneuver, ordered by the commodore, would put all seventeen ships in range of Blackrock at the same time, but to do so, it would add almost a full standard day to the travel time. Hollis knew damn well that an extra day of travel time meant one more day for word to leak out, one more day for the pirates to prepare for their arrival.

Her crew knew something was wrong. She could sense it in the air. Honestly, they would have been singularly imperceptive not to have guessed something—she knew she had nowhere near her first mate's ability to affect bland unconcern, whatever the circumstance, and nor did Emmett. Even Foster was noticeably more short than usual with their orders. But it wasn't like it had been on the voyage out to the *Agate*. Her crew, it appeared, had decided she was to be trusted, and seemed willing enough to put their fate in her hands. And that was perhaps more disconcerting than anything else.

But they didn't know everything. They didn't know the reason Hollis never went anywhere without an escort, or the reason for the worry in her first and second mates' faces as they watched her.

And, two days later, it appeared even that hadn't been enough.

She glanced down at the small needle tucked into the scrap of fabric in her hand.

Two days into the voyage, and someone was trying to kill her.

At least this time they'd tried poison, rather than a knife.

She had to deal with this, sooner rather than later. She couldn't afford the uncertainty, and she couldn't afford a distraction, not going into a battle like this one.

She gave a rueful sigh, her heart pounding hard and fast against her ribs.

Foster and Emmett would be furious. But she couldn't, at present, see a better option—she was the target, and therefore she was likely the only one who'd be able to draw her would-be killer out.

Best to get this over with.

Carefully, she tucked a stun-pistol into the pocket of her jacket, the metal of it cold against her palm. Then she pushed the door to her cabin open.

The young midship officer posted there sprang to attention. "Captain," she said quickly.

Hollis shook her head. "At ease, officer." She paused. "You didn't see anyone enter my cabin by any chance, did you?"

"No, Captain." The young woman looked on the verge of terror at being addressed by her captain, and Hollis managed a small smile.

"Thank you. Stay here, if you please. If anyone comes looking for me, I'm going down to the officer's quarters to speak with Mate Price. Don't let anyone into my cabin in my absence."

"Aye, Captain."

Hollis turned and made her careful way towards the lift.

When she stepped into the officers' mess, every head in the crowded room turned to her. Emmett, who was sitting with a group of senior officers over a game of whist, sprang to his feet and crossed over to her, concern on his face. "Captain?" he said, coming up to her. "Is anything wrong?"

She sighed. "I'm not sure," she said in a low voice. She glanced around, and raised her voice loud enough to carry. "I'm looking for Mate Price. Are they here?"

Emmett gave her a questioning look, but shook his head, a wry expression crossing his face. "You'll find Price in their quarters, I believe," he said.

Hollis raised her eyebrows, glancing around the officers' mess.

Emmett grinned. "Captain. If you've ever caught Price taking a break, you're ahead of me. Damn good officer, but they're going to work themself into an early grave at this rate." He paused. "Shall I ask someone to fetch them?"

She shook her head, keeping her voice pitched loud enough to be overheard. "No need. I'll go find them. The exercise will do me good."

Again, he gave her that questioning look, but she shook her head minutely.

Some part of her wanted to ask him to accompany her. But better that he stay here, and make it clear to everyone that she was alone.

The ship's corridors were all but deserted, and Hollis had to force herself to keep from glancing over her shoulder at every sound. She reached Foster's door without incident, but she could feel the cold sweat beading on her forehead.

She tapped on the door and waited.

"Come in," their muffled voice came at last, and Hollis pushed the door open.

Foster was seated at the small table, charts pulled up in front of them. Their elbows were on the table, a mug of coffee apparently forgotten in front of them, forehead creased in concentration. They glanced up as she stepped inside, then their eyebrows jumped and they shoved back their chair. "Captain?"

"Please, Mate Price, I'm not as fragile as all that," she said, gesturing them back into their seat.

Foster was already standing. "Sit down, Captain. What's happened?"

She shook her head, but took the proffered seat. "I wanted to speak with you about the mission." She paused. "I'd expected you to be in the officers' mess."

Foster sighed and pushed aside the mess of charts and calculations. "I thought I'd best memorize the charts and the new navigational specs, and it's not quiet enough in the mess to let me think."

Hollis studied them. "You're off duty, Foster. Surely you can study charts later?"

They glanced at her, a wry expression on their face. "Captain. I'd thought you, of all people, would understand."

She raised her eyebrows, waiting. At last, they sighed and gestured to the charts. "Greene can go gamble in the officers' mess, because if he makes a mistake in one of his calculations and someone catches it, they'll let him know and he'll fix it and no more will be said. But Greene is from the Level, and he's gone through the Academy. Those of us who aren't from the Level? Who haven't been Academy-trained? We don't have the luxury of making mistakes."

Hollis nodded slowly.

She remembered well enough the feeling—the desperate, never-ending quest, not only to be competent, but to be unimpeachable. To work yourself to the bone to avoid giving anyone even the faintest hint that you had a weakness that could be exploited.

But Foster had never been anything but calm and collected. Hollis had never sensed from them the desperation she'd always felt, deep inside herself.

And it was only now that she wondered if they simply hid it better than she had.

"Very good, Price," she said at last.

Foster was still watching her. They shook their head, still wearing that wry smile. "I'm sorry, Captain. It's not you. I suppose it's just habit by now." They brushed a weary hand across their face. "Now. What did you want to discuss?"

Hollis pulled her chair closer to the table, grimacing at the sharp stab of pain the movement brought. "I believe you've looked through the mission report we received this morning on liftoff, no?" she asked, her voice loud enough to be overheard.

Foster nodded, frowning.

Hollis sighed. "I don't like it. There's no plan in place in case of a pirate counter-attack, and I'm not confident that they'll roll over and show their bellies as easily as Commodore Webb seems to assume they will."

"Not with Mad Dog in charge, they won't," Foster muttered, half under their breath.

"Exactly." Hollis's voice was grim. "I'd like our crew drilling on the guns and prepared for a ship-to-ship engagement, should it be necessary. But I wanted to speak with you before I took the matter to Greene." She paused. "What do you know about Commodore Webb?"

Foster leaned back in their chair, a thoughtful expression on their face. "He's been a commodore for long enough that I think he's given up hope of advancement," they said slowly. "But as far as I know, he's never been a particularly ambitious man. Captained a ship for a good thirty years, and I think they promoted him only because there was no good reason not to. No scandals on his record, at least nothing public, but no notable successes, either."

Hollis shook her head in frustration. "Why would he not expect the pirates to fight back? And why the hell did Admiral Usher not back this mission? I went through everything I have access to, and I couldn't find out who in the Admiralty ordered this to go ahead. If the pirates had been more active than usual, I could maybe understand it. But this? I can't figure out what's behind it, or why. And as far as I know, having records like that classified is highly irregular—from everything I was told in the Academy, most routine missions have open information-access to the captains and officers."

Foster was still frowning. "That's the other thing I've been wondering about, Captain. I told you that the crew's records had been classified unavailable. That's unusual. But there's more to it than that—nothing about this mission is available, not the political side of it, not the personnel side of it. And the parliament meetings where it was discussed are all closed."

Hollis slapped her hand down on the table in frustration, then sighed, closing her fist. "It's times like these I wish to hell I'd paid more attention to Level politics back in the Academy."

Foster glanced at her with a small smile. "Well, if you're right, this is more political than either of us thought at the start of it all." They shook their head. "I agree with you—best to keep the crew sharp, and keep a weather eye open for any sign of things going wrong."

"I'll speak with Greene tomorrow, then," said Hollis. She hesitated a moment, then pulled the folded piece of cloth carefully out of her pocket and laid it on the table. Foster glanced down at it, then up at her, confusion in their face, and she pulled the folded cloth back to reveal a needle, glinting dully against the rough fabric.

"What's that?" they asked after a moment.

Hollis sighed, lowering her voice. "I found it tucked into the back of my chair," she said. "I ... tested it for poison."

Foster's expression had gone sharp with concern. "And?"

She nodded silently.

Foster swore, shoving back their chair. "God's sake, Captain, you could have led with that! Who had access to your cabin? Do we have any ideas?"

Hollis put a quick finger to her lips and gestured Foster back to their chair, glancing at the door.

Slowly, their eyes never leaving hers, Foster took their seat again.

When they were seated, Hollis leaned forward, speaking quietly enough that Foster had to lean forward as well to hear her. "I've taken your advice, and there's been someone with me at all times since launch. But I didn't set guards over my cabin, although I suppose I should have. This happened after we launched, I'm certain of it." She blew out a short breath. "The issue, Price, is that whatever this is, I think it has to do with this mission to Blackrock."

Foster ran a hand through their hair, but, thank God, kept their voice down. "The issue, Captain, is that you're going to be killed if we don't figure this out! I'm not entirely sure how you're not seeing that."

"Of course I see that," she snapped in a whisper. "Believe me, I have no desire to die, and I shall take all suitable precautions. But I happen to believe the wellbeing of the navy overrides my personal self-interest. I assumed you felt the same." She paused. "I suspect that whoever left this was waiting to see if they'd succeeded in killing me. I made no secret of the fact that I was coming to talk with you, and your cabin is far enough out of the way that they'd have a good chance of following me. I have my stun pistol with me. I hope they'll be worried enough about our conversation that they'll try to kill me on my way back. That will give me at least an even chance to find out who this is and what they want."

Foster's expression had gone instantly grim. "It'll be easier if you have backup," they said curtly, shoving back their jacket to reveal their own stun-pistol. "I'll call ahead to Greene to have sailors armed and ready in case something goes wrong. In the meantime, best not to wait until whoever it is manages to come up with a solid ambush plan."

Hollis nodded, pushing back her chair. "Thank you, Mate Price," she said, raising her voice again. "I shall certainly look into this further."

"Very good, Captain." Foster's voice was impressively bland, but she knew them well enough to hear the tension under it. "Please let me know if you need anything further from me."

"Of course." She stood, wincing a little at the movement.

Her hand was clenched around the stun-pistol in her pocket, her entire body tense as she pushed the door open and stepped out into the corridor. She almost expected a shot to ring out the moment she came into view, but instead, the sound of the door closing behind her was loud in the silence.

She could hear her own heartbeat in her ears, loud enough that she wished, irrationally, that it would quiet enough for her to listen.

But she couldn't afford to hesitate, and make whoever this was suspicious.

She turned and started down the corridor towards her cabin, making no effort, this time, to keep the pain from her posture or hide how her steps faltered.

She'd made it almost to the lift when she heard a sound from behind her.

She whirled, pistol in hand, then dived to the floor, biting back a grunt of pain as an energy blast sang over her head. She caught a confused glimpse of running figures, and she yanked up her stun pistol and fired at the closest. They staggered, but kept coming, and she fired again. The figure dropped, almost on top of her, then a second person grabbed her by the arm. Hollis gasped in pain, the pistol slipping from her fingers as she was dragged to her feet. The sharp tip of a knife skittered against her ribs, and she could feel her attacker's breath hot against her ear.

Then they stiffened, their grip on her loosening. She staggered, catching herself against the wall, and fumbled for her energy pistol, bracing herself for another attack … but it didn't come.

When she turned, a man in a petty officer's uniform was slumped on the ground, blood spreading in a bright stain across his shirt. Foster stood behind him, panting, a bloody cutlass in their hand and blood spattering their shirt and the white cuffs of their sleeves.

"Sorry, Captain," they said. "I couldn't get them with the stun pistol without risking hitting you, and if I'd missed, they'd have slit your throat and be done with it." They gestured to the ground, where a woman, also in an officer's uniform, lay limp. "I think that one's still alive, though, so we'll have someone to question."

Behind Hollis, a small group of armed sailors rounded the corner at a run, Emmett in their lead, his pistol drawn. He came up sharply at the scene, glancing between her and Foster. "Captain, Price. Are you alright?"

Hollis nodded, straightening with an effort.

Foster caught Emmett's eye. "I'll escort the captain back to her quarters," they said grimly. "I don't know if there's anyone else waiting, and I'd like to be sure. Can you handle this?"

Emmett nodded. "I'll ID the dead man, and get the woman somewhere secure." He turned to Hollis. "I'll notify you when she's conscious—I assume you'll want to interrogate her?"

"Yes. Thank you, Mate Greene." Now that the fight was over, Hollis's head was spinning with the pain.

Foster gestured to two of the sailors, and they fell into step behind Hollis as Foster took her arm.

She was grudgingly grateful for it—she doubted she'd have been able to walk without staggering.

At Foster's direction, the sailors scoured her cabin for any sign of additional tampering. Hollis watched, leaning on Foster to keep from swaying on her feet. Foster's expression was impassive, but she could feel the tension in their muscles.

At last, the sailors stepped outside, leaving the two of them alone.

"Well," she said, sinking into her chair with a groan of relief. "At least now we may get some answers."

Foster gave her a look. Their lips were pinched tight, their posture noticeably tense.

She sighed. "Price. If you have something to say, may as well say it."

They shook their head, and slowly took a seat across from her. "Captain. I don't mean to be disrespectful, but you were almost killed. Again."

"I took a risk, but I'd thought it through—"

Foster gave a sharp shake of their head. "I don't think you understand." They paused, as if searching for the words. "Do you not see this crew, Captain?" they said at last. "You've sailed before the mast. You know what it's like below decks, and how many cruel, and vicious, and incompetent captains are employed by the navy. Then here you come—a woman from the Stacks. A woman who'd have every right to lord her success over her crew, and you don't. You treat the sailors like humans, you run a strict ship, but not a cruel one. But that's not all—you stood up to Mad Dog. You volunteered to go with your sailors onto a dying ship, you got yourself cut to ribbons trying to rescue crew when you could have told them to leave the sailors and go after the weapons, or easier still, to back off and let Mad Dog have the *Agate*. Then, from what I hear from Greene, you volunteered to stay on the *Agate* to keep from turning ghost and harming your sailors, and when you realized saving the skiff may mean sacrificing the *Verity*, you were willing to let the skiff die, yourself on it." They paused. "Or so Greene tells me. I was, as you know, unable to receive your communications." Their tone had taken on a stiffness that told her that the matter was still something they'd very much prefer not to discuss.

They sighed. "Can't you see it? That's the stuff legends are made of. And the fact that the Admiralty clearly has it in for you only makes you more appealing for the sailors before the mast." They leaned forward. "I'd not say anything, but I think you don't realize what these sailors are willing to do for you. They'd walk into a bay full of ghosts if you ordered it, because they know you'd do it too. That's more power than most captains have. And when you put yourself in danger—it's not just you you're putting at risk. They'll run into danger after you to save you, and they won't think twice about it."

She watched them for a moment.

Foster believed what they were saying. She could see it in the set of their posture, the resigned expression on their face.

It was absurd on the face of it. But there had been something about how the crew had watched her—how Foster and Emmett had watched her …

She scowled, suddenly uncomfortable. "I'm only doing my duty as a naval captain," she snapped. "And if my crew would follow me into a bay full of ghosts, they're only doing their duty as crew. I don't know how you were trained, but my superior officers expected my life and death given to them as a condition of my position, whatever that position may be."

Foster sighed, dropping their head wearily. "And you never fought them on it."

"I swore my life to the navy when I signed up. That was hardly something I was going to renegotiate."

At last, Foster raised their head. "Even after everything they did to you? Even after how they treated you, you still believed they deserved your loyalty?"

Hollis was almost surprised at the quick rush of anger that washed through her. "They all assumed that because of where I was born, I was worth less," she hissed. "I was less loyal, less trustworthy, less capable of making sacrifices. Surely they believed the same of you?"

She leaned forward. "But I will be damned to hell if I prove them right."

Foster was quite a long moment, studying her. "Even if it kills you?" they asked at last, softly. "Because what I told you about your crew wasn't just words. There are people who'll die to save you, and you'll be condemning them too."

"That would be their choice," said Hollis, her tone frigid.

Foster raised their eyebrows, then huffed out a soft, humourless laugh. "Of course, Captain." They rose, their face dropping back into its usual bland, competent mask. "Now, if you're open to my advice, I believe it would be wise to set a watch at your door before you go to sleep tonight."

12

Silas

By the time Silas had stripped out of his Level clothing and was back into his shipboard kit, and had passed the information they'd found on the fleet over to Gracie, Ari was already changed and out on deck, calling out orders over the comm. He could hear the strain in her voice, and she barely glanced at him as he came out on deck, just gestured him to the pressure room with a jerk of her thumb.

He didn't mind, honestly. His muscles were still tight from the shock of being back at the Academy, however briefly, and he was trying, very hard, not to think about it.

Ari, he assumed, would be doing the same.

When at last they'd left the Stacks behind, and he'd finished resetting the pressure gages, he found Ari on the main deck. "Ari," he said, "Captain said she'd send on what we had on the fleet back to the captains on Blackrock." He hesitated. "She … asked me to go through the documents we stole. She thinks there might be something there she can use."

"Yeah," Ari said after a moment. She still looked paler than usual, and she didn't quite meet his eye. "Told Freddie and the others you wouldn't be available. Figured that's what Captain'd have you doing."

He paused. "Ari, listen—"

She turned on him. "Get below, damn you!" Her voice was tight.

He glanced at her face, then sighed and turned away towards the crew's bunk.

It was empty, thank God, and he sank down on his hammock.

His hands shook as he pulled up the documents on his comm.

The documents he'd run off with, weeks before, were the transcripts of the trials.

These documents contained the evidence.

This was where the details behind the faulty FTL drives were laid out in brutal detail, the documents that showed exactly how his parents had died. This was the information the navy would have killed him for, rather than let it get out.

And he was suddenly not entirely sure he wanted to know what was inside them.

He wasn't sure how long he'd been reading. His muscles had stiffened, and there was a dull ache in his back where he'd slumped down on his hammock. But he couldn't bring himself to care.

The words scrolled on the holo-page in front of his face, glowing dimly in the darkened crew's quarters.

He was certain that if he closed his eyes, the words would glow behind his eyelids, stark against his vision. He could shut off the documents floating over his comm. He wasn't sure he'd ever be able to stop the words scrolling through his mind, stamped into his brain and pushing ghostly fingers through his memories and into his imagination.

He'd known the bare facts of how his parents had died—a naval accident that had taken out an entire fleet of ships of the line, due to a flaw in the FTL drive.

But somehow, he'd imagined … something other than this.

They'd died screaming. There were documents that explained exactly what effect the catastrophic failure of the FTL drive would have had on the bodies of the sailors on the ships that had been lost; atoms pulled apart, bodies vaporized, but slowly enough to allow their nerve endings to send signals to their brain, slowly enough to let the agony and the horror of the whole thing register, slowly enough to let them die screaming. An agonizing, horrific, unthinkable death, but somehow that wasn't the worst of it.

The worst of it was the bland, dry documents that laid out the decision-making process. The impersonal warnings that safety procedures were being ignored, that safety tests weren't coming out clean. The terse replies. The impassioned pleas, increasingly frantic, from the experienced technicians. The warnings of what exactly would happen should the FTL drives be released without further testing. The notes threatening legal action, defamation suits, should word of any of this be leaked to the press.

The testimony afterwards—bland, insincere regret.

The graph of distributed profits, before the FTL company went bankrupt from the scandal.

He felt sick to his stomach, emptied. Hollowed out, somehow.

He'd grown up with stories of his parents' bravery, their heroic deaths in the tragedy. The traitorous vice-admirals who'd sabotaged the ships, on the payroll of the Rosette System. And he'd believed them. He'd believed every word. He'd taken orders that had originated with people whose names he'd seen on these documents— their terse responses refusing the testimony of their own experts that the FTL drives were not ready. And he'd believed, every moment that he'd done it, that he'd been honouring the memories of his parents, rather than spitting on their graves.

Gracie had asked for the technical details of the fatal flaw in the FTL drive, to use for whatever it was she was planning. He'd found them quickly, prominent in the reams of evidence that had been presented to the military court behind closed doors.

But even after he'd found them, he couldn't seem to stop reading. He couldn't seem to pull his eyes from the screen, even though part of him wanted to, even though part of him was screaming and dying along with the thousands of naval sailors who were lost in the disaster.

"Sil?"

He looked up with a start, and it took him a moment to recognize Gracie's voice through his comm.

He fumbled for the button to answer her, his fingers thick and clumsy. "Captain?"

There was a moment's pause, then Gracie's voice again, still mild, but this time with a touch of concern. "You alright, lad?"

Again, it took him a moment to remember how to answer. "I'm … fine," he said at last. "Everything's fine."

It was a lie, and Gracie would know it was a lie, but he wasn't sure, at this point, what the truth was. He wasn't sure how to articulate what the long, unending, relentless stream of words had done to him.

He wasn't sure he knew.

He'd seen, back in the navy, sailors sliced wide open, wounds that would kill them in minutes, who didn't seem to realize what had happened to them. Who, for a few merciful moments, didn't seem to feel the pain of the wound that would kill them. The chief medical officer on the first ship he'd served on had told him once, half in jest, that if a sailor was injured and screaming, she wasn't worried. It was when they didn't scream that she worried. Because if you were hurt badly enough that your brain couldn't process what had happened— it meant something was seriously wrong.

That was how he felt, right now.

"You got through those documents?" Gracie asked.

"Aye, Captain." His voice sounded strange in his own ears.

"Well then. Why don't you come up and show me what you have?"

"Aye, Captain." He pushed himself upright, trying not to let himself think. Trying not to let himself take in what he'd read.

He wasn't sure exactly how he made his way to Gracie's cabin. He was certain, somehow, that when he sat down, he'd managed to compose his expression into something fixed and emotionless.

She watched him a moment without speaking. He'd come to expect that from Gracie. But this time he hardly noticed.

The knowledge of what he'd read was humming under his skin, buzzing in his brain like adrenalin, his muscles shaking with it.

"Find what you were looking for, lad?" she asked at last.

He nodded brusquely and pulled a note up over his comm, sending it to hover over her wrist comm with a flick of his fingers.

She glanced over it quickly. "You got me what I asked for, right enough." She looked up, and there was something far too perceptive in her gaze. "And you went back to the Level. Back to the Academy, I hear tell. So." She paused. "You rethink your loyalties, Sil? You haven't sworn onto my crew for more'n this quick hop to the Level, and there're a hell of a lot of ships of the line waiting back on Blackrock to blow us into space dust. Can't say as I'd blame you if you wanted to part ways, or at least to lay low until things settle a bit and you and I can discuss those documents we agreed on. If you'll stay on, I'll be happy to have you. But you'd best know—I'll be using this information you gave me to strike back against those naval ships. You willing to come with us, use this against the navy as killed your parents and mine? This'll have to be your own choice—I won't force you." Her mouth quirked into the hint of a smile. "Known you long enough that I'm not sure I could if I wanted to."

Silas met her gaze without flinching. His voice was oddly steady. "I'll sign onto your crew again, if you'll have me. You gave me your word you'd look over my documents, but I'm willing to wait on that. And in the meantime—" He leaned forward, resting his forearms on his knees, his eyes never leaving hers. "In the meantime, Captain, if you'd like to take down the ships of the line—all I ask is that you show them as little mercy as they showed you."

She raised her eyebrows, considering him. At last, she nodded. "Well, Sil. Looks like you and I are after the same thing."

13

Hollis stood on the bridge, her hands clasped behind her back, her jaw clenched, watching her navigator tap in the coordinates of the next jump.

Her head ached dully. She wasn't sure she'd slept more than an hour in a stretch since they'd killed one of her would-be assassins and captured the other.

The woman had refused to talk. Hollis, Foster, and Emmett had all taken turns questioning her, but she sat in the corner and refused to say a word. And with the approaching battle with the pirates, Hollis hardly had the attention to spare for the prisoner.

There hadn't been any more attempts on her life, at least. But she still found herself waking from nightmares of a hand around her throat, a knife glinting in the moonlight, raised over her head.

Just as often, she woke from nightmares of Mad Dog's laconic voice through the *Verity's* comm. *"Best pray to whatever you pray to for mercy. Because you'll get none from me. I know what your navy does to pirates when you capture us. And I swear to you, Captain of the Verity—you'll be begging for a fate that easy."*

Whatever Commodore Webb knew about Blackrock, Hollis was willing to wager every credit chit she owned that he'd never gone up against Mad Dog. Hollis had heard stories of the woman all her life, and even then she'd managed to underestimate her. And she knew, in her bones, that the pirate captain wouldn't sit idly by while the navy sent a fleet to bomb the *Sweet Jenny's* berth, without fighting back.

"Coming out of jump in three. Two. One. Coming out." The navigator's voice rang through the bridge, and Hollis braced herself unconsciously for the disorienting sensation. Around them, the rest of the ships of the line flickered into view on the *Verity's* screens.

"Very good, Wilkes," she said brusquely. "Prepare to jump again on the *Resolve's* signal."

She stared at the screen in front of her, watching along with her navigator for the signal.

The next jump would put them in range of Blackrock.

The commodore had decided they'd jump in close, rather than jump at a distance and run in the remainder of the way. It meant they'd be able to start firing almost immediately, but it also meant that they'd have no reconnaissance of the surrounding space. It was entirely possible they were jumping directly into a trap.

The signal flickered across the *Verity's* comm screen, marked with the commodore's code.

"Wilkes. Jump on the *Resolve's* signal," Hollis snapped.

"Aye, Captain," said Wilkes, her eyes glued to the screen. "Jump on my count. Three. Two. One. Jumping."

Hollis braced herself against the quick rush of disorientation as the FTL drive engaged. "Very good, Wilkes," she said. "Your bridge. I shall be on the captain's deck preparing the crew, and then I shall be in my cabin preparing my weapons."

"Aye, Captain," Wilkes murmured, her attention fixed on the screens.

Hollis turned and strode off the bridge, tapping her comm through to Greene's line. "Mate Greene," she said. "Please assemble the crew. We'll be coming out of jump in range of Blackrock within three hours."

When Foster tapped at her door, she looked up with a start. "Yes, Mate Price?"

"Captain. Wilkes asked me to inform you that we'll be coming out of jump in the next fifteen minutes."

Hollis closed her eyes.

A bright thrill of excitement pounded in her blood, despite every damn misgiving she'd had about this mission from the get-go.

She was captain of her own ship. They were going up against the pirates at Blackrock, and her pistol was clean and her cutlass was sharp and her crew was ready for action, trained on the guns to Emmett's exacting standards.

"Thank you, Mate Price," she said, pushing back her seat. "I'll be up directly."

Foster was waiting for her as she emerged from her cabin, and they kept pace with her as she made her way down the corridor to the lift. As much as she hated it, the ratlines were still absurdly outside of her current abilities, but the wait for the lift always felt like a thousand burning needles pricking under her skin.

Foster waited beside her with no visible impatience, because of course they did.

She drew in a deep breath, and forced herself not to scowl in their direction.

They tempered their pace to match hers as she made her slow

way to the bridge, stepping in just a fraction behind her, as always.

The eyes of the entire bridge turned on her as she came in, but she ignored them, crossing over to the screens.

"Wilkes," she said after a moment. "Please broadcast the count for coming out of jump across the ship."

"Aye, Captain," said Wilkes, her voice short with nerves.

"Officer Harris." Hollis tapped her comm through to the weapons master. "Have the guns up and the crews ready to engage the moment we come out of jump. Greene will count you down."

"Aye, Captain," Harris said through the comm.

Hollis turned to where Emmett was standing, his brows drawn together, face tight with worry. "Mate Greene. Have the secondary gun crews prepared to relieve them in case of injury or death. Please also have armed crews at every airlock, prepared to repel boarders. We don't know what we're coming into, and I'd like to be ready for any circumstance."

"Aye, Captain," said Emmett. He strode out of the bridge, and she watched him go.

"Coming out of jump in five minutes." Wilkes's voice over the ship's comm was loud enough, almost, to make Hollis start.

She nodded without speaking, and kept her gaze fixed on the screens. Her heart was pounding quick in anticipation.

"Captain. The gunner crews are at the ready, and there are crews stationed at each airlock, under the command of one of the petty officers, to repel boarders." Emmett's voice floated through her earpiece.

"Thank you, Mate Greene," she said.

"Coming out of jump in one minute."

Beside her, Foster's posture was tense. She knew, without looking, that they were watching the bridge crew, scanning the screens for any sign of trouble. The position of first mate carried with it the responsibility for the running of the ship, and she'd never seen Foster be anything but perfectly competent.

"Coming out of jump on my count. Three. Two. One. Coming out."

The ship shuddered just a little, the disorienting jolt as the FTL drive disengaged, and the black of space reformed around the ship, visible through the plex windows and written across the ship's screens. Around them, the rest of the fleet flickered into view, phasing back into running space within firing range of the small, rocky moon that held the pirates' stronghold, caught in the orbit of a massive, deadly gas planet.

Hollis found she was bracing herself unconsciously for a rapid-fire burst of pirate weapons, for ships swarming out of the channels in the porous rock of the moon that served as docking bay ports for the pirates—but none came.

The scene around them was almost eerily still.

"Captain Ives." The voice came over the ship's comm, the imperious tones of Commodore Webb. "Into formation, if you please. Fire on my signal."

"Aye, Commodore," she said, tapping the comm. She turned to Wilkes. "Bring us into position." Her breath was still coming quick and short, adrenalin humming in her veins.

She watched on the ship's screens as the *Verity* moved into position on the starboard edge of the formation. The other ships were moving ponderously into position as well, into a formation that would allow them to concentrate fire in the most efficient manner on their target—the ugly black bulk of the moon that held the pirate settlement.

"On my mark." The commodore's voice over the comm was loud

in the silence of the cabin. "Three. Two. One. Fire at will."

"Mate Greene," Hollis snapped at the same time, and she heard his barked order over the comms. The *Verity* shuddered with the release of the broadside, the missiles arcing towards the pitted moon. The ships around them were releasing their broadsides as well, the shots showing on the *Verity's* tracking screen as a flurry of brilliant bursts.

"Again!" Emmett barked, and the ship trembled with another broadside.

A few endless minutes later, she could see through the screens the first round of missiles impacting on the surface of Blackrock.

Hollis found she was braced unconsciously for a rumble of counter-fire from the moon's surface—surely the pirates had some form of surface weapons, even if they weren't a political collective they'd certainly cooperate enough to maintain a surface defence—but there was nothing. No answering fire, no flash on the *Verity's* screens.

"They must have gone underground," Foster murmured, low enough that only she could hear. She could tell by their tone, though, that they were as uneasy about this as she was. "It's possible that they're waiting out the damage in the deeper caves. It would be the intelligent thing to do—we don't have the weapons to penetrate that deep, and the mission doesn't include landing ground troops."

Hollis nodded. "Possible, yes," she said, her own voice as quiet as theirs. "But do you honestly believe Mad Dog would take the cautious route when there's a chance to hit back against the navy?"

The second round of missiles hit. Hollis was clenching her jaw so tightly it ached.

"Captains," came the commodore's voice through the comm. "It appears we won't be facing counter-fire. In the circumstances, we shall proceed to do as much damage to the moon and its infrastructure as possible. With that aim, please move the formation forward three points and continue firing."

"Aye, Commodore," Hollis said, the response coming automatically.

Her stomach was tight with a mix of anticipation and dread.

Maybe the commodore was right. Maybe the pirates had no intention of fighting back.

But she couldn't quite make herself believe it.

The ships of the line moved as a body, the entire formation shifting in and closer to the moon's surface.

"Fire at will," came the Commodore's voice through the line, and Hollis relayed the command to Emmett. Again, the ship shuddered with the release of the broadside, and, a minute later, the crackle of the impact against the moon's surface sparkled on the *Verity's* screens.

Hollis was never entirely certain, afterwards, if something had caught her attention, something her conscious mind hadn't had the time to parse, or if some intuition had screamed out a warning, but she was already turning, mouth half-open to shout out an order, when the blast rippled out from the surface of the planet.

"Back!" she shouted. "Wilkes, get us back, now! Greene, get the sailors to anchor in, we're pulling back!"

Her navigator was already hunched forward, her hands flying over the controls. Vaguely, Hollis could hear the others in the bridge shouting, hear the engineer yelling something, and then the wave of the blast hit, throwing her to the ground.

Alarms blared, the bridge in complete chaos, and she shoved herself to her feet, ignoring the knife-blade of pain. Wilkes slumped over the controls, blood pouring from a gash across her head, and the sensors were going wild. Hollis staggered over and pushed the unconscious woman out of the way, yanking the controls back, and the *Verity* shuddered and jerked, the controls fighting against her grip.

She cursed. "Price! Find me a goddamn technician, and tell them to switch us over to auxiliary power. That was a goddamn electromagnetic pulse. Our main running engines are dead, and we need to get the hell out of here."

"Aye, Captain." Foster's voice was tight with strain, and they turned quickly out the door.

"Ghost!"

Hollis spun at the panicked shout, yanking out her sparker.

Wilkes' crumpled body lay where it had fallen.

And above it, her fully formed ghost.

Hollis choked out a curse as the ghost's hand closed around the shoulder of the nearest bridge crew. The woman's terrified scream cut off as the ghost's teeth ripped out her throat, sending blood spraying across the deck in a scarlet arc.

The body fell to the deck, and the ghost sprang at another of the crew.

Hollis shoved herself forward, sparker glowing.

One of the junior navigators had jumped forward as well, their sparker jabbing through the ghost from the other side. The ghost spun on the man, its clawed fingers tearing through his chest, reaching through the white bone of his ribcage to the soft organs within. He fell to the deck screaming, a horrible, gurgling sound— then Hollis's sparker found its mark.

She stepped through the fading blue plasma of the dispersed ghost, jabbing her sparker into the haze forming over the dead man's body, then turned.

The young bridge officer was lying in a red pool of blood, head tipped back at an unnatural angle, but there was no telltale blue haze around her body.

Hollis sagged with relief, gasping for breath.

The bridge was in chaos, people shouting, screaming, the deck slippery with blood.

She straightened with an effort. "Belay that at once!" she shouted over the noise. "Is this a ship of the line, or a damn circus? You're naval sailors, bloody act like it! Get to your damn posts and wait my command!"

"Captain! Power switching over to auxiliary!" Foster snapped over the comm.

"Acknowledged." Hollis slid back into the dead navigator's seat and shoved the switch over, and the *Verity* steadied a little under her hand.

She let out a quick breath of relief as the ship pulled back, the auxiliary running engines humming with the sudden increase of strain.

Then they steadied, and Hollis finally had time to glance up at the screens.

The other ships of the line were floundering, the formation shattered by the electromagnetic pulse of the explosion.

"They must have set it to go off when our explosives hit deep enough," the junior navigator said, her voice low and frightened.

Hollis nodded without speaking.

They'd managed to pull out, switch over to auxiliary, but the *Verity* had been on the starboard edge of the formation, out of the main path of the burst. Not all the other ships had been so lucky.

There was a creeping numbness settling over her.

There was no way the pirates should have had weapons like that. Those were military-grade, stronger than she'd ever seen. There was no way anyone on Blackrock should have been able to get their hands on that caliber of weapon. And even if they had—the pirates would have needed a precise knowledge of the composition of the fleet, and the weapons they'd be using, in order to set the trap that precisely.

"We're out of range of another burst," she said at last, dropping her hands from the controls. "Take the controls, Officer Davis. And get a medical officer in here to see to the injured."

"Aye, Captain," the junior navigator murmured, slipping into place as Hollis stood. Someone else was muttering into their comm, presumably calling in a medic.

Hollis's muscles still tingled with the strain, her body tight with adrenalin, but the bridge had calmed—the officers still grim-faced and pale, but the panic gone.

Then, from the corner of her eye, she caught a flicker on the screens.

She swore and strode over to them. "Officer," she snapped to the technician. "Pull up the diffraction scanner, if you would."

The man leapt forward to do as she asked.

All of them stared at the screen as ship after ship after ship flickered into view.

Pirate ships.

Hollis swore, the sound loud in the sudden utter stillness.

It had been a trap, after all. And now the pirates were coming in to collect their prize.

14

There was a moment of stunned silence in the cabin. Then Hollis tapped her wrist comm and snapped, "Greene! Crews on the weapons and the shields, get them firing!" She didn't wait for his response, just hit the ship's comm. "Commodore," she said, her voice sounding oddly calm in the wild chaos of the ship. "Pirate ships, approaching the fleet from the stern. They're cloaked, but visible with a diffraction scanner."

She could already see through the screens other of the ships of the line, those that were still functional, at least, turning broadside to the approaching pirates, so she couldn't have been the only one who'd seen the threat.

"Ready and waiting your orders, Captain," said Emmett a moment later.

"Hold fire until my command," said Hollis. She was on her feet again, supporting herself against the control table, her eyes fixed on the screen. Adrenalin pumped through her veins, steadying her hands and pushing the searing pain of her weeks-old injury to the back of her mind.

The pirate ships were splitting up, and in a moment she could see their strategy—cut off the ships that had taken the worst damage from the electromagnetic pulse and take them apart while other pirate ships kept the rest of the fleet busy in self-defence.

She cursed under her breath.

This strategy had Mad Dog's name written all over it.

But she'd gone up against Mad Dog before, and lived to tell about it.

She narrowed her eyes, studying the screen, tracking the movements of the ships.

A couple smaller pirate vessels were coming for the *Verity*, but their courses weren't straight on. Clearly, they didn't know how badly her ship had been damaged, and they didn't want to take chances.

"Captain. There's a ship within firing range," Emmett said through the lines.

"Hold your fire, Greene," she said tersely. "Let them get closer. Keep on the shields, but don't show them our heavy weapons."

There was a moment's pause. "Aye, Captain," he said at last.

The ship drew closer. Hollis watched it, her teeth gritted.

"Captain, they've opened fire on us with their heavies." Emmett's voice was strained.

"Acknowledged. Hold your fire." Somehow, she managed to keep her voice calm. "Foster, please keep me informed on the level of damage we're taking."

Shots blossomed out from the first pirate ship, and Hollis watched them through the screen, felt her ship shudder at the impact.

This wasn't the *Sweet Jenny*, though. The *Sweet Jenny* was a legend. This pirate ship didn't have the power to take a ship of the line apart without getting in range of her heavy weapons.

It hung back a moment, and another pirate ship joined it.

"We're taking damage to the shields, captain," came Foster's voice through her comm.

"How long can the shields hold?" Hollis asked brusquely.

"With this level of firepower? Maybe twenty minutes. But if they get in closer with their light weapons, it'll be less."

"Acknowledged." Hollis could feel the grim thrill of it seeping through her muscles. "Emmett, send them a warning shot from the light weapons."

"Aye, Captain." A barrage of shots hummed out from the *Verity*, just out of range of the pirate ships.

The ships seemed to have finally decided that the *Verity* was badly enough damaged, because they came in closer, just out of range of her light weapons, increasing the strength of their barrage.

"Mate Greene," Hollis snapped through the comm. "Have the gunners on the heavy guns lock in their aim. Prepare to fire on my order. Keep the gunners on the light weapons firing in the meantime."

"Aye, Captain." Emmett's voice was thick with relief. "Gunners locked in," he called a moment later.

Hollis studied the scene in front of her.

The pirates were sitting just out of range of the light weapons, firing their heavies at the *Verity*. From the volume of shots coming their way, they'd pulled power from their shields to give more power to their guns.

"Fire!" she snapped.

Greene barked the command, and the screen lit with yellow streaks of energy.

The pirate ships jerked and bucked under the barrage, too close in to pull back out of range.

"Greene. Fire at will," she called.

The volume of shots from the *Verity* increased. One of the pirate ships was pulling back, but the other seemed to be having trouble, the *Verity's* shots impacting against its shields, shoving it back by main force.

It exploded, a quick burst of light swallowed up instantly by the surrounding black.

She could hear the whoops of the gunners through her comm, but the *Verity's* weapons fire didn't let up, following the remaining pirate ship until it was out of range.

"Shall I put the gunners on the missiles, Captain?" She could hear the repressed jubilation in Emmett's voice.

"No," she said. "Hold fire. Wait my command."

She studied the screen quickly.

The *Verity* had gotten off lightly. She'd been uninjured, and near the edges of the battle.

Pirate ships were swarming the commodore's ship, the *Resolve.* They were focused on the ships near what had been the centre of the formation, and from the looks of it, the naval ships didn't have the firepower to fight back.

But there were a handful of other ships near the edges who seemed to have gotten off as cleanly as the *Verity*.

Hollis stepped over to the ship's communicator and tapped through to the two-hundred-crewed ship that had been beside her in the formation. "This is the captain of the *Verity*, paging the *Destiny*," she said through the comm.

"This is the captain of the *Destiny.*" The woman's voice was tight with panic.

"Captain," she said. "I think if you and I perform a pincer maneuver, we can bring the *Resolve* out. How are your guns?"

"Guns are functional," the woman said after a moment. "Heavies have taken damage, but we can still shoot, and the light guns are undamaged."

"Shields?"

"Our shields are at full power, other than the pirate damage we've taken since the fight."

Hollis let out a short breath of relief. "Very good. On my mark." She turned to the internal ship's comm. "Mate Greene. We will be going in. Please have the gunners ready on the shields."

"Aye, Captain." By this time, his voice was calm, as clipped and businesslike as she'd grown accustomed to.

The captain of the *Destiny* had been right—her ship's guns, although not as strong as the *Verity's*, were enough that between the two ships, they were able to push back the pirate ships around the *Resolve*. More ships called in through the com as they went, and soon there was a half-formation of them, doing the brutal work of pushing the pirates back. Besides the initial ambush, it didn't appear that the pirate ships had a cohesive strategy, and soon enough the pirate captains began to pull their ships back.

Hollis stayed at the bridge, holding herself upright with almost nothing but willpower as the battle raged on. She refused to leave the bridge, and she refused to sit, because she had to be able to stride between the screens, call out over the comm, shout instructions to the navigator or to her first and second mates.

The pain in her gut had become a background noise, sometimes faded, sometimes rising to drown almost everything else, and there was a reddish haze over her vision, the muscles in her hands cramped from gripping the edge of the control panel to keep herself upright. When Foster finally came up to join her, they took one look at her and caught her elbow surreptitiously.

Hollis realized, with a vague sense of surprise, that she'd been about to fall over.

"Captain," said Foster in a low voice. "Please for the love of God sit down."

She wanted to protest, but at this point she was so exhausted she wasn't sure her mouth could form the words, even if her brain could form an argument.

"Thank you, Price," she said instead, her voice coming out weaker than she'd anticipated. Foster pulled a seat over, and she sank into it with a sigh of desperate relief she couldn't hold back.

Foster pulled up the screen, tilted so that it was easily visible from where she was sitting.

"How are the shields?" she asked.

"They'll hold." Foster's voice was as polite and proper as always, and it was only the clipped tone in it that told her how exhausted they must be.

She looked back at the screen, and her first mate's gaze followed hers. "I think we have them running," Foster said.

"I should hope so." Hollis could hear the strain in her own voice, but she was too tired to try to mask it. "How many sailors have we lost?"

"We lost one section of the gunners, when the pressure went in their compartment," Foster said, after a moment. "And we have a few dozen injuries from the ship's gunfire."

Hollis swore. A section gone meant they'd lost at least twenty sailors.

Twenty people who'd put their lives in her hands, and who'd died following her orders.

Sickness rose in her stomach, winding together with the lancing pain, but she shoved it down ruthlessly. She'd have time to deal with that later.

Foster sent her a sympathetic glance, then turned to face the screen again.

Most of the injured ships had been pulled clear. They'd watched the *Merit* explode before their eyes, the pirates turning their guns frantically on the massive ship of the line as its rescuers approached.

She wouldn't think about it right now, the loss of life, the destruction. They still had work to do.

But by some miracle, they were pushing the pirates back. The ambush hadn't turned into an utter disaster. And right now, perhaps that was the most she could ask.

15

Gracie

Gracie watched Silas from the corner of her eye as she studied the note he'd sent over to her wrist comm, detailing what he'd found.

They were only a few hours out from Blackrock. The *Sweet Jenny* would have missed the ambush, although she'd prepared the other captains for that possibility. But if this information was what she hoped it was …

Silas reached in his pocket and dropped the remainder of the chips onto her desk, pushing them across to her, and stood abruptly. His hand gripped the edge of the desk, his posture tense.

She half expected him to start pacing her small cabin. Instead, he stood where he was, but the tension vibrating through him was enough to set her teeth on edge.

"What is it, lad?" she asked at last, pushing the note to one side and looking up at him.

His face was pale, and there was a sharp hurt under the anger in his expression that gave her a sudden pang.

She'd been the one to send the boy back up for these documents.

And she'd known exactly what he'd find.

The truth, yes. But he'd been raised in the navy. That had been his life, as much as it had been hers, before she'd been accused of treason.

And she could still remember the horrible, hopeless, unthinkable disorientation of that moment—of realizing the thing she'd given her life to had betrayed her. That the rock she'd built her whole self around had melted like sugar in water, leaving her groundless and lost.

She'd done the same to him. She could see it in his face, and she'd heard it in his voice when he'd told her to show them no mercy.

It hadn't been her that betrayed him. The Level and the navy had done that all on their own. But she'd been the one to open his eyes to it, in a way that was irrevocable and unretractable, and she couldn't hide from the fact.

But, a small part of her whispered, it couldn't have possibly been any more cruel than what he'd done to her. It couldn't have possibly been more cruel than opening up wounds she'd thought were healed, or at least scarred over, and exposing the raw, bleeding flesh underneath. She'd thought she'd come to terms with her banishment. She'd thought she'd come to terms with her life, with what the Admiral had done to her, what the Level had taken from her. She'd reached a place where she could be at peace.

Jenny, laughing up at her, eyes sparkling. "We'll do it, Grace. Once we graduate, we'll be admirals before you know it. They'll tell stories about us to the cadets, and we'll laugh about it in our admiralty offices."

"Side-by-side offices, of course." She'd been laughing too, she couldn't help it when Jenny laughed.

"Of course." Jenny's face had gone serious with an effort, but her eyes still twinkled with merriment. "I'd hardly accept it otherwise."

Gracie watched her—the cool shadows shaping her face, contrasting with the bright spark of her gaze, the brilliance of her white-gold hair, the quiet, calculating intelligence of her. She shone like a star, distant and beautiful and perfect, and yet somehow, still, Gracie's.

It caught in her throat sometimes, threatened to choke her, how much she loved this woman. How much Jenny had become her whole world. How everything she'd wanted and dreamed of and worked for paled next to this one woman.

She'd die for Jenny. She'd said it a hundred times, half in jest, but it was true. She'd do anything—anything at all—for Jenny Usher. It was a truth she knew in her bones. She'd burn the world and walk through the flames. Because losing Jenny would be like losing the star she charted her course by, and somehow, deep down, she knew she wouldn't survive it.

She closed her eyes against the stabbing, twisting pain of the memory.

With her promise to Silas to look over the documents he'd brought, she'd gained herself a weapon. And she'd lost any pretence that she could carry on with her life as it was, skirting around the edges, harrying the navy when they sent out their ships. She'd lost any pretence of caring how many of their people she'd take down in order to take down the Admiral.

She'd lost any pretence she could live in a world with Judith Usher, without one of them dying for it.

There was an ache in her chest, a tight, suffocating pain that had become so familiar over the years that she scarcely noticed it, sometimes.

But now she thought, perhaps, that it might kill her.

She shook her head ruefully, and glanced at the lad in front of her.

Look at the two of them—hurt, angry, lashing out.

But she, at least, was old enough to be strategic about it.

He still hadn't spoken. At last, he shook his head, dropping his gaze. "They knew, Gracie," he said, has voice so quiet she had to strain to hear it. "They knew what they were doing when they sent those ships out. And not one of them ever paid for it. Not a one of them. They didn't pay for it, because every damn person on the Naval High Command was complicit. They let it happen." He glanced up, and she could see the fury, barely controlled, in his gaze. "Every damn person in the navy is complicit in this, and I'll do whatever you need me to to help take them down."

Gracie drew in a long breath, pushing back the guilt. "Thank you, lad. You've done plenty for the moment. Now, get along with you. I think Freddie was looking to get the joint seams greased."

He gave her a short nod and turned away, his footsteps sharp off the deck.

She sighed, watching after him.

Freddie'd be good for him right now—she'd set him a task that would leave him too tired to think afterwards, and Gracie knew well enough what a mercy that would be.

After a moment, she tapped her comm. "Temple. Come to my cabin, if you please."

"Aye, Captain," he answered almost immediately. "Be there in a moment."

She turned back to the note Silas had sent her, skimming through it as she waited.

There was a knot of grim anticipation forming in the pit of her stomach.

This was exactly what she'd hoped it would be.

She looked up as Temple stepped into the room—a small man, with olive skin and a mild expression. "Captain? What is it?" he asked.

She smiled. "Temple. I'd like you to look at something for me."

He frowned, but came around to the edge of her desk. She turned the note towards him, then pulled up another on her comm and set it to hover beside the first. "You recognize that tech?"

He was still frowning, but he nodded slowly. "Aye, Captain, that I do. Them's the specs we got from the ship as picked up the classified naval broadcast, isn't it?"

She nodded. "And what about this?" She gestured at the specs from the classified documents Silas had given her.

Temple looked them over, eyebrows raised. At last he looked up at her. "Not sure what you're showing me here, Captain, but this is the same technology. A bit older, but you can see it's based off the same design."

"What you're looking at is the specs of the FTL drives that went up in the Starfire naval disaster," she said softly.

There was a moment of silence. Then she could see the understanding dawning on Temple's face. "They used the same basic concept in their navigation equipment," he said slowly. "They modified the design and incorporated it into their nav systems. Can see how that'd be useful, but I wouldn't have thought they'd have dared."

She nodded again, her smile widening just a touch. The knot in her stomach was tight enough she could feel it, hard and heavy in her gut. "Aye, they did that." She paused. "Didn't send Sil and Ari up to the Level just for information on the fleet. We needed that information, yes, and I figure our friends back at Blackrock have already put it to good use, but that wasn't the only thing. I asked Sil to get me these documents, because I figure we may be able to do more than just take down a couple of naval ships, at the price of a few of ours." She tapped the specs, leaning forward. "They fixed up the problem that led to the FTL drives failing, then they used the tech for their nav equipment. But if someone was to replicate the error that caused the disaster, and was to enter it back into the nav systems …"

He stared at her for a moment. Then, slowly, he smiled, the expression sharp and ruthless.

She'd known Temple for years. She knew damn well that under his mild mannerisms, he was as brutal and ruthless as she was. There wasn't a sailor on her crew who didn't hate the Level, Temple more than most. And now she saw in his face that he'd understood exactly what she was saying.

"Aye, Captain," he said at last. "I believe you might have the right of it there." He paused, calculating. "Need to get access to the nav equipment on one of their ships—fleet flagship would be best. But if we could program something that'd insert the error there, figure we could design it so it'd replicate across the entire fleet when they sent out the jump codes. Figure that'd about do what we'd need it to."

She leaned back in her seat, still smiling, just a little. "Can you do it?"

He nodded, brows already creased in thought. "I can. I'll get Jumper to help me on it, lad's a natural at this sort of thing, and Freddie'll help if we need her. But as I said, to put it to any use, I'd need access to one of the ships of the line as is using the new nav equipment to send out jump codes."

Gracie smiled again. "I'll take care of that, Temple. There's a fleet of naval ships just outside of Blackrock. We're—how long? A handful of hours away, I think."

He nodded.

"Figure they should be working their way out of the trap we set them around now. Cleaning up, counting the bodies. Won't have a lot of energy for worrying about boarders from a ship as they didn't expect. And then, when they've come out one way or the other, and set their nav equipment to take them back to the Level with their tails between their legs …"

Temple grinned, the expression sharp and vicious. "Then I guess we'll see how the navy deals with a second Starfire."

16

Judith

Admiral Judith Usher dropped her face into her hands with a weary sigh. The holo-images hovering over her desk were burned into her retinas so that she could probably have read them with her eyes closed, if she'd cared to.

It was long past the time most of the Admiralty had gone home to bed, and the offices were dark and silent. It had been hours since she'd heard footsteps and voices in the corridor outside her office.

She was exhausted. Her eyes were sandy with lack of sleep, and her body felt heavy and sluggish, but her brain was spinning too quickly to allow her to rest.

There had been another set of classified documents stolen from the archives.

The first time it had happened, she'd thought little of it—whatever Silas Hunt had found there, and whatever his reasons for stealing them, the documents weren't current records, and she had too many other things to worry about.

But the second time had caught her attention.

And when she'd pulled up the records and examined what documents were stolen, her blood had run cold.

Starfire. Every document that had been taken had to do with the Starfire disaster. The first documents, the ones that Officer-Candidate Hunt had stolen, were the records of the trial. The second set were the reams and reams of evidence and records before and after the fact.

There was a reason the documents were classified—a scandal of that size would sink more than a few powerful politicians, and ruin family names with the money and influence behind them to rock the Level to its political foundations.

Then there was her suspicion that Hunt had somehow been lured away by Gracie.

If Gracie had been behind all this—she couldn't imagine anything good coming of it. And the fact that it was happening now, just after the fleet had left for Blackrock—a mission Gracie knew about, and had had time to prepare for—couldn't be coincidence. Could it?

This expedition to Blackrock had the potential to end in disaster. She'd known that the moment it had been suggested. She'd tried to talk the politicians out of it, but, with the typical arrogance of those who had no experience whatsoever in the matter at hand, they'd dismissed her complaints. She could have fought it harder. But there was too much at stake at the moment for even something like the action against Blackrock to be worth upsetting the delicate web of favours and persuasion she'd managed to weave over the past months and years.

But this—these stolen documents made a trail that led straight to Captain Mad Dog.

She closed her eyes, trying to recall every detail of her meeting with Gracie, the look in the woman's eyes when she'd told her about the planned attack.

She couldn't have come up with an effective counter-offensive in that short of time, could she? Even if she somehow managed to set a trap, it would hardly do more than delay the navy, and it would sacrifice far too many pirate crews. Gracie was many things, but reckless with lives on her own side wasn't one of them—no matter how many good naval captains and sailors she'd happily shoot down.

She could send a warning through the emergency channels to Commodore Webb.

For a moment, her hand hovered over her dictation machine.

Then she lowered her hand, shaking her head.

She was being paranoid.

But it had only been a few days since she'd seen Gracie. And she hadn't remembered how the woman could still haunt her, how the memories of her could drag Judith's attention away from her duty, make her second-guess every decision. How Gracie could colour every thought, until Judith was never fully sure if the thought was her own, or some reflection of Gracie.

She couldn't afford this. She couldn't afford to split her focus because of old guilt, and nebulous fears of a woman she'd once loved.

And that was what she was doing. She knew damn well that, although he may not be a military genius, and she may not entirely share his political views, Commodore Webb was competent for an expedition like the one to Blackrock. Her fears over the mission were born of a combination of the past weeks of strain and exhaustion, and the sight of Gracie again, after all these years.

But dammit ... she wasn't sure. She couldn't be sure.

She tipped her head back against her chair.

She was so tired. She was so tired, and the work in front of her seemed endless, and the survival of the Level and the Stacks and every ship and resource planet in its boundaries hung on her neck like a yoke, and she couldn't afford a distraction. War was coming. Every briefing she received told her it was coming, and soon, but it was next to impossible to convince a politician who wanted nothing more complicated than arguing over the latest finance proposal in parliament to focus on something that would disrupt their entire world. She'd had to fight for every scrap of resources she'd been given, every security briefing, every chit of funding for a new captain or a new ship, and she was more and more convinced that somewhere in parliament—maybe somewhere in the Admiralty itself—there was someone on the Rosette System's payroll, doing everything they could to sabotage her efforts. There were nights, like this one, where she felt as if she were dragging the entire parliament behind her singlehandedly, the effort enough to kill her.

She sighed, pushing aside the holo-notes with a flick of her wrist.

The work would still be there in the morning. And her mind was cobwebbed too thick with memories to allow her to be effective tonight.

Sleep would help.

She pushed herself slowly to her feet, feeling far wearier than her years should account for. When she stepped out of her office and closed the door behind her, the sound echoed in the empty corridors—aside from the night security, she was the last one to leave the building, yet again.

Her footsteps were loud in the stillness as she made her way down the empty corridors and down the three flights of stairs to the ground floor. She could have taken the lift, but there was an instinctual part of her that wanted to move, as if perhaps she could outrun the ghosts in her head if only she was moving.

The guard at the door straightened at her approach, saluting smartly. All the guards here knew her by now, and knew her habits when she was working on a particularly intractable problem.

"Admiral," he murmured, and she nodded in return.

If her mind hadn't been fixated on ghosts already, she might not have noticed the faint glow wafting from the dark corner of the street.

Not entirely uncommon to get ghosts around the Admiralty buildings, close as they were to the port district. The peacekeepers were vigilant enough during daylight hours, but nights, when there were fewer important people about, they were less meticulous.

The guard must have seen her stiffen, because he spun.

The ghost's attention snapped to him, and it drifted closer, mouth opening to reveal the jags of blackness that could tear flesh from bone.

It bore the shape of a young woman, dressed in an officer's uniform, her face sharp and proud, posture challenging.

For just a moment, Judith's heart lurched in her chest, her brain shaping the stranger's face to one that was far, far too familiar …

The ghost lunged. Judith stepped forward at the same moment, igniting her sparker in a practiced motion, and plunging it into the thing's side.

For a moment, the three of them stood frozen. Then the ghost melted into a fading coil of blue mist.

The guard was gasping, his own sparker held in a trembling hand. "Thank you, Admiral," he said at last, his voice shaking.

Judith pocketed her sparker, her heart pounding hard and strange in her chest, and gave a brusque nod. "Best stay alert. You won't always get a warning."

He nodded, and she saw the sick pallor of his face as he tucked the sparker carefully back into its holster.

She didn't look at him as she stepped past him to where her transport waited.

She'd known the ghost hadn't been her dead lover. She'd seen Gracie days earlier, and this ghost looked, not like the Gracie she knew now, but like Grace as she had been, Before.

But she hadn't hesitated. Not an instant.

Her driver had the interior of the transport heated, but she couldn't shake the chill from her bones.

When she got back to her apartment, she barely had the energy to climb the steps and divest herself of her uniform before falling into bed.

"My sweet Jenny. I thought I might find you here." Judith looked up as the door to her second-mate's cabin swung open and First Mate Grace Madox stepped inside, her usual devilish grin on her face, the typical swagger in her step.

Judith found she was smiling despite herself. She couldn't seem to help herself around Grace—charming, brash, impossibly confident, as if the Level and everything on it belonged to her and her alone.

She hadn't been able to help herself since the first time she met the woman two years back, on this very ship.

"I'm in the middle of my work," she said, trying to sound snappish, and failing utterly.

Grace grinned, stepping closer, leaning into Judith's space so that Judith could smell the musky-sweet soap she used. "My sweet, sweet Jenny," she said, lowering her voice to a rough whisper. "I have news. Thought you might want to hear it."

Judith tried to lean back, tried to collect herself against Grace's intoxicating nearness, but Grace rested an arm against the back of her chair and leaned in closer, eyes sparkling, smile playing around the corners of her mouth.

"What is it, then?" She hoped she didn't sound quite as breathless as she felt.

Grace's free hand ran along Judith's hairline, tugging a lock of hair loose from her regulation ponytail and twisting it between her fingers. "Looks like the captain changed his mind. There'll be two recommendations to the Academy this year."

"I ... I thought—" Judith swallowed, and tried again to focus on the words, not the warmth of Grace's hand in her hair, the undisguised heat of her gaze. "I thought he said he didn't want to lose his first and second mate at once, that was why he wanted to recommend you this year, me the next."

Grace threw back her head and laughed, hopping up to sit on the edge of the table, somehow without untangling her hand from Judith's hair. "He did. And I told him that if he thought that, he'd have no candidates for the Academy this year, on account of I'd tear up the recommendation myself."

Judith stared for a moment, then shook her head ruefully.

A recommendation to the Academy was the most coveted prize a captain could bestow upon a promising petty officer. And Grace would have thrown it away without a second thought—Judith knew well enough the threat hadn't been an idle one.

"One of these days you'll go too far," she chided.

Grace laughed again. "For you, Jenny? I'll always go too far. Besides—" she grinned. "They wouldn't dare do anything to either of us. You're a genius. And me? I'm brilliant. They'd not dare do a thing."

Jenny laughed despite herself.

This had always been Grace's way—from their first clashes as the youngest two captain's mates in the recruiting pool, both with their egos and their reputations to uphold, to their tentative truce, to the day when Grace had pushed her up against the wall of the ship beside the captain's quarters and kissed her dizzy and breathless, her brash disregard of the naval rule against romantic relations between a ship's officers as thoughtless and reckless as everything else about her.

The captain was aware of their relationship, almost certainly. But Grace seemed to bear a charmed life. She was just as brilliant as she claimed, hotheaded and difficult and stubborn and utterly brilliant, a talent the navy couldn't afford to lose.

"And if you're wrong, Grace? If they throw you out?"

"Then I'd turn pirate, and kill captains and burn ships and take down the Level itself to woo you, my sweet Jenny." She was laughing, and the light from the sun, streaming in through the porthole, cast her in a pool of light so that she seemed to almost glow, brilliant and luminescent. Her face turned serious, and she cupped Judith's chin in her hand. "I'd do it, Jenny," she whispered. "I'd burn the system to the ground for you."

And looking into her eyes, Judith had no doubt at all that she would.

She leaned forward and let herself fall into Grace's kiss, the feel of Grace's hands tangling in her hair and running down her ribcage and catching her hips.

It should feel dangerous. She knew, instinctively, that Grace was dangerous— the intensity of her, the way she loved like a fire burned, reckless and hot and wild, the brilliant, restless genius of her. But instead it was a heady intoxication that set her floating, laughing and giddy and breathless.

She'd damn herself, gladly, for this woman beside her.

Judith woke with a start, her breath coming shallow and too quick, her cheek pressed against the smooth fabric of her pillow.

Gracie Madox was dangerous. She'd always been dangerous, she'd never let a mission like this one to Blackrock go by without trying to strike back.

Grace Madox was dangerous …

She pulled up a note with trembling hands.

She'd send through a warning. She had to—to tell Webb to look out for Gracie and the *Sweet Jenny*. To watch for whatever the woman had planned, because she had something planned.

She cursed and closed her eyes, trying to steady her breathing.

It was a dream. It had just been a dream, a memory.

After a moment, she shut down the note with a quick gesture, and rolled over, staring up into the darkness.

This was paranoia. She'd sound mad if she sent something like that, in the middle of the night. She'd look unhinged, and there were already too many wolves circling her, sniffing for any hint of weakness they could use to take her down. She couldn't let Gracie distract her. That's all this was, a distraction pulled from her dreams or nightmares of Mad Dog Gracie Madox, and she wouldn't let it fool her into taking command of the Blackrock mission.

The voice from her dreams mingled with the voice in her memory, older and harder, but still, unmistakably, Grace. *"I'll kill you one of these days, Jenny, or you'll kill me. Hardly matters, though, does it? That's why you came."*

It did matter. It mattered desperately. The Level hung on the brink of war, and Judith was the only one in position to keep them safe, harangue the politicians and bureaucrats into providing the funds and training, recruit and vet captains who'd be able to innovate and adapt to new strategies.

But there were nights still, nights like this, when she lay restless in her bed, tossing and turning, chasing sleep that wouldn't come, that she thought, perhaps, she'd still damn herself for Grace.

17

"Coming out of jump on my count." Temple's voice was crisp. "Three. Two. One. Coming out."

Gracie closed her eyes against the familiar feeling that strummed through her body every time a ship entered or exited an FTL jump, and breathed out softly. "Thank you, Temple," she said, her eyes fixed on the screen.

As the ship's sensors reoriented to sub-lightspeed, the familiar surroundings of a few hour's run time from Blackrock appeared on the screens. She smiled, just a little, as the dots on the screen filled in.

"There they are," she murmured.

The site was a mess. She could see, from here, the faint glow on the screens that marked the debris fields from shattered ships. Some were small enough that they must have been pirate crews. But at least two were far too big for any pirate ship on Blackrock.

Temple glanced over at her. "Which ships you reckon they took down?" His voice was grim.

Gracie shook her head without speaking.

It looked like the naval ships had taken out at least half a dozen pirate vessels, maybe more.

But if they'd simply sat back and let them fire on Blackrock until its surface had been reduced to a heap of slag, there would have been more deaths. Even if they'd managed to get off Blackrock, or get to the deep caves, there'd have been far, far too many casualties, and that was only counting the casualties from the battle. If the settlement itself had been destroyed, many, many more would have died afterwards.

Life on Blackrock wasn't like life on the Level. When you were living one step away from the edge, it didn't take much to push you over—loss of a ship, loss of a position. An injury that meant you couldn't fly for a few weeks or months, so your captain replaced you with someone who could. Loss of the savings you'd been scraping together over the years. Anything was enough to tip you over the edge when you lived that close to it, and she knew well enough the desperation that drove people to piracy.

At the least, this meant they'd made their deaths more costly than the Naval High Command had anticipated.

"Looks like your strategy worked out," Toothpick murmured, watching the screen.

"Aye," Gracie said quietly. "That it did. But it was a damn sight more expensive than I'd like."

"Took down two ships of the line," her first mate said, his voice mild.

She turned to smile at him, letting the tips of her teeth show. "Well, Toothpick. I guess we should make sure those deaths count, since it looks like we have the chance to, no? I figure taking down the other fifteen ships at once should do the trick."

He smiled back, and there was a spark of hatred in the expression.

"Figure it might, at that, Captain."

Gracie studied the screen in front of her for a long moment. "Best get Sil and Ari and Jumper up here," she said at last. "I'll want their thoughts on this."

Toothpick nodded and tapped the comm, and Gracie frowned at the screen in front of her.

There was still some scattered fighting on the edges of the fleet's formation, but it was already dying down. Even if she'd had a mind to, the *Sweet Jenny* wouldn't come in quick enough to make a difference, and truth be told, there was no difference to be made against fifteen fully-crewed ships of the line now that the element of surprise had been lost. Their strategy had been born of desperation, and she'd had no illusions about what they'd be able to accomplish.

They'd taken down two ships of the line, two-hundred-crewed at least, unless she was much mistaken. Perhaps it wasn't as much as she'd hoped, but it would cost the navy. And that, in the end, had been the objective. She knew damn well they'd never have been able to take down the entire fleet. But they'd injured them, and hopefully once the remainder of the pirate ships had jumped out, the remaining naval ships would be paying more attention to licking their wounds and calculating the damage than watching for a shielded ship slipping into their formation.

The door to the cockpit slid open, and she glanced up as Silas stepped inside, followed by Ari and Jumper.

She saw how Sil's eyes darted to the screen, and she saw how his posture stiffened at the unmistakable debris fields. For a moment, his face went pale. He didn't say anything, though, just drew in a breath and straightened, a grim cast to his expression.

"Sil, Ari, Jumper," she said, turning in her seat and surveying them. "Called you up here because I'm going to need your help with something."

"What is it, Captain?" Ari's tone was clearly trying to be light, but Gracie could hear the strain under it.

That, she did feel bad about. She'd known the girl had painful memories of the Level. And she'd known that Ari'd do what she asked regardless.

But she'd needed this information. And the haunted look on her second mate's face was only one reason more that what they were doing now was worth it.

She turned to Silas. "Sil," she said. "You still have your naval uniform you came out in?"

He frowned at her. "I … believe I do. Ari brought it on board, and I believe it's stored in my kit."

She nodded. "Good lad. And you had a spare jacket, didn't you?"

His frown deepened. "I did."

"You think it'd fit Ari?"

He glanced over, considering. "It might. I'm broader in the shoulders than she is, but she's around my height." He turned back to her. "What are we doing, Captain?"

She smiled. "Looked through that information you got me, Sil. And I figure we can put it to use after all. But we'll need to be on board a naval ship to do it."

His eyebrows shot up, and she chuckled. "Come, lad, you just disguised yourself as a Level gentleman. This can't be more difficult than that."

He glanced at her, then back to the screens. "How—" He broke off his sentence and nodded grimly. "You're right. Whatever happened here, they're not going to be paying too much attention, are they?"

"Don't guess as they will," she said mildly.

He hesitated a moment. "My jacket isn't the standard uniform they wear shipboard," he said at last. "But I think we can make it work, at least so that if someone isn't looking too closely, we'll blend in."

Gracie nodded. "Jumper?" she said, turning to the boy and signing along with her words.

He signed back an acknowledgement.

"You and Temple got what I needed programmed in, yes?"

Jumper nodded, his hands moving rapidly in response. *Got the programming done. Should only take one person to set it into the system.*

"Good. I want you on the weapons, in case the navy sees us." She turned. "Temple? You think you could kit yourself up like a naval sailor before the mast? Sil'll know his way around the ship, and him and Ari'll be able to keep attention off you if needs be. But I'll need to send someone who knows what they're doing with the tech."

"Aye, Captain, believe I can," said Temple quietly. "Let me chart out a course to get us in close, then I'll go scrounge something up. Officers' uniforms are different, yeah, but not much difference between the sailors at the bottom of the pile, be they merchant or navy or pirate."

Gracie nodded at him. "Thank you, Temple. Chart us a course, and I'll bring us in." She turned to Silas. "Sil. That's the other reason I wanted you up here. Figure you know your way around a ship of the line, and figure that'll make it a hell of a lot quicker to get what we're after. I want to take us in to the flagship, if I can. But I need to know if you can get Temple where he needs to be on that ship."

Silas studied the naval formation a moment, then pulled up a note on his comm. "I recognize the vis-tag," he said. "That's the *Resolve*. Three-hundred-and-fifty-crewed. I haven't sailed on her, but I had to memorize the layout of every ship of the line in the Academy. I'll be able to get Temple wherever he needs to be." He paused. "Captain," he said at last, voice quiet. "I won't ask what we're doing, not right now."

She heard in his voice what he didn't say. He wouldn't ask, not because he would disagree, but because he would agree regardless. And he wasn't sure he could bear it.

"Won't tell you anything you don't want to be told, lad," she said, her tone matching his.

"I'll ask for all the details when we get back. But right now, all I need to know is what Temple needs, and how long we'll plan to be on board."

Gracie nodded, glancing over at Temple. He frowned. "Need to get to the control room," he said at last. "Shouldn't take more'n a minute or two from there."

Silas nodded. "That, I can do." He turned to her. "Now, if you'll excuse me, I'd best get changed and get Ari my old jacket."

"You do that, lad," she said. He turned, but she could see the lines of strain in his face as he went, and the tightness around his eyes.

"Got the course charted," said Temple after a moment, turning. "Ship's yours, Captain. I'll go get changed myself. And—" He glanced up at the screens. "Don't look like they've picked up on our shielding. Don't figure as they'll be looking for someone coming in, not right now. No sense to it, strategy-wise, so I don't figure as they'll waste the ship's power on doing scans as would pick us up."

Gracie nodded, and slid into the seat Temple had vacated as he stood. "You do that, Temple." She glanced at the screen again. "We should be in range in just under two hours."

18

Hollis

It was a solid twenty-four hours between the time they'd come out of jump and when they sent the last of the pirate ships on their way.

Every sailor aboard the *Verity* was exhausted, Hollis could see it in their eyes and their postures. She'd finally given in to Foster's insistence and sat down, barely taking enough of a break to swallow the pain tablets Archibald had sent up for her—she'd told him to give her only as much as would keep her functional, balancing on the knife-edge where the painkillers offset the cloudy-headedness from pain enough to make up for the fog the painkillers themselves set in her brain.

She was so exhausted, though, that it hardly made a difference.

Even Foster's normally straight pose was wilting a little, the weariness apparent in the set of their shoulders and the tight lines at the corners of their mouth.

But they'd won.

It had been a bloodier victory than any of them had hoped, but they'd managed to pull the flagship out of the swarm of pirates before it was taken down. Another ship of the line had been lost, and two more were limping badly—they'd likely be unable to use the FTL jumps back to the Level, and Hollis expected that the commodore would order them to abandon ship, evacuate the sailors onto the other ships of the line, and tow the broken hulls far enough not to be in immediate danger from pirates while they were repaired. The *Verity's* guns were almost disabled from overuse, and they'd lost yet another gunner compartment—a pirate ship had come around behind the wreckage of one of the destroyed ships of the line, heavy weapons firing and locked on before the *Verity* could get a clear shot. They hadn't breached the hull, but in the panic of firing back, one of the *Verity's* heavy guns had exploded, killing three of the sailors. Two of them had gone ghost, and before the survivors could get word out in the chaos, everyone in the compartment was dead, ripped apart with the vicious brutality that marked ghost-killings.

But it was over. That was all she'd let herself think of for now.

There was something nagging in the back of Hollis's mind, a fact that she knew was important, but in the fog of strain and exhaustion, it kept slipping maddeningly out of her grasp every time she tried to catch it, leaving her with nothing but a vague sense of unease.

"Captain." It was Archibald, through the comm. "As your chief medical officer, I must recommend that you get some sleep. I'm surprised you've held up as long as you have, but I'm warning you, at some point you will actually collapse."

Hollis stared stupidly at her comm for a moment before she remembered how to hit the button to respond. "Thank you, Officer Smyth," she said. "I shall set the watches, as we are no longer under active attack. And then I believe I shall take your advice."

There was a snort through her comm that was far too sarcastic to be fully respectful, but she ignored it. "Mate Greene," she said through his line. "I believe the emergency has passed. Please set the sailors on watches, and get the second watch below to their hammocks. Coordinate with Officer Smyth to organize the med bay into watches as well, and keep a skeleton crew on the guns at all times in case the pirates have another trap planned."

"Aye, Captain." Emmett's voice was thick with weariness.

"I'll take first watch on the bridge, Captain," said Foster, at her elbow. "You go below, and you can relieve me at next watch."

Hollis bit down the protest that wanted to rise in her throat—there wasn't, in fact, any good reason for it. Foster was perfectly capable of running the ship, and she was fully confident in their judgment.

And once again, the relief of knowing that she could trust her first and second mates hit her with a force that was almost enough to make her sag, and tightened her throat painfully.

"Thank you, Price," she said, pushing herself gingerly to her feet. She swayed for a moment before she caught her balance.

Foster came over to stand next to her. "Captain," they said in a low voice. "The section where we were holding the prisoner was breached. We didn't see her body—it's possible she escaped. Until we find her, be careful, and don't go anywhere alone."

Hollis stared at them for a moment, waiting for the words to penetrate her exhausted brain. Then she almost laughed. "Thank you for the warning, Price, but at this juncture, I'm not certain what she can do that the bloody pirates haven't already tried."

Foster gave a terse nod. "I've informed the petty officers to be on the lookout for her, and in the meantime, I've hand-picked a security detail for you. You should be safe enough at present, even if she's still alive."

Hollis nodded, too weary to answer.

A moment later, a sailor was beside her. "Captain," they said, eyes wide and nervous.

Hollis bit back a scowl—the youth looked terrified enough as it was—and instead nodded her thanks, swallowing down the bitterness of it in her throat. She made her slow way down to her cabin, supporting herself on the young sailor's shoulder, until finally they'd left her to stand guard in the hallway and the door had clicked shut behind them. Then she dropped onto her cot with a groan, weariness weighing on her muscles like lead.

She lay gingerly back, closing her eyes and waiting for the blessed relief of sleep. But despite her utter exhaustion, sleep wouldn't come. There was that nagging sense, in the back of her head, of something forgotten, something vitally important.

She tried to roll over onto her side, and the motion pulled at her injury, bringing tears of pain to her eyes. She lay where she was a moment, breathing shallowly and trying to force her exhausted body and brain into submission.

She had to remember. There was something that she needed to remember, and she couldn't for the life of her think of what it was ...

The faces of the sailors she'd lost paraded before her closed eyes. She hadn't known all of them, but she'd recognized most of the names when Emmett had given her the report.

Two of them had been on the skiff with her, when they'd run in fighting the black hole's gravity to rescue the sailors from the *Agate*. They'd volunteered, risked their own lives to save the lives of fellow sailors who were strangers to them. And now they were dead, both of them. One killed by the loss of pressure, the other ripped to shreds by the ghost of a crewmate.

The sight of the ship of the line, flaring into a brilliant explosion, then gone—utterly, abruptly, with no trace left but a cloud of ever-expanding debris.

There was a detail she'd missed. It was slipping at the edges of her consciousness, teasing her with its presence, never quite fully formed enough to grasp.

But at last even the nagging worry, the half-formed fear twisting uneasily in her stomach, wasn't enough, and she drifted into a restless sleep.

She woke with a start, gasping, and it took her a moment to reorient herself to her surroundings. Her heart was pounding so quickly she felt like she'd been running, the sudden burst of panic enough that she almost could ignore the pain of her injury.

She fumbled for her comm. "Mate Price," she snapped into it, her voice cracked and rough with sleep.

"Captain?" Foster, at least, sounded alert enough. "What's wrong? You should be sleeping."

"Where's the *Sweet Jenny*?"

There was a moment's pause. "Captain?" asked Foster at last, cautiously.

"Damn you, Price, answer my question! Where the hell is the *Sweet Jenny*?" Her hands were clenched into fists, and she could feel her fingernails cutting into the flesh of her palms.

"I'm ... not certain, Captain. I don't recall seeing her," Foster said at last.

"Ask Greene." Hollis's words were coming out short and harsh. "I need to know where the hell Mad Dog is."

"Aye, Captain," said Foster, their tone switching to its usual competent efficiency. "I'll ask Greene, and I'll ask the navigator to see if she can track it."

There was a moment of silence on the comm, and Hollis closed her eyes, hoping against hope that she was wrong.

But she was all but certain she wasn't.

She should have been able to see the *Sweet Jenny*. Her vis-tags were impossible to miss, unless Mad Dog had a reason for hiding her. But there was no reason for hiding her that Hollis could think of, not after the trap had been sprung.

And she should have been able to see it. The *Sweet Jenny* had guns that could take down the shields on a ship of the line, Hollis had experienced that herself. There was no way a ship like that should have been hard to spot.

"I have Greene and the navigator checking the ship's records for sight of the *Sweet Jenny* during the battle," Foster said a moment later. They paused. "May I inquire what this is about, Captain?"

Hollis pulled in a quick breath. "Mate Price. We both saw what Mad Dog was willing to do when we were trying to bring in the *Agate*. She was willing to tie her ship and her crew to a dying ship, as long as she was bringing the *Verity* down with her. Do you think she'd sit this out?"

There was another moment's pause. "You think—" Foster began, their voice thick with a sudden unease.

"She's out there, Price. If the *Sweet Jenny* wasn't in the fight, then there's something that Mad Dog's planning that we're not seeing. This isn't over yet."

When Foster spoke again, their words were clipped, sharp with strain. "I'll let you know as soon as Greene has something for us," they said. "In the meantime, I'll let Greene know to have the sailors on alert."

"I'll be on the bridge in a moment," Hollis said, trying to keep her voice measured. "Mad Dog is planning something. I don't know what it is, but I'm damn well not going to let her take us this time."

"Aye, Captain." There was a note of dread in Foster's voice that echoed the dread coiled in Hollis's stomach.

19

Silas

Silas stood at the airlock doors, his entire body stiff with tension.

The naval uniform that had once felt as comfortable as his own skin sat strangely on his shoulders, heavier and more confining than he remembered. He hadn't put it on since he'd joined up with the *Sweet Jenny* almost a standard month ago.

Ari stood beside him. She hadn't quite regained her equilibrium since they'd returned from the Level, but she was affecting an air of jaunty unconcern, and he wasn't going to call her bluff. His coat sat a bit big on her shoulders, the buttons of it straining a little over her chest rather than cut to fit as most uniforms were. But it was enough that they'd pass in low light or at a distance, and with luck that was all they'd need to do. Even on a three-hundred-and-fifty-crewed ship of the line, most of the petty officers knew each other by appearance, even if not by name. Best not to get close enough to give anyone a chance to ask questions.

Temple stood beside them in his pirate's kit. He'd been right enough, though—below decks on a naval ship, he'd hardly stand out.

"You ready?" Gracie asked, looking them over with a critical eye. "Should pass well enough, I think. Temple, you have what you need?"

Temple nodded. "Aye, Captain."

"Good. Get in the skiff, then, I've got a mag-lock hooked on so we can pull you in quick-time if you need it. But I'd rather we didn't need it."

Silas nodded.

The tension ached up his muscles, squeezing at the base of his skull.

He didn't know what Gracie was planning with the information he'd got her from the Level. If he sat down and thought about it long enough, he'd likely be able to figure it out, and for that exact reason he had studiously avoided doing just that. The previous evening, he'd found Ari tucked away in the engine room after watch. When he'd joined her, she'd produced a flask of rum she'd smuggled in from somewhere, and the two of them had proceeded to get drunk enough that they could ignore the demons that had followed them back from the Level.

Gracie must have known, but she hadn't said anything, and he was grateful for that, at least.

He knew the bare bones of what Ari's demons were. He still wasn't sure he could name his, because that would involve summoning a hundred more.

So instead he'd got drunk the night before, and spent the day scrubbing and polishing for Freddie until his hands were raw and his fingers swollen and sore, and now he was going to smuggle the three of them onto a naval flagship to do something, the substance of which he only didn't know because he'd intentionally avoided figuring it out.

He smiled humourlessly to himself.

Wouldn't his superior officers be proud of him, if they saw him now. Wouldn't his aunt and uncle, who'd raised him. They'd never let him call them "mother" or "father," and he'd spent every moment of his life knowing, through every part of him, that he had a mother and father who'd been killed doing their duty to the Level and the navy, and that that was exactly what was expected of him. That being killed in the line of duty was no tragedy, but an accomplishment second only to living up to what his parents never had a chance to do.

His parents, who'd died screaming. Who'd died in agony, because of the very people he'd spent his life venerating. Perhaps, if there was such a thing as an afterlife, his parents would be proud of him after all. But he couldn't quite picture it. He had no memory of them, and the story he'd been told—two tragic martyrs, whose deaths, among thousands of others, had been the impetus for the treason trials and the rash of hangings—were burned too deeply into his psyche for anything as coarse as facts to get in the way.

He wasn't sure even now, if his aunt and uncle had known the truth, if it would have changed anything for them after all. They lived and breathed the navy, his entire family did. It was the family profession, practically a tradition. Something that was burned into their psyches as much as the legend of his parents was burned into his, and just as difficult to excise.

His aunt and uncle would have cried at his funeral if he'd been shot down. Hell, they'd likely been told he was dead already—he knew well enough how close-mouthed the navy was about defections —and they'd already cried for him, tears of pride as much as sorrow. But if they were to see him now, alive?

He shook his head and shoved the thought away. He'd deal with it later. He'd deal with all of this later, this wasn't the time for it.

Maybe there'd never be a time for it. Honestly, he could live with that outcome.

"Come on, best get going," he said brusquely, and started for the small skiff.

Temple set the course, and Silas piloted them in. After the frantic chaos of piloting through the grav field of a black hole, it was almost disorienting in its simplicity.

"Got the shielding up, so they shouldn't see us come in," Temple muttered as Silas followed the course he'd set into the nav screen. "Going to come in at the cargo compartment, and I have a lock-break as should get us inside."

Silas nodded, not taking his eyes off the screen. From the corner of his eye, he could see Ari, her hand tight around the butt of her pistol, a small, grim smile on her lips.

Then they were there, and the skiff jostled a little as he lined it up with the exterior of the airlock on the cargo hold. "Sealed on," he said at last, taking his hands from the controls.

Temple stood and crossed over to the skiff's airlock door. He tapped it open, and maneuvered a pirate's lock-pick onto the exterior door. The devices were clumsy, and not much use in a battle —they took too long to unlock the airlock doors, unlike the noisier, but quicker, lock-hammer. Quiet enough, but you were likely to find a squadron of enemies carried in front of the door waiting for you to get it open if you weren't careful. But he'd glanced over the specs Temple had shown him earlier, and cross-referenced them with the diagram in his mind, and agreed that it was unlikely anyone would be waiting behind this particular airlock.

At last, there was a *click* as the lock pick finished its work. "You ready?" Temple asked, glancing back at them. His expression was grim.

Silas glanced at Ari, standing next to him. She was wearing a dangerous grin, her hand tight on her pistol.

Silas smiled without humour. "I think we are," he said, drawing his own pistol.

Temple drew his pistol as well, and gestured them back out of the line of fire. Then he pushed the airlock door cautiously open with his free hand.

The airlock slid up, and Silas found he'd braced unconsciously, waiting for a barrage of shots. But none came, and at last Temple peered out through the entrance and beckoned them forward.

Once they were assembled in the empty cargo bay, Temple slid the airlock door closed loosely, without locking it, and turned to Silas. "I got us in. Your turn, lad."

Silas nodded without speaking and stepped forward. He glanced around, orienting himself, then started for the exit to the cargo bay. They got out of the cargo bay without incident, and Silas glanced up and down the thankfully empty hallway.

They were in the belly of the ship. If the *Resolve* was trying to recover from a pirate attack, it would be busy up in the med bay and by the engine room. If they kept close to the cargo hold and took the ratlines up, he was pretty sure he could find them a passageway that would let them avoid notice, at least.

"Come on," he said with a jerk of his head. "This way."

He'd been right—the corridors were mostly deserted as they made their way through the passageways that crossed between the cargo bays. But once they'd shimmied up the ratlines past the crew quarters and onto the main deck, they ran into more and more sailors—one or two at first, then more.

From the corner of his eye he saw Ari's hand tighten on her pistol in its holster, but none of the sailors paid them the slightest attention —the colour of the jackets he and Ari wore were enough, it seemed, cut notwithstanding, to keep from drawing immediate attention, and Silas could see the haunted, haggard looks on the faces of the sailors they passed, some of them limping and blood-spattered, all looking as if they hadn't slept in days.

He fought down the sickness twisting in his stomach.

He'd been in enough battles shipboard to know that feeling in his bones, the sick, haunted horror of seeing shipmates shot down beside you, watching someone you'd grown up beside torn to pieces by the vicious ghost of a friend.

He drew in a breath and fought down the sharp bite of sympathy.

Gracie was right, after all. They were fighting a war with the Level. The sailors here were collateral damage, just as much as the pirates that had died. Neither he nor Gracie had started the war, but he would be damned if he rolled over and let the Level kill more good sailors without at least fighting back.

The crowds got thicker as they approached the control room. Temple came up beside him and said in a low voice, "Are we going to be able to get in there, lad?"

"I can get us in," Silas said, biting off the words. Temple eyed him, but at last he nodded and fell back.

"What you planning, Sil?" Ari whispered from his other side.

"With luck, it'll be empty," Silas said grimly. "If not, I'll drop a percussive explosive in the corridor nearest the airlock. It'll be enough to get everyone temporarily evacuated, I think, and they shouldn't be suspicious—there were enough sailors there preparing to repel boarders that I doubt anyone'll see it strange that a percussive got left behind.

Ari nodded. "Not bad," she said, grinning. It wasn't her usual grin, but it was closer than he'd seen it since Gracie had told her she was going to the Level, and he found himself grinning back, just a little, despite himself.

"What the hell are you doing here, sailor?"

Silas looked up sharply, the barked command engaging something automatic in his brain so that he snapped to attention without thinking.

"I'm sorry, Officer. I was just on my way to bring Sailor Temple here to the command room. They asked for help on the controls."

The instinctual reaction seemed to reassure his questioner, at least. The woman studied him suspiciously for a moment, then sighed, her shoulders slumping a little, her entire posture broadcasting weariness. "Get on with you, then. Sooner we can get out of this hell-hole, the better for all of us."

"Aye, Officer. Thank you, Officer,"

She waved him past, and he grabbed Temple by the arm. "You heard the officer. Come on with you, quick-time. We don't have time to waste." He made his tone sharp and imperious, the tone he'd heard all too often from officers directed at the sailors below decks.

"Aye, Officer," Temple muttered, casting Silas a surly glance that, Silas guessed, was only partially assumed.

"Come on with you, none of that," Silas snapped, dragging him forward. He didn't let go of the man's arm until the officer was out of sight around a corner. Then Temple jerked his arm free and scowled at Silas.

"Got into character a sight too easy for my liking, lad," he grumbled.

Ari was clearly trying, not very hard, to hold back her amusement. "What, Temple? Gonna talk to your superior officer like that?"

Temple turned his scowl on her, and Silas again found himself grinning reluctantly.

When they reached the command room, Silas groaned. It was crowded with sailors, officers and technicians both.

"What do you need?" he whispered to Temple.

Temple looked over the room with a calculating air. "Going to need it empty, I'm afraid," he said, turning back to Silas at last. "The program I'll need to get into's in the middle of the damn room. Ain't going to be able to do anything inconspicuous, not with the setup like it is." He shook his head. "Bright side, should be easy enough once I'm in."

Silas let out a short breath. "I'll get it clear for you. Hold tight. Ari, you stay here with him. As soon as the room's empty, get him over there and stay with him. It'll look less suspicious if someone catches a glimpse of the two of you if there's a petty officer keeping an eye on things."

Ari nodded, a familiar, dangerous glint in her eyes. "Guess I can do that. And if we do get caught, guess we'll figure out if these Level sailors bleed as red as the others I've killed." She paused. "Call in if you get in trouble. I know the damn navy told you your life ain't worth spit, long as you're doing your duty, but Gracie'll have my hide if I let one of her crew die without I tried to do something about it."

Silas nodded, something he refused to examine tightening his throat. "Just get Temple in there and do what we came to do. I'll be fine."

He stepped out of the room and into the bustling chaos of the hallway, shoving his way through towards the door which, if his memory was correct, led to the nearest airlock to the control room. He'd have to plant the percussive farther into the ship than would be entirely expected, but everyone here was exhausted and under pressure, many of them injured. With luck, they wouldn't be paying too much attention.

He stepped around a corner, where the edge of the wall would shield him from view, and reached into his jacket, pulling out the percussive that he'd stashed there earlier. Then he stepped out into the rush of the corridor, and a few steps farther along, let the percussive slip from his fingers.

He gave himself ten seconds before he hit the controls.

The blast of it knocked him off his feet, throwing him sideways into the wall. When he lifted his head, everyone in a ten-metre radius was on the ground, and as he scrambled to his feet, the alarms began to wail, a sharp, piercing sound that set his teeth on edge and grated up his spine.

"Get everyone out!" he shouted, hauling another sailor up by the arm and pushing him on his way. "Get everyone out, evacuate the control room. Probably just an accident, but we don't damn well have the sailors to afford to lose more if it isn't."

People were staggering to their feet around him, and there must have been something about the ring of command in his voice that made people obey automatically.

Once the people around him were started down the corridor in the right direction, he strode back towards the control rooms. "Everyone out," he snapped, grabbing a sailor who was running towards the room. "We're getting everyone out until we figure out what the hell that was. Come on, help me get them clear."

The man glanced over at him, panic on his face, and turned to help.

By the time Silas reached the control room, it was all but empty. He grabbed the last of the stragglers, turned her bodily around, and shoved her down the hallway after the others, and she went without argument.

"You have maybe five minutes," he hissed through the closed door. "That's all I can give you, and we're sure as hell not getting another chance after this."

Temple grunted an acknowledgement from inside, and Silas walked quickly down the corridor the way he'd come, as if checking for stragglers.

They'd figure out what had happened soon enough. But he could at least make sure no one stumbled over them by accident.

At last, what seemed like hours later, although it couldn't have been longer than a couple minutes, the door behind him slid open. He spun, his hand going to his pistol on instinct, and Temple and Ari stepped out.

"We got it," Ari whispered. "Now let's get the hell off this ship."

Silas nodded and started forward at a quick pace, Temple and Ari falling in behind him.

People were starting cautiously back into the abandoned corridors, and somewhere behind him he could hear someone shouting orders. He put his head down and walked faster—no point in letting someone recognize him as the one who gave the order to evacuate.

He caught a glimpse of a figure in front of him just before he ran into them, and he jerked his head up, stopping just in time.

The woman stared at him, and he cursed under his breath.

It was the same officer who'd stopped him earlier.

"What the hell are you doing here?" she snapped.

"Just getting these two evacuated," he mumbled, trying to keep his head down.

"What—" She cut off her words abruptly, and he chanced a quick glance up, then had to bite back another curse.

"You're the officer I ran into earlier," she said, a suspicious note in her voice. "What were you doing in there?"

"I brought this man up to help with the controls, and when they were evacuating, I went in to get him back out again," Silas said through his teeth, even though he knew by now there was no point.

He felt sick to his stomach.

Her eyes narrowed. "You're not wearing a regulation uniform. Nor is she." She gestured to Ari, behind him.

"Just please let me pass," Silas said, still through his teeth. "I'd like to get this man—"

There was a pistol in her hand, pointed at his head. "I don't know who the hell you are, or what you're doing, but you're coming with me until we figure it out." Her words were cold. "I lost fourteen sailors from my division in that battle, and I'm not taking a chance on losing more."

From the corner of his eye he caught Ari's movement. The officer's pistol swung towards her, and the woman took a couple of steps back. "Leave your hands where I can see them," she growled, swinging the pistol back and forth between the two of them. With her other hand, she reached to tap her comm.

"No!" Silas snapped, lunging for her.

Time slowed; he watched her swing the pistol towards him, and there was a brief, clinical moment where he knew he'd die, but it hardly seemed to matter. He'd stop her from getting word out, that was the important thing, and it would give Ari time to take her down in the confusion.

Then he was shoved out of the way, and he hit the corridor wall hard even as he heard the soft hiss of an energy pistol shot.

For a second he couldn't quite figure out what had happened, or whether or not he'd been hit, and there was the hiss of another shot, Temple's grunt of pain.

Then he was on his feet, and his brain made sense of the scene—Temple, crumpling to the ground, blood soaking his shirt. The woman standing with her pistol raised, face set.

He acted before he could think. Hell, he knew, in some part of his mind, that he was still trying not to think, that he'd been trying not to think since he had opened the data chips he'd stolen from the Level.

He grabbed the officer by her shoulder and spun her around, yanking her back against his body. Then he jerked his cutlass free with his other hand and slit her throat, her blood freckling his face and drenching his jacket sleeve.

He shoved the limp body away and turned back to Temple, crouching beside Ari where she'd rolled the man over. His face was bloodless, but his eyes were still open, his face twisted in pain.

"Come on, let's get him out of here," Silas snapped, and between them, he and Ari lifted Temple and sprinted for the exit.

They got to the skiff without further incident. Ari's face was pale, her jaw set, and she carried her pistol loose in her hand. Silas supported Temple, who slumped against him, shaking with pain, as Ari shoved open the door to the cargo room, then pushed open the airlock door. It was still unlocked, thank God, and the skiff still attached, and he half-carried Temple across the space and settled him onto the cramped floor of the skiff, pulling off his jacket to tuck under his head.

"You stay with him, I'll get us back," Ari snapped. Silas nodded, still crouched beside Temple. The man was unconscious by now, his eyes closed, his head lolled back, and Silas touched the sparker in his pocket.

If Temple died, he'd need to be ready to disperse the man's ghost before it could fully form.

"Hold tight, we're leaving." Ari's voice was sharp with strain. He heard the click of the airlock door closing, then the hiss of the skiff door doing the same. Then Ari slid past him into the pilot's seat, and the skiff pulled away from the side of the *Resolve* and shot back towards the *Sweet Jenny*.

20

Hollis

Hollis was shaking with pain by the time she made it up to the bridge. She hadn't had the time to wait for Foster to send someone, though, hadn't had the time to walk slowly.

"Captain?" Foster began, turning as she entered.

She cut them off sharply. "Have you heard back from Greene?"

Foster frowned, and there was a tightness in their expression that told her they were as worried about this as she was. "Mate Greene just informed me that he's gone through the records of the battle. At least from the *Verity's* vantage point, the *Sweet Jenny's* vis-tags didn't show up on the screen at all.

Hollis closed her eyes and steadied herself against the back of a chair, cursing.

She'd gone up against Mad Dog before. There was no way the woman would have taken off and run at an approaching naval battle. The trap the pirates had sprung had Mad Dog's signature on it. But there'd been no sign of her in the battle.

"Can you put word through to the other ships, please? Ask them if they have any record of the *Sweet Jenny?*"

"I've already done that." Foster's voice was grim. "I don't have all the reports back yet, but the ships that have gotten back to me report no record of the *Sweet Jenny's* vis-tags on their histories." They paused. "She could have been shielded. Or it's possible she scrubbed the vis-tags well enough that the ship didn't show up."

Hollis shook her head. "If she'd been shielded, she'd still show up on the records. I'm certain Greene, at least, was thorough enough that he checked that. And the *Sweet Jenny's* shape is distinctive enough that Mad Dog wouldn't be able to completely scrub the vis-tags—the shape of her would be enough to tag her."

Foster had turned back to their screen, and now they glanced up at her. "I have reports in from two more ships," they said. "They were on the other side of the formation from us. No record of the *Sweet Jenny.*" They blew out a quick breath. "I'm still waiting on a handful of reports, but the ones I have back were spread out through the battle." They looked over at Hollis. "I think we have enough information to be certain that wherever Mad Dog was, she wasn't here."

Hollis hesitated a moment. Her heart was pounding, tension tightening her stomach so the pain there was a solid, constant burn.

"Put me through to the *Resolve*, please," she said at last. "And in the meantime, tell Mate Greene to put all the crew that are currently on watch on high alert, and to get himself down here."

"Aye, Captain," said Foster, turning to the communications panel.

A moment later, she heard the commodore's irritated voice through the ship's comm. "Captain Ives? What's happened? Your first mate indicated this was an emergency."

"Commodore," she said, stepping closer to the comm and trying to hold back a gasp of pain at the movement. "The pirates aren't through with whatever they're planning. We need all ships on full alert."

He was silent a moment. "Ives?" He said at last. "What the hell are you playing at? The pirates took us by surprise, but we made sure it cost them. And we sent them running, I had my officers tracking the ships. There weren't any that stayed behind."

"That's precisely the problem," she said through her teeth. "The *Verity* has no record of the *Sweet Jenny* during the battle, and nor do any of the other ships I've been in contact with. Mad Dog wasn't there."

"Surely that's a good thing." There was no disguising the impatience in the commodore's tone now. "If Mad Dog decided to save her own skin and leave the fight to the others, I hardly see—"

"Commodore. Have you gone up against Mad Dog before?" The thick haze of exhaustion clouding her brain, and the sharp panic of the situation, stripped the words of any sense of diplomacy, and she had to bite back a curse. Beside her, she could see Foster's minute flinch.

"Captain Ives." The commodore's voice was cold. "You forget your place."

"Mad Dog wasn't in the battle, because she has something planned. Some trap. I know her, I've gone up against her before. She won't leave this, Commodore. She's not one to let others fight her battles, and she's not one to let naval ships of the line come after Blackrock without fighting back. Please. We need every ship on high alert until we figure out where the hell the *Sweet Jenny* is."

There was a long silence. Even her own bridge crew had turned to look at her, and in the sudden quiet, Hollis realized how loud she'd been speaking.

She narrowed her eyes and glared at the comm screen. Her heart was pounding so quickly she could hear it in her ears, feel it in her fingertips.

"Ives, you are being unreasonable. Hold your position and stand down, that is an order."

"I'm trying to stop a disaster while it can still be prevented!" Hollis snapped. Her head was spinning, and the adrenalin that had gotten her from her cabin up to the bridge was buzzing through her brain sharp enough that her legs felt oddly unsteady, her knuckles white where she was clutching the control desk.

"You believe we are in imminent danger because you are unable to verify the location of one pirate ship." The commodore's tone was thick with sarcasm. "And you're demanding that I order the entire fleet on full alert." His face came into view over the screen, and he glared down at her.

"Please, Commodore," she muttered. Her entire body was made of pain, and she was barely holding herself up, but he had to understand, she needed to make him damn well understand.

He studied her for a moment, then turned to Foster. "Mate Price." His tone was clipped. "Your captain suffered an injury in your last posting, correct?"

Foster's eyes flicked to Hollis, then away, but their expression remained polite and impassive. "Aye, Commodore," they said. "Our chief medical officer cleared her for duty, and Admiral Usher agreed and gave the order for her to serve."

The commodore snorted. "Get me your chief medical officer on the line, at once."

Again Foster hesitated, just the barest instant. Then they dipped their head. "Of course, Commodore."

A moment later, Archibald's face appeared on the screen. He was frowning, his jacket spattered with blood, hands gloved. "Mate Price?

What did—" Then he seemed to notice the commodore, because he stopped abruptly.

"You're the *Verity's* chief medical officer?" Webb snapped.

Archibald nodded. "Aye, Commodore."

"Very good. It appears your captain is suffering ill effects from her injury. I will be charitable, and assume it is that, not a desire to be court-martialled, that is compelling her to refuse to follow my orders. Therefore, I am instructing you to take her down to the medical bay and give her the appropriate sedatives to calm her condition."

Archibald stared. "Commodore—" he began at last.

"That is an order," Webb snarled. He turned to Foster. "Mate Price, the ship is under your command in the meantime. I trust that you, at least, are capable of following instructions. My fleet is demoralized, I have two damaged ships that I need to get back to the Level and two others destroyed outright, and every ship here is injured and every captain trying their hardest to keep order. The last thing we need is panic over an imagined danger. I must maintain discipline, and your Captain Ives seems too distressed to be able to follow orders. Her status will be re-evaluated when we return to the Level, but in the meantime, I am promoting you to acting captain."

Hollis finally jolted out of her shock. "Commodore—" she began. The world was spinning, the panic and adrenalin racing through her veins almost enough to stop her tongue.

The commodore turned on her. "Captain Ives. You will be silent."

"Commodore, Captain Ives isn't—" Archibald started.

"Officer, you will take her down to the med bay and restrain her as necessary, or I will order that she be thrown in the brig. From the looks of her, that may well be a death sentence. And you'll be joining her there, along with any other officer who refuses to carry out my orders." He turned back to Foster. "Acting Captain Price. See it done. I shall watch to ensure my orders are carried out, as it appears the *Verity* is a veritable nest of mutiny."

Hollis closed her eyes a moment. "Price," she said, her voice toneless. "The commodore has given an order, and it behooves us to obey it."

At least Foster would be in command. They wouldn't be able to warn the other ships, perhaps, but they, at least, would be watching out for whatever death-trap Mad Dog intended to spring on them.

For a moment, she wasn't entirely sure Foster would obey.

"Mate Price," she snapped, rallying the last of her strength. "You have been given an order."

"Aye, Captain," Foster said, the response almost automatic. They hesitated the briefest second, and for just that second, Hollis could see the helpless fury in their face. But when they turned to Webb, their expression had smoothed over into its normal bland respectfulness. "Aye, Commodore." They turned to the screen beside them. "Officer Smyth. Please send someone to escort the captain to the med bay."

Archibald's jaw was clenched hard enough that Hollis could see the muscles standing out on it, but they only said, "Aye, Mate Price. I'll send up a stretcher in a moment."

"Thank you, Smyth." There was an unmistakable tightness to Foster's expression.

Hollis stood where she was, propped up against the control desk, and for a moment she wondered, almost hysterically, if she'd simply topple over before the stretcher reached her. She wanted to grab Foster by the shoulders and shout at them that they needed to figure this out or more sailors would die, that whatever Mad Dog had planned, if the attack that had taken down two ships of the line was merely a diversion, whenever it came, it would be destructive beyond their wildest imagination. But she couldn't, not with the commodore looking on.

She could only pray that Foster understood, that they hadn't also taken her words as fever-ravings.

And so she simply stood where she was, and waited. And when the stretcher Archibald had sent appeared, with two junior medical officers supporting it, she didn't fight. There would have been no point. She simply lay down on it, as she was instructed.

She could feel the eyes of her bridge crew on her, see again that momentary flash of fury flicker across Foster's face. But right at this moment, there was nothing any of them could do about it.

The commodore's face was still on the screen when Hollis was carried into the med bay. "The sedation, if you please?" he snapped, as Archibald approached the stretcher warily.

Archibald looked up. "Commodore, I think we can secure her without—"

"I have given you a damn order!"

Archibald drew in a long breath through his nose. "Aye, Commodore," he said at last. He turned to Hollis, and she could see the worry and strain on his face. "Sorry, Captain," he whispered.

She felt the sting of a needle on the inside of her arm, and the world went dark.

21

Silas

By the time they reached the *Sweet Jenny*, Temple was breathing in short, painful gasps. His face was waxy, blood soaking his shirt despite the pressure Silas was holding against the wound. The shot had hit him low in the side, but it was high enough up that the man's lung was probably punctured, and Silas could hear it in the rattle and wheeze of his breath, see the blood bubbling around the corners of his mouth and staining his teeth.

Ari had called in ahead, and when the airlock door slid open, Vee and Gracie were waiting at the entrance. Vee strode inside and crouched beside Silas, her face grim. "Toothpick, Jumper, going to need help getting him to the med bay," she called over her shoulder, then she pushed Silas gently out of the way and examined the wound.

"What happened?" Gracie had come up behind them, her own face as grim as Vee's.

"Energy pistol," said Ari shortly. "Sil slit the throat of the one as did for him, leastways."

Vee glanced up at Silas, her gaze taking in his blood-soaked shirt. "Any of that blood yours, lad?"

He shook his head. "The shot was meant for me. Temple got me out of the way. This belonged to the one who shot him." He waited for the flash of condemnation in Vee's eyes, but she just turned back to the wounded man, peeling back his makeshift bandage gently.

When he looked up, Toothpick and Jumper were standing over them with a hover-stretcher.

"Help me get him up, lad," Vee said, getting to her feet. "Don't have much time, from the sounds of him." Between them, she and Silas maneuvered the unconscious Temple onto the stretcher, then she gestured to Toothpick and Jumper. "Get him down to the med bay, I'll be behind you. Need both of you with me, most likely."

They started off, Vee striding along beside the injured man. Silas was half-tempted to start after them, but Ari put a hand on his arm. "Leave it, Sil. Vee don't like people getting in her way when she's working. She'll call in if she needs help."

He nodded without looking at her, and stared after the stretcher. His jaw was clenched tight enough that his head ached with it.

Gracie stood beside them. Silas could feel the tension from her, but when she spoke, her voice was as mild as ever. "Sil, Ari. What happened?"

"We got in, did what you asked," Ari said. Her tone was muted, and he could hear in it how worried she was. "Sil distracted the officers while Temple'n me were in the control room. Worked well enough, but we ran into an officer on the way back who didn't see things our way. Tried to shoot Sil point-blank, and Temple jumped her. She got off a shot, and then Sil slit her throat and we brought Temple back."

Gracie glanced at Silas. "Will they be suspicious of boarders, you think, finding her?"

He hesitated, then shook his head. "On a normal day, I'd say yes. With sick and wounded everywhere, it's more likely they won't have the time or sailors to worry about it until things have calmed down." He paused. "Captain. This was my fault."

She raised her eyebrows. "How so?" She paused, then gestured them over with a jerk of her head. "May as well talk in the cockpit. More comfortable there, and I'd just as soon be somewhere I can see if we're running into trouble."

Silas fell into step behind her, Ari following.

The guilt of it sat in his stomach like a rock. One more thing he couldn't quite bring himself to think about.

He couldn't hold it off forever. One day, everything he was pushing back would come crashing down over him, and he wasn't sure, honestly, if he'd survive it. But not yet. He couldn't afford that yet.

When they reached the cockpit, Gracie slid into her usual seat and gestured to the pilot's chair. "Got Freddie on the weapons while Vee's got Jumper down in the med bay," she said. "Ari, you think you can handle piloting in the meantime? Not hurt, are you?"

"I can pilot." Ari's words were terse, but it was more worry than anything. "Not hurt, me."

Silas stood where he was for a moment, then at last he sank down into another chair. Gracie studied him for a long moment, and he couldn't bring himself to meet her gaze.

"Your fault, was it, Sil?" she asked at last.

He nodded. "She recognized I didn't belong on the ship. Temple got shot trying to get me out of the way." He was speaking through his teeth.

Gracie quirked an eyebrow at him. "You figure he shouldn't

have?"

"No!" Silas snapped. "He's our damn navigator, and I've seen how good he is. I'm … what the hell am I, a glorified cabin boy? I'm disposable, Temple isn't."

From the pilot's seat, Ari snorted. "Told you, Captain, navy messed with the boy's head."

Gracie was still studying him, a hint of humour twitching at the corners of her mouth. "You're my crew, Sil. Don't take kindly to people killing my crew. Temple did what any of my crew would have done, that's why they ship with me." She shook her head. "Can't speak for every pirate crew. Hell, probably plenty out there that make the navy look clean. But not a one on the *Sweet Jenny'd* cut a crewmate's line to save themself, if I thought they would they wouldn't be here."

Silas closed his eyes and forced himself to breathe slowly.

"Vee's a good doctor, she's pulled people out of worse before," Gracie said quietly. "Don't give up on Temple just yet. But for what it's worth, lad, I'd be just as worried if it was you down in that med bay. You signed onto my crew. Ain't going to let you walk yourself into a pistol shot on account of what you were fed as a boy in the navy."

"Aye, Captain," he said dully.

"Ari? You said you got done what I asked?"

"Done and dusted," said Ari, attempting a grin.

"Good." She turned to Silas, and there was something unexpectedly compassionate in her tone. "Got to talk to Ari about next steps, lad. That'll mean discussing what we've done. You don't want to hear, may be a good time to go clean yourself up, find Freddie and ask her to find a task for you."

Silas tried for a wry smile. It came out weaker than he'd intended, but at least he managed that much. "No, Captain," he said. "I'm sailor enough to know what I've done."

She nodded, still studying him. Then she turned to Ari. "You know the gist of it, don't you, lass? Sil, what you and Ari brought me from the Level in those documents was more or less what I hoped it'd be. See, reason the Level's new tech looked familiar to both of us was, we'd both spend our share of time reading over the records from the trial. There was a bug in the programming for the FTL drives when they sent out the Starfire fleet, caused them to malfunction mid-jump. That's what caused the disaster. Don't have to mention what came after—you know that well enough. Pinned it on treason, they did, when the real reason was mismanagement in the ranks, people who thought to line their pockets with no regard for the lives it'd cost. Be that as it may, they took the FTL drives out of the ships. But looks like they didn't give up on the technology. Weren't going to be able to put it back in an FTL drive, I guess, but from the looks of it they found a use for it in the nav systems."

Silas listened impassively, but tendrils of dread were winding around his chest.

Gracie paused, watching him, and there was a look in her eyes that was almost sympathy.

"We replicated the bug that caused the FTL drives to malfunction, didn't we?" he asked. "You got the specs of it off the documents I brought back."

Gracie nodded.

Silas closed his eyes.

He knew well enough what this would do.

A full fleet of ships. Fifteen naval vessels left of it, well over three thousand sailors, if he was any judge.

"You alright, lad?" Gracie's voice was quiet, but harder than he'd ever heard it. "Because if you ain't, don't need to stick around for it."

He'd been the one to bring her the information. He'd been the one to sneak Ari and Temple onto the ship to plant it, and in the process, he'd slit the throat of a naval officer whose only crime was doing her job.

Not that it mattered. She and all her shipmates had been doomed the moment Temple stepped out of the control room—a bright wash of devastation that would leave their bodies strewn across the vastness of space at the pressure of their navigator's hand on the FTL controls.

He felt like he might vomit.

But was this really any worse than what he'd already done? He'd already betrayed the navy. He'd saved Gracie's life, when it was a choice between her life and the lives of everyone on the *Agate*. He'd gone onto the Level to steal documents, he'd taken advantage of Lawrence's loyalty to get himself and Ari away, knowing full well what he was carrying with him and what he planned to do with it, killed an officer of the navy for the crime of protecting her ship.

It hardly seemed to matter. Finding those documents had turned the solid ground he'd built his life around to mist under his feet, and he'd been in freefall ever since. If there was a hell, he'd long since damned himself.

There was only one thing he was certain of now. He was going to take the Level down. He was going to stop it from hurting anyone else like he'd been hurt. And a war meant casualties, there was no escaping it.

"No," he said distantly. "No, Captain. I'm fine."

He could feel her eyes on him, but he kept his fixed on the screen.

"Ari," Gracie said at last. "Get the scanner running, pick up what you can of their broadcasts. Best we know when to expect it. They're a naval fleet, so I'm guessing they'll all jump at once. Figure we ought to know when it'll happen. Moment they're gone and out of our way, we can get Temple back to Blackrock where he can be taken care of proper."

"Aye, Captain," said Ari.

"They won't die in pain, if that's what you're worried about, Sil," she said. "Temple and Jumper managed it so they'll die instantaneous."

Silas nodded, without speaking.

"You wanted to declare war on the Level," she said. "I wasn't convinced we could do it, when you first came to me. But if we take out an entire fleet, saddle the Admiral with a second Starfire—I think that may be enough to take down even Admiral Usher. And if we take her down, figure there aren't too many as won't topple along with her."

Again, Silas nodded.

His stomach was a hard knot, and the tension in his shoulders ached down his spine. But he wouldn't take it back. He couldn't.

He'd asked for Gracie to take down the Level, and she was doing it. There was no quarter given or taken in a war like this. And if he'd damned himself, at least he'd see the Level and those who'd been living on the fat of the Starfire disaster dragged to hell with him.

"I did, Captain," he said quietly. "And I don't regret anything I've done."

It was the truth. But it didn't take away the taste of vomit in the back of his throat as Ari scanned through the channels and picked up the naval broadcast line, waiting for the flagship to give the order that would take down the fleet.

22

Hollis

"Captain."

Hollis felt as if she were swimming through mud, her mind thick and unresponsive.

"Captain!"

She blinked her eyes open, and a hazy shape took form in front of her.

She muttered something incoherent, and the shape moved, adjusting something over her head. "Captain Ives?"

The figure over her bed consolidated into a person at the same time as the fragmented memories snapped back into place. She jerked upright, then doubled over, squeezing her eyes shut against the lance of agony the movement sent through her and cursing through her teeth.

"Steady on, Captain, you're not cured yet, dammit." Archibald's voice was thick with concern.

"What the hell happened?" Hollis hissed in a sharp whisper, the moment she was able to speak again.

Archibald's face was grim. "I had my orders to sedate you, and if I didn't do it, you'd end up in the brig. I may not hold with the commodore's methods, but he was right on one thing—you wouldn't have lived through that, not in the shape you're in right now. Although," he added under his breath, "if it was possible to survive on nothing but sheer bull-headedness, I suppose you might have lived through it after all."

Hollis closed her eyes, her stomach sinking in sudden dread. "What happened?" she asked. "How long has it been? Did Mad Dog —"

Archibald held up a hand. "Easy, Captain. It's been—" He checked his timepiece. "Half an hour, give or take. The commodore has ordered the ships to prepare for a jump back to the Level, but it'll be a few minutes yet. They're still loading the sailors off the disabled ships." He paused. "I followed the commodore's orders, like I said, since it was that or lose a patient. But I reversed the sedation the moment the commodore cut off the call." He shook his head. "Took you this long to wake up, and I don't doubt it was at least as much the fact you haven't slept in thirty-six hours as it was the sedation. But now that you're back among the living ..." He tapped his comm. "Mate Price. I think there's someone here you'd asked to talk to."

There was a tap on the med bay door an impressively short time later. When Archibald pulled it open, Foster stood there. Their face was drawn and pale, their uniform more rumpled than Hollis could ever remember seeing it. The relief on their face at seeing her, though, was utter, and completely unmistakable. "Thank God," they said, stepping quickly inside and closing the med bay door behind them. "Captain, are you alright?"

"I'm fine, Price, what the hell's going on out there?"

They shook their head tightly. "Mate Greene and I have been scanning through everything the screens have picked up. We've had to do it quietly to keep the commodore from noticing, but I've picked up something, I think."

"What is it?" Hollis made as if to stand, but Archibald pushed her back down.

"Stay there, damn your eyes," he snapped. "Do you want to be conscious, or not?"

"I've got it here," Foster said, crossing over to crouch beside her. "Look." They pulled a note up on their comm, and Hollis glanced through it quickly.

"There," Price said, and then she saw it. A small dot on the far edge of the screen, well out of range of the battle.

"That's her?" she asked. "Are you certain?"

Foster nodded grimly. "It's her. Took me a while to run all the vis checks under the shielding, but I'm certain of it. But watch this." They tapped the note, and the scene moved. Hollis squinted at it, frowning. Then she saw the tiny shape detach from the *Sweet Jenny*. She sucked in a quick breath as it latched onto the side of the *Resolve*, dread coating her stomach. But it detached again what must have been a few minutes later, returning to the *Sweet Jenny*. The ship pulled back, out of range of the sensors, and the note flickered still.

She looked up into Foster's pale face. Their expression told her that they had no more idea what had happened than she did.

"Have we heard an alarm from the *Resolve*?" she asked.

Foster shook their head. "This was about ..." they glanced at their timepiece. "Forty minutes back. If they'd planted something on the ship, we'd know by now."

Hollis closed her eyes, trying to force her foggy brain to function.

What the hell was Mad Dog playing at? It was something, she'd known there was some reason that Mad Dog had held off in the battle. But what? It couldn't be something as simple as taking down the *Resolve*. After the battle with the pirates that had taken down two ships of the line and disabled two more, Mad Dog would never settle for something so anticlimactic. Taking out the commodore and the flagship would be something, yes, but not enough for someone like Mad Dog Gracie Madox.

"Why the flagship?" she murmured. "It was in the centre of the formation. She risked running the skiff through the fleet's sensors, and bringing the *Sweet Jenny* in close, for what? If she'd wanted to take down as many sailors as she could, there's three-hundred-and-fifty-crewed ships on the outskirts of the formation. So why this?"

Foster shook their head. "I've been trying to figure out the same thing," they said, their voice clipped and grim and exhausted. Hollis realized, abruptly, that while she'd had at least an hour or two of sleep, Foster hadn't been spelled off since the beginning of the battle.

She squeezed her eyes shut.

What was she missing? What the hell was she missing that Mad Dog had seen?

"Besides the commodore, what does the flagship have that the others don't?" she said, half to herself. "What would Gracie need on the flagship?"

"It's the communications centre," Foster said slowly. "If she'd wanted to disrupt communications—"

"But she didn't, did she?" Hollis said. "The commodore had no trouble communicating with us."

The wry look on Foster's face told her everything she needed to know about how they felt on that subject.

"And even if it had happened after, Archibald told me that the commodore gave the order for the fleet to be ready for jump in the last few minutes. So if she meant to disrupt the communications, it didn't work." She paused. "Unless … unless she didn't want to disrupt the communications." Horror was building in her gut, hot and heavy, the memory of that awful, hopeless moment when she'd been told of the mag-lock Mad Dog had sent back with the skiff, and realized, abruptly and irrevocably, that the pirate had doomed them all. "Unless she wanted the jump to go ahead, for some reason." She pulled in a quick breath, fighting the fog in her brain, trying to force her thoughts into clarity. "Unless there was some way she sabotaged the jump. But how could she …"

"The programming," Foster snapped, standing abruptly. "The flagship sends out the jump coordinates to every ship of the fleet. If Mad Dog found a way to sabotage them somehow …"

Hollis closed her eyes against the dizzying wave of dread. "That must be it. Price, that has to be what she did. The ships cannot jump, not until we have time to figure out what the hell she did with the jump coordinates. Whatever happens, the fleet cannot begin the jump."

23

Foster cursed, low and harsh. "There's no way you or I will talk the commodore into delaying the jump," they said. "If he realizes you're conscious right now, he'll throw you in the brig with Smyth, Greene, and me to keep you company, and send one of his own over here to captain the *Verity*."

"I know," said Hollis grimly. "But we can't let them jump."

Foster hesitated, then blew out a short breath. "If there's an error in the code, it'll be something discoverable, but I somehow doubt the commodore will listen if it comes from any of us on board here. He already thinks we're next-door to mutineers. Is there any captain in the fleet who might listen if you could get through to them?"

Hollis grimaced. "As you may be aware, Price, I wasn't exactly a popular candidate in the Academy." She paused a moment, then shook her head. "The *Consolation's* first mate may listen to me."

Foster's eyebrows shot up. "Excuse me, Captain," they said after a moment, "but isn't that Lucian Ainsley? The man you almost killed in a dual in the Academy?"

Hollis gritted her teeth. "Yes, it was. But he didn't rat me out afterwards, which was honestly more than I expected. He may listen.

But from what Smyth told me, we won't have time for Ainsley to run the diagnostics, even if he does agree to do it. Didn't the commodore give orders to jump in the next few minutes?"

"I'll tell the commodore we had a malfunction, and we need time to repair her," said Foster grimly. "I'd guess there's at least a fifty percent chance he sends one of his own technicians over to take a look, and once that happens we've lost the ship. But that should give Ainsley time to run the diagnostics."

Hollis stared at them. "Price," she said at last. "I wasn't aware when I first met you that you were willing to risk a court-martial on such a regular basis."

"I'm not!" Foster's tone was frayed. "But I'm not usually serving under someone who runs quite so bullheadedly into danger at every damn opportunity!"

Hollis felt a pang of guilt, but she crushed it ruthlessly. This was the survival of the entire fleet.

"Very well, Mate Price," she said brusquely. "You do that. I shall contact Ainsley."

"I'll get you a line through the ship's comm," said Archibald grimly. "And let's pray to God or Our Lady of the Ghosts that you get through in time."

Lucian Ainsley's tone, on hearing Hollis's voice, was less than pleased. "Ives?" he snapped. "What the hell do you need?"

"Listen, Mate Ainsley," she said through her teeth. "I have reason to believe that the pirates have sabotaged our FTL jump."

He paused. "You …" he began. Then he snorted. "Try someone more gullible. I know you hate me, but this is low even for you."

"I don't hate you," she snapped.

"You almost killed me!"

"You didn't give me a choice!" Her words rang out in the med bay, and a couple of the medics turned to look at her curiously. She lowered her voice. "I swear to you, I would not have contacted you had it not been an emergency. And I'm currently putting my own damn life on the line to do so. Have you ever known me to lie?"

He hesitated. At last, reluctantly, he said, "What do you want me to do?"

"I need you to talk your captain into running diagnostics on the jump code the flagship sent out. I have visuals that the *Sweet Jenny* sent a skiff to the *Resolve*, then left a few minutes later. I suspect they sabotaged the codes, but I can't prove it myself. The commodore is … disinclined to listen to me at present."

There was a long moment of silence. "Send over the visuals," Ainsley said at last. "I'll speak with my captain."

Hollis closed her eyes in relief. "Thank you."

"I'm not doing this for you, Ives."

"I don't give a damn what you're doing it for, it's a chance to save the damn fleet," she bit out. "My own first mate is currently risking a court-martial to give you time." She paused, pulling up the visuals Foster had sent through to her, and sent them on to Ainsley. "There. I trust that's sufficient proof?"

A moment later, he whistled low. "I suspect I can make my captain agree to run scans if I show her this," he said. "I'll keep you up to date on the results."

The line clicked off, and Hollis sagged on her cot. At last, ignoring Archibald's worried look, she forced herself to sit up straight, and tapped a line through to her first mate. "Price," she said. "Ainsley has agreed to go through the codes the flagship sent out."

"Thank God for that," Foster's voice was tight with strain. "I was worried the commodore would have me hanged for treason on the spot when I told him we'd had mechanical issues. Greene backed me up, but the commodore is going to send someone over the moment he has time to spare. It's not going to put off the jump long—he's already determined that the ships that do not have damage will make the jump, and he's currently deciding how many ships he'll leave back with the injured ones. But it's something, at least. It's bought us maybe ten minutes." They paused. "Best pray that Ainsley runs the scans quick-time."

"Captain. Please at least lie down while you're waiting news. It won't change whether the answer comes back good or ill." Archibald's voice bore the weary patience of one who was accustomed to his pleas falling on unheeding ears.

If the pain in Hollis's gut hadn't been enough, at this point, to have her seeing stars, she may not have obeyed even then. But it was, and she lowered herself reluctantly onto the bed, her teeth gritted so hard they ached.

She couldn't tear her eyes from the timepiece over the door.

Three minutes.

Five.

From the ship's comm Archibald had brought her, she heard the commodore issuing orders, the acknowledgements of the captains preparing for an FTL jump.

Seven minutes.

Nausea churned in her stomach, and there was an odd, feverish cast to her thoughts that made her wonder, distantly, if there was some truth to the commodore's diagnosis. This entire thing felt like some fever-nightmare, where everything was unreal and at the same time both much too close and impossibly far away.

"Prepare for jump in two minutes. Captains, instruct your navigators to follow my count." The commodore's voice was sharp and brisk.

Hollis closed her eyes, muttering a prayer. Her cutlass had been removed when she'd been transported down to the med bay to be sedated, and she didn't even have a buck-knife to slit her thumb, but she assumed she'd bled enough recently to satisfy even Our Lady.

24

The broadcast Ari had pulled up was crackly and unclear, but understandable if you were listening closely enough.

Silas couldn't seem to pull his attention away from it.

He noticed, from the corner of his eye, that other members of the crew had drifted into the cockpit as well, until it was crowded, but he didn't dare pull enough of his attention away from the broadcast to notice who'd come and who was still left behind.

He'd agreed with Gracie that together, they'd take down the Admiralty. And she was right—this would do it. This would destroy the careers of hundreds of self-satisfied bureaucrats and admirals, and it would reopen the conversation about the Starfire disaster that had changed the course of his life and Gracie's. It might, even, allow them to show the documents he'd stolen, and let everyone on the Level see what the Admiralty had done, and what they'd covered up.

And to do that, they were going to kill thousands of innocent sailors.

Perhaps "innocent" was too strong a word. Perhaps Gracie was right, and every person who signed onto the navy owned their sins in the same way the navy had always insisted every person who signed up for piracy owned theirs, circumstances notwithstanding. But he'd grown up in the navy, dammit. He'd seen, first-hand, who these sinners were—his friends. His lovers, his family—people who were more his family than the aunt and uncle who'd raised him. Innocent they might not be, but they were just people, in the same way Ari and Freddie and Jumper were just people. In the same way Temple, lying on the point of death in the med bay, was just a person. They hadn't asked for this war. But they'd suffer for it, nonetheless.

"Prepare for jump in two minutes. Captains, instruct your navigators to follow my count." The commodore's words were brusque and businesslike, and there was no suspicion in them. They must have found the woman he'd killed on the *Resolve,* but it seemed they hadn't connected it to pirates. And why would they have? The pirate ships were gone, most of them jumped far enough away that they'd not be a danger. The trap had already been sprung. There was no reason to suspect what Gracie had done.

He'd agreed to this. Temple had almost died for this. Temple had almost died because he was trying to save Silas's life. He'd agreed, and he wouldn't take it back, even if he could. The Level navy needed to be cleaned out. It needed to finally, finally pay for the sins it had hidden for so long, and he knew well enough that meant bloodshed. You couldn't take down corruption like this without bloodshed, and he'd always known, even when he'd tried not to, that most of the people dying would be people who had no involvement in it.

"One minute. Wait my count."

He'd damned himself, and he knew it, and the thought made sickness twist in his stomach, guilt clawing its way up his throat. He'd damned himself, and Gracie had damned herself, if she wasn't already damned for what she'd done as a pirate. He didn't know anymore. He wasn't sure, anymore, what was right and what was wrong. But he knew well enough that once this happened—once he, himself, was complicit in a second Starfire—that was something he could never take back. That was something he could never redeem himself from. He'd grown up hearing about his duty. He'd grown up being told what he was born to do. And he'd betrayed that, over and over and over. Every time he'd chosen his own life, the lives of the pirate crew who had become, against all odds, his friends, over his duty to a navy that would have hanged him, he'd betrayed that duty.

Perhaps, after all, he didn't deserve redemption. Perhaps he never had. And perhaps it was only right that he would destroy himself, just as certainly as he'd destroy the naval fleet, the moment the order came to jump. Perhaps, in some perverse way, he'd finally found a way to fulfil the duty that had been injected into his veins since he was too young to remember or question. Perhaps this was the final sacrifice—himself, his morals, his duty, his chance for redemption, his very damn soul—in pursuit of something greater.

"Commodore! Wait! Hold the count!" The woman's voice was sharp with fear, and the very unexpectedness of it jolted Silas out of his revery. "This is the captain of the *Consolation*. Hold the count!"

He turned, automatically, to where Gracie sat.

Her posture had stiffened, and he saw at once that she had no better idea than he did what this was about.

"Captain?" Ari said, her voice tight with strain.

Gracie gestured her silent. "Just keep the broadcast going, lass." There was a tension behind her mild tone that told Silas she was more angry than she was willing to show.

"Hold!" The commodore barked the command. "Captain

Edwards. What is it?"

"Commodore, I think we should speak privately. This is an urgent and sensitive matter, and it's regarding the jump codes."

"Ari, who is this Captain Edwards?" Gracie's voice was loud in the sudden stillness.

"Don't rightly know, Captain," said Ari.

Gracie nodded, eyebrows raised in an inquisitive look. "Why don't you find out everything you can on her, then?" she asked. "I'd like to know where this sudden suspicion came from. Didn't get close to the *Consolation*, and there's no reason why she'd have cause to check the jump codes. In the meantime, Jumper, you get on another broadcast channel. Look through the ones from earlier, and any private messages you can find. I'd like to know what the hell is going on." Her voice was sharp and clipped and businesslike.

Jumper nodded, face grim, and stepped over to where Ari was frowning over a scrolling list of holonotes.

No one spoke, but Silas could feel the tension through the cockpit, mirroring the tension singing through his entire body. He'd been shoving his own emotions back for so long that he hardly knew what he felt right now, hope or dread.

Then, at last, the commodore's barked-out command echoed over the broadcast, sharp enough that it was clear even through the fuzzy captured signal. "All ships, hold! Repeat, all ships are ordered to hold!"

Silas let out the breath he'd been holding, a sickening rush of something that could have been despair, or bone-melting relief, washing through him so strongly that he swayed a little on his feet.

They'd lost. Somehow, the commodore had discovered what they'd done, and they'd lost. Everything he and Ari had done to get the documents to Gracie, Temple, lying unconscious in the med bay with Vee working frantically to keep him alive, for nothing.

There wouldn't be another Starfire after all.

He felt like the ground had been cut out from under his feet.

He'd doomed himself. He'd taken hold with both hands of the thing that would make him, finally, unredeemable—only to have it dissipate from between his fingers like mist.

He'd been saved. Against his will, despite himself, he'd been saved.

"Captain." Ari looked up. "Have the info you were looking for. Edwards captains a two-hundred-crewed ship, graduated the Academy seven years ago. No connection to pirates, and we haven't gone up against her in the past. Nothing I can find ties her in with Starfire, either."

"What about her first and second mates? Anything there?" There was still that simmering anger under Gracie's tone, but there was a dark interest in it as well.

Ari grinned tightly. "Figured you'd ask that. First mate is Lucian Ainsley, graduated from the Naval Academy six months ago. This is his first posting. Looks like there was some sort of mark on his record in the Academy—caught him duelling or some such, but they let him graduate anyway. No record of a ship he served on going up against the *Sweet Jenny*, no history with Starfire. Same for the second mate, Nolan Berton, although he graduated a decade ago."

"Wait," said Silas suddenly. "Lucian Ainsley? I heard about that. He was almost killed in a duel, and everyone said it was Hollis Ives who all but killed him. He wouldn't admit it to the Admiralty when they questioned him on it, and that almost got him thrown out, but he had a family name behind him. If he'd ratted out Hollis, she'd have been out before they had time to convene a hearing. But there were rumours enough in the Academy at the time, and the other candidates left her alone after that."

Gracie turned to him, interest burning in her gaze. "Hollis Ives," she said thoughtfully. "Seems we can't go a month without hearing her name." She glanced over at Ari. "I didn't check which ships of the line were sent out in the fleet. Is the *Verity* part of it?"

"Aye, Captain." Ari's tone was grim.

Gracie hummed quietly. "Hollis Ives. She's a clever woman, seems like." She turned, and Silas realized that the rest of the crew in the cockpit, other than him, had been keeping an eye on Jumper.

He cursed himself, and resolved to damn well do better about that.

"What did you find, lad?" she asked.

Jumper's fingers flew in rapid signs, and Silas followed along as best he could. He'd been devoting more time to studying the Stacks sign language that made up most of Jumper's vocabulary, but he'd been distracted enough in recent days that he'd let his studies slide a bit. He could still pick up enough, though, that he could parse the meaning.

Found something … earlier broadcast … Ives … you need to hear.

"Go ahead then, lad, play it for us," said Gracie, in her usual mild tone.

Silas closed his eyes and tried to get himself back under control. He wasn't entirely sure how Gracie could take their defeat with such equanimity. His entire body was shaking with tension, his muscles weak with accumulated strain, his brain humming with adrenalin.

But then, he realized suddenly, this had been Gracie's life. He'd been quick enough to condemn her as a coward when he first met her, but she'd been doing this for twenty-five years—scraping by, pulling herself and her crew out of obscurity by main force, swallowing insult after insult and defeat after defeat, watching the woman who'd testified against her on false charges rise to become the most important figure in the Admiralty. If she hadn't, she'd never have survived as long as she had.

He'd wanted a lion, someone brave enough to roar in the faces of the hunters that shot at it, and he'd found a fox. And the fox had survived, raiding the edges of the Level, nipping and biting and never quite letting them rest easy, for over two decades before Silas had discovered the secret he'd found in the archives. She'd lived with it that long.

Jumper tapped the broadcast line, and a voice came through that Silas recognized instantly.

Hollis Ives.

"Commodore. The pirates aren't through with whatever they're planning. We need all ships on full alert."

There was a moment of silence, then the commodore's voice. "Ives? What the hell are you playing at? The pirates took us by surprise, but we made sure it cost them. And we sent them running, I had my officers tracking the ships. There weren't any that stayed behind."

"That's precisely the problem." There was an undertone to Hollis's voice that spoke of something beyond exhaustion, but her words were sharp. "The *Verity* has no record of the *Sweet Jenny* during the battle, and nor do any of the other ships I've been in contact with. Mad Dog wasn't there."

"Surely that's a good thing. If Mad Dog decided to save her own skin and leave the fight to the others, I hardly see—"

"Commodore. Have you gone up against Mad Dog before? Mad Dog wasn't in the battle, because she has something planned. Some trap. I know her, I've gone up against her before. She won't leave this, Commodore. She's not one to let others fight her battles, and she's not one to let naval ships of the line come after Blackrock without fighting back. Please. We need every ship on high alert until we figure out where the hell the *Sweet Jenny* is."

They listened in silence as the commodore stripped Ives of her post and replaced her with her first mate.

Silas found he was leaning forward, jaw clenched.

He'd never known Hollis personally, only heard the rumours of her in the Academy, and seen how she'd reacted when she'd gone up against them a month previous. It had been, by all accounts, her first command.

Somehow, she seemed to have both gained the ire of the commodore, and the loyalty of at least her first mate and chief medical officer, in that short time. For a moment, he was almost certain that Mate Price was going to disobey a direct order.

And he couldn't help a wince of sympathy when he heard the chief medical officer of the *Verity* agree, at last, to sedate his captain.

The recording clicked off. Gracie was frowning thoughtfully, but when she opened her mouth to speak, Jumper made a quick gesture. *Not all. There's more.*

His fingers danced over the controls for a moment, and another recording crackled to life.

"Commodore. This is Acting Captain Price, of the *Verity*. Regret to inform you that we seem to have suffered a mechanical incident. We will not be ready to jump on schedule. Request that you delay the jump until we have time to figure out what's going on."

The commodore's cursing through the line indicated exactly what he thought of his newly promoted Acting Captain.

Jumper's fingers moved on the controls again, and a new voice came out.

"Ives? What the hell do you need?"

"I have reason to believe that the pirates have sabotaged our FTL jump." Hollis sounded more dead than alive at this point, her voice ragged and exhausted. "I swear to you, I would not have contacted you had it not been an emergency. And I'm currently putting my own damn life on the line to do so. I need you to talk your captain into running diagnostics on the jump code the flagship sent out. I have visuals that the *Sweet Jenny* sent a skiff to the *Resolve*, then left a few minutes later. I suspect they sabotaged the codes, but I can't prove it myself. The commodore is … disinclined to listen to me at present."

There was a moment of silence, then the voice that must have been Lucian Ainsley responded, with a note of resignation. "Send over the visuals. I'll speak with my captain."

The recording ended.

That was eight minutes before Captain Edwards called in to the commodore, Jumper signed.

For a few moments, there was silence in the cabin. There was a thoughtful expression on Gracie's face, but there was danger there, too.

Silas closed his eyes.

He couldn't get the sound of Hollis's voice out of his mind. *"I would not have contacted you if it wasn't an emergency. And I'm putting my own damn life on the line to do so."*

It wasn't just her life she'd put on the line. She'd put her first mate's and her chief medical officer's reputation, and likely their lives as well, on the line with hers. Because despite the fact that she'd been betrayed by the navy, perhaps even more thoroughly than he had, she'd chosen her side. And she'd been willing to sacrifice innocent lives to do it.

He didn't agree with her. He couldn't. There were too many good people in the navy who would be sacrificed to cover up corruption, over and over and over, too many good sailors and officers, like himself, like Hollis, who'd be fed to a machine that would crush them, with no regard for morality and no accountability, if the corruption wasn't brought into the light, the perpetrators of it brought down.

But she'd done what she'd done, risked her life and the lives of people whose only crime was loyalty to their captain, to do it. She'd stopped the massacre of the naval fleet. She'd saved her own soul.

And in the process, she'd somehow, inadvertently, saved his as well. The edge he'd been about to plunge over had been fenced, abruptly, and he'd been pulled back from the step that would have lost him to himself, forever.

He wasn't sure if he was furious, or grateful.

He closed his eyes.

In the end, it didn't matter. It didn't matter why she'd done it or how he felt about it, it didn't matter if he agreed with her or with what she'd done.

If Gracie's plan had worked, and the fleet had gone up—once he'd been complicit in a repeat of the same disaster that had killed his parents and seen him raised an orphan, he'd have doomed himself to a path he'd never come back from. He'd seen it as inevitable.

And it wasn't. Whatever Hollis Ives had or hadn't done, she'd done that, at least. By snatching it away, she'd shown him it had never been inevitable at all.

It was his choice. It had always been his choice. And whatever he did next, it was his own goddamn choice.

"Hollis Ives," said Gracie at last, that thoughtful note in her tone. "She's just as clever as the Admiral gave her credit for, it seems." She turned a little in her seat and glanced over her assembled crew. "And now, I suppose, we'll need to decide what to do about her." She paused, glancing back at the screens. "They haven't jumped. But they can't, now, and they're at least a day, if not more, from help. They're stranded, and they can't use their navigation equipment to get home. We could put a call out to the rest of the pirates, bring them back. It'll be bloody, but enough of the ships are injured that we might shoot a few more of them down yet."

"Captain. Wait." Silas was almost surprised to hear his own voice. He hadn't, consciously at least, decided to speak at all.

"Yes, Sil?" Gracie turned to him, eyebrows raised, calculation in her gaze. "What is it?"

"Captain." His voice was grim. "I told you I planned on taking down the Admiralty with you. I won't go back on that. It needs to be taken down. But this is playing the navy's game, spending the lives of the Level sailors before the mast and sacrificing our own."

"This is war, Sil. Don't reckon you can win a war without innocent people getting hurt. And I ain't sacrificing Temple's life to save a few naval sailors—figure you know me better'n that. No chance of getting him back to Blackrock, not with the navy fleet sitting there, and now that they know we're here? They track us jumping for the Stacks, they'll have every naval ship left over waiting for us when we come out of jump."

He sighed, closing his eyes for just a moment. "I know. This is war. But I have an idea. We can still get Temple somewhere safe. We can still take down the Admiral, without killing pirates and a thousand Stacks and resource planet sailors to do it. We don't have to get our hands as dirty as they're willing to get theirs."

She was still watching him, and he could feel her gaze pierce clear through him. But at last, she nodded slowly. "Alright, lad," she said. "Ain't going to say I care much for the navy, but if you can give me a way to save pirate crews, I'll hear you out. Let's hear this plan of yours."

25

Hollis

"Captain. Would you be so kind as to come to the bridge? I'll send someone down for you, but I have a question I believe you may be able to assist me with." There was a tone in Foster's voice that made Hollis shove herself upright, hissing out a curse between her teeth.

She managed to slide off the medical cot and catch herself before she landed on her face on the floor, ignoring the dirty looks Archibald was sending her direction.

True to Foster's word, by the time she'd managed to straighten and clear her head, a young midship officer was at her elbow, the same one, if she recalled correctly, who had helped her to her cabin earlier. Foster was clearly unwilling to let Hollis's condition become common knowledge on the ship, and Hollis was absurdly grateful.

By the time she reached the bridge, her muscles were trembling, sweat standing out on her forehead, but her mind felt clearer than it had in a long time. The sharp panic of the last few minutes had cleared away the cobwebs of exhaustion, and it had been long enough since the sedation that it, too, had cleared her system.

At last, she sank into a chair on the bridge that the young midship officer brought her, letting out a quick, involuntary gasp of relief.

The other officers on the bridge were studiously ignoring her, their gazes fixed on their controls. She was impossibly grateful for it. If there was to be a charge of mutiny, best it stayed with her and Foster, although Archibald was almost certain to be implicated as well.

"Acting Captain Price," she said, once she'd recovered her breath.

She caught Foster's minute flinch at the title, but the expression they turned on her was as respectful and impassive as ever. She'd known them long enough now, though, to see the worry under it.

"Captain," they said, crossing over to her. "I do apologize for the trouble, but as things stand, I can't leave the bridge. I was hoping you would have some insight into a recent development."

She heard the words they weren't saying. They needed her advice, and they didn't dare ask it over the comm channels for fear they'd be checked, sooner rather than later.

"Of course, Acting Captain," she said. "I'm happy to be of assistance."

Foster crouched next to her seat, pulling up a readout on the screen in front of her. "Captain," they said in a voice low enough to avoid being overheard. "Look."

She frowned at the screen they were showing her.

Then she sucked in a quick breath. "That's the *Sweet Jenny*."

"I know." Foster glanced around quickly, then lowered their voice. "She's still out there. And she must have figured out by now that the jump isn't going ahead."

"Which means she knows the ships are at least temporarily stranded," Hollis finished, unease stirring in her chest. "I don't think this is over yet."

Foster gave a quick shake of their head. "I'm inclined to agree with you. Mad Dog is the closest thing to a leader the pirates have. She may not have a title, no, but they'll listen if she calls them in. And I'm not certain we'll last another battle against pirates, not damaged as we are, and not with the *Sweet Jenny* thrown into the mix. We took far too many losses last time, and that was without Mad Dog. With the ships stranded like this ... I don't like what the commodore did. But he was right on one thing, at least—I think there are more than a few here who are on the edge of panic."

Hollis closed her eyes and breathed in through her nose, then blew out a calming breath. "Have you informed the commodore yet, Acting Captain?"

"God's sake, Captain, please don't! It's bad enough from the commodore without you doing it, too!"

She turned to stare at Foster, and they dropped their head wearily into their hands. "I'm sorry," they said, and she could hear the ragged exhaustion in their voice. "No, I haven't informed the commodore yet. I wanted to speak with you first."

Hollis turned back to the screen, glowering at it as if it might tell her the secret of what Mad Dog was planning if she stared at it long enough.

Then she saw it.

She cursed. "She's doing it on purpose. Look where she is on the screen—in range of our scanner, but none of the other ships will pick her up." She closed her eyes a moment. "She must have figured out it was the *Verity* that stopped the jump. And now she's sending a message."

Foster was frowning at her. "What message do you think she's sending, then?"

Hollis almost laughed. "She's letting us know she's there. And she's letting us know that if she decides to, she can call back the other pirate ships."

Foster was still watching her, their face still creased in a frown. "Why?"

Hollis managed a grim smile. "I'm not sure. But I suspect she's giving us an option—go after her, or watch her take down the fleet."

Foster stared at her for a moment, then cursed, low and angry. "We can't take down the *Sweet Jenny*. If she wants us to come after her, it's to lead us into a trap."

Hollis nodded. "I know. But if we keep her busy long enough, then the fleet gets away. I think that's her bargain—us, or them."

Foster stood abruptly, pacing over to their own screen and then back. They closed their eyes, running a weary hand over their face. "What should we do, Captain?"

Hollis was still watching the screen.

There was a strange, lightheaded exhilaration pulsing through her, flooding through the fear and exhaustion. "We go after her." She pushed herself upright. "We go after her, and let her try to bring the *Verity* down. The *Verity* is a ship of the line, and Mad Dog may be clever as hell, but we stand a chance. And even if she shoots us down —we've still won. We've given the rest of the fleet a chance to get back to safety."

Foster drew in a long breath. "You'll sacrifice your crew."

Hollis closed her eyes. Her heart was still pounding with that same strange exhilaration. "Ask them, then," she said. "You're Acting Captain. Ask them. Ask them if they're willing to face death to save the fleet. Because these are my sailors, and they've done this before. Back in the Adrian Sector, they put their lives on the line to save the crew of the *Agate*. Just now, they put their lives on the line to save the flagship. And they'll do it again. I'd wager my rank on it, whatever that's worth."

Foster was watching her, ruefulness and frustration mingling on their face. "You're right, Captain," they muttered, almost to themself. "They're your sailors. And here you are, standing on the bridge, half-conscious, defying your commanding officer's orders, ready to throw yourself into the jaws of death yet again. How the hell could they do otherwise?"

She held their gaze. "Ask them, Price. The command will have to come from you. I won't force you into this."

Foster gave a humourless laugh. "You wouldn't have to, would you?" They turned on their heel and strode over to the comm.

Hollis watched them with an air of odd detachment as they requested, in their usual steady tone, for Emmett to assemble the sailors on the main deck. Then they stepped out towards the captain's deck. They cast a glance back at her as they went, but she couldn't read it.

She sagged back into her seat, closing her eyes.

"Captain?" It was the junior navigator.

Hollis forced her eyes open with an effort. The woman was watching her, eyes large and frightened. "Captain, is it true? Are we going to go after Mad Dog and let her shoot us down?"

Hollis studied the woman for a moment. "I have no intention of allowing Mad Dog to take my ship or my crew," she said at last. "But there's a chance there'll be nothing I can do to prevent it. And if you knew we couldn't prevent it? That we'd run the risk of losing our ship, but saving the fleet? What would you say then?"

The woman closed her eyes, and Hollis saw the bob of her throat as she swallowed. "I'd say I'll follow you, Captain Ives," she said, her voice quiet.

From the main deck, she could hear the quiet rise and fall of Foster's voice, although she couldn't make out the words.

Her first mate was doing this for her as well. She'd known them long enough to know that. They wouldn't have made this choice on their own, let alone presented it to the crew.

But she couldn't very well do otherwise. Mad Dog had been trying to take down an entire naval fleet, thousands of sailors and officers with their ships. And Mad Dog had given her the opportunity to prevent it, and possibly lose her crew for it.

"Captain." She looked up abruptly to see Foster standing beside her. They gave her a brief smile, but there was no humour in it. "The crew will go after Mad Dog if you ask it of them."

She hesitated the briefest moment. Then she nodded. "Very good, Price. Contact the commodore, if you would, and request his permission."

The commodore's acquiescence was curt and brusque. "Damn your eyes, Acting Captain Price," he grumbled. "I'd lay good money your Captain Ives is behind this. But I won't say no—we're stranded, and God knows we need the help. Likely save me from hauling the both of you in front of a court-martial when we get back to the Level, at any rate."

"Thank you, commodore," said Foster, their tone still impressively calm despite the ragged exhaustion under it.

They turned back to Hollis.

She gave a short nod. "May as well get on with it, then," she said. "And we'll see if I read Mad Dog right."

26

"Well," said Gracie quietly, her eyes fixed on the screen in front of her. "Looks like you were right after all, Sil. Looks like your friend Captain Ives was clever enough, or stupid enough, to pick up on your message."

Silas stood behind her, looking over her shoulder at the screen. Sure enough, the dot that was the *Verity* had turned, and was coming after them.

His stomach was tight, his hands clenched at his sides.

They were going to take down the *Verity*. He was going to help Gracie shoot down Hollis Ives, who'd fought her whole damn life to get where she was, and her ship and her crew with her.

But she'd made her choice, and so had he. She'd chosen the navy, and he'd chosen to take it down, and he knew well enough that both of them were convinced the choice they'd made was the right one.

He was going to take down the navy that had killed his parents and was willing to sacrifice a hundred sailors like Hollis Ives in its insatiable appetite for glory and wealth and reputation. Taking down the fleet would have done it, and killed thousands of sailors in the process. But if they played it right, taking down Hollis Ives could do the same thing. The first commissioned officer from the Stacks. The woman Admiral Usher herself had thrown her backing behind. Hollis Ives, already with a charge of insubordination hanging over her head the moment the commodore returned to the Level, who'd recklessly taken her three-hundred-and-fifty-crewed ship after the *Sweet Jenny*, and who'd be shot down doing it. If anything could shake the Naval High Command's confidence in the Admiral, it would be that. If Gracie could use that defeat to embarrass the Admiral badly enough, it could bring all the rest of her decisions into question. And with the information on the two batches of documents Silas had stolen—perhaps they could turn the tide against the Level still.

And despite the fact that Temple was still in the med bay, hovering between life and death, despite the grim, haunted look in Ari's face and the cold ruthlessness in Gracie's expression—Silas would talk them into doing this with as little bloodshed as possible, if he could.

Hollis was willing to sacrifice herself and her crew for the navy. And he was willing to sacrifice himself and his future to bring it down, but he wasn't going to sacrifice his soul, not this time.

Hollis had, at the very least, shown him he had that option.

Gracie turned to glance at him. "Are you ready then, lad? Let's see how Hollis Ives navigates a jump with compromised nav equipment, shall we?"

Silas nodded, his expression grim. "Aye, Captain. I'm ready."

27

Gracie

Gracie drew in a long breath, trying to pull herself back from the blind fury that wanted to consume her.

Hollis Ives was a product of the navy that had created her. She was a tool, that was all, albeit a clever one.

But Temple was lying in the med bay next to death, and Ives was currently standing between the *Sweet Jenny* and safety, and Gracie had neither the time nor the patience to worry about the well-being of one of Judith's willing tools.

Silas was right—much as the anger burning inside her called for blood and destruction, they could kill Hollis Ives without sacrificing more pirate crews, and that, at least, was a good thing. They may well need every pirate crew she could get onside once this had started in earnest.

"Ari," she said, glancing over at the girl. Ari's jaw was set, and there was a concern on her face that told Gracie just how worried the woman was. "You're piloting. Sil, you get on the charts. They taught you that in your Academy, I assume?"

"Aye, Captain." The lad's expression was fixed as well, his face still pale. Neither he nor Ari had had time to so much as change from their blood-spattered naval uniforms, and for a brief, incongruous moment, Gracie almost smiled at the irony of the situation—her cockpit piloted by two uniformed Levellers, who, in a different life, could have been standing on the bridge of a ship of the line like the one they were planning to shoot down.

"We'll run thirty minutes out, then do a short jump," she said, pushing her calculations to hover over Silas's screen. "Put us down here. Let's see how our Captain Ives handles an FTL jump without her nav equipment." She gave a humourless grin. "Or perhaps we'll get lucky, and her navigator will slip up, and we'll see if Temple's hack worked after all."

Ari gave a distracted nod, glancing over at Silas. "Get me the coordinates, Sil, soon's you can."

"Aye," he said, bending over his screen.

Gracie watched them for a moment, then stood. She could trust Ari to run the ship straight, and she had no doubt as to Silas's abilities, now that she was confident he'd not question her orders.

"Call me on the comm before you go into jump," she said. "I'm going to check on Temple."

She stepped out of the cockpit and strode quickly to the edge of the deck, sliding down the ratlines with the ease of long practice.

Vee was waiting for her in the med bay, face grim.

"How's he?" Gracie asked brusquely.

Vee tipped her head towards the cot. "Not good, Captain. I can keep him alive for now, I think. But ain't going to do much more less'n I can get somewhere with proper supplies."

Gracie followed the woman over to the cot.

Temple lay there, skin an unhealthy grey, tubes over his mouth and nose, an IV hooked up to his arm and cords and sensors over his body.

Her stomach twisted to see him like that. He'd been her pilot for more years than she could remember off the top of her head, and he was a good man.

She'd lost crew before. It was an unavoidable part of her chosen profession. But she refused to accept the inevitability of it like most pirate captains did. She wouldn't give the Level that.

She'd given them everything else. She'd given them so much, and they'd taken it all—her life, her career, her identity, her family, the only woman she'd ever loved.

She wouldn't give them her crew, not without a fight. She'd never give them that.

"Is there anything we can do?" she asked, forcing herself not to look away from the wounded man on the cot. She owed Temple that much, at least.

From the corner of her eye, she saw Vee shake her head. "Not 'less you can get us back to Blackrock. Or better yet, to the Stacks—the hospital there'll treat him. I know Neon, worked with her before. Knives'd be able to save him no problem, and even if she's not there, there're other surgeons she's trained. We could save him if we got back to the Stacks. But that ain't happening with that naval ship on our tail, is it?"

Gracie shook her head grimly. "It won't, at that. But I don't plan on having them follow us for long."

Vee studied her for a moment. "Didn't think you would, Captain," she said after a moment. "And the lad? He's not making a complaint?"

Gracie shook her head, a hint of a smile forming on her lips. "No. Lad was distraught about what happened to Temple, but I think he'd have been alright with it either way. Turning pirate, the boy is, and that ain't a bad thing. Figure he'll be an asset after all."

Vee nodded slowly. "Figure you may be right," she said. "Didn't think much of the lad at first, but you're right—he's officer type if I've ever seen it. What Ari says, he knows plenty about the navy that'll be useful."

Gracie nodded. She let her eyes run over Temple's still form one last time before she turned for the door. "I'll get you a passage back to the Stacks soon as I can," she said, her voice grim. "Figure it'll take more than one naval ship to stop that."

Vee nodded, already turned back to her patient, and Gracie stepped out of the med bay. Her jaw was clenched tight enough that the tension radiated up her skull and gathered in a knot at the back of her head.

She'd be damned if Hollis Ives would cost her her navigator.

By the time she returned to the cockpit, Ari and Sil were bent over the jump calculations. Ari glanced up briefly as she entered, and Sil gave her a quick nod, but didn't look up.

She hid a smile, and stepped over to study the screen over Ari's shoulder.

The naval ship was close enough behind them that she knew Ari had kept them in range on purpose—weren't many ships that could match the *Sweet Jenny* for running speed, and none of them were naval ships of the line.

At last Ari straightened in her seat, leaning back a moment to stretch out her back before hunching forward again. She glanced up at Gracie, almost involuntarily, and when Gracie gave her a brief nod, she turned back, placing a hand loosely over the FTL controls. With her other hand, she tapped the ship's comm. "Going into jump on my count." Her voice was clipped. "Three. Two. One. Jumping."

There was the quick disorientation of an FTL jump, but Gracie was accustomed enough to the feeling that she hardly had to brace.

Silas was bent over the charts, his forehead creased in a scowl of concentration. At last, he tapped something through to Ari's screen and sat back, closing his eyes a moment. When he looked up, his eyes found Gracie's. "How's Temple?" he asked quietly.

The lad was a sailor through and through, someone who'd have had a captain's posting a few months out, more than most likely. But there was a desperation to his voice that she recognized, and the blood smeared across his forehead and soaking through his shirt, the pallor in his face, made him look somehow younger than she knew he was.

"Vee'll keep him alive, lad," she said, her tone matching his. "Meantime, you'n me and Ari'd best figure a way to get him somewhere that'll do more than keep him from dying."

Silas nodded, turning back to his controls, but she could see the tension in his posture.

Silas

"You ready, Sil?" Ari's voice was grim. "Because figure we're both about to get real busy in a minute here."

"I'm ready," he said, running his hands reassuringly over the controls.

He could still feel the residual adrenalin from his time on the *Resolve* humming through his body, the stiffness of drying blood crusting his shirt, but he didn't have time to focus on any of it.

Ari was right. The coordinates Gracie had set had them coming out right in the outer pocket of a debris field. Temple could have put them down perfectly, and hell, he'd known Ari long enough to guess she knew damn well what she was doing as a pilot. But this sort of jump took absolute precision, and even if they hit it straight on, they may not last the first minute or so afterwards.

"Coming out of jump on my count. Three. Two. One. Coming out." Ari snapped.

He tightened his hands on the controls as the ship came out of jump, then swore, yanking back on the controls to avoid a piece of debris bigger than the *Sweet Jenny* directly in front of their cockpit.

He heard Ari's involuntary curse from beside him, but he couldn't focus on that right now, because every scrap of attention he could spare was devoted to keeping them from blowing themselves into space dust.

A smaller bit of debris glanced off the ship's shields.

"We're hit," Freddie snapped through the general line. "Another like that and we'll lose shields."

He didn't have the attention to answer her, focused on keeping them on a course that would lead them through the worst of the debris without a direct hit that would take out any of the vital ship's systems.

"Jumper," he snapped, yanking his attention off the screen for just long enough to hit the general comm line. "Need you on the guns. I'll mark the ones I need you to take out, and you'd damn better hit them right on or we're not making it out of this in one piece."

Jumper's staccato acquiescence through the comm was reassuring, even though Silas only caught perhaps one out of three words.

He tapped the screen quickly with his free hand, marking the debris coming up he was pretty sure he wouldn't be able to steer them out of, and a moment later, the sharp burst of shots from the *Sweet Jenny's* guns appeared on his screen, momentarily lighting the black.

Tension sang through his muscles, his knuckles white as he clutched the stick.

Another smaller piece of debris glanced off the ship, and he could hear Freddie's cursing through the line, but he couldn't pay attention to it right now.

The path he'd chosen would get them through the debris field with minimal damage, and he was almost certain that they'd not lose anything vital, but if Jumper didn't manage to take out the massive meteoroid in front of them …

The shots were still streaking out, impacting against their target with no noticeable effect, but dammit, they were too close, he didn't have time to chart them a new course …

The meteoroid glowed, the bursts of energy igniting the core of it, and, as if in slow motion, the entire thing shattered like dropped glass.

The weapon bursts turned to the largest of the fragments, and Silas barely had time to snap through the line, "All power to the shields and brace!" Then they were in the middle of it.

He had to hold himself back from flinching at the chaos around them, and the *Sweet Jenny* shook and jolted, the shields glowing as they dissipated the energy of the hits …

Then they were through, and Silas dropped bonelessly back in his seat, his entire body weak with relief.

"Not bad, Sil," came Gracie's voice, and he looked up to see that she'd come to stand over his shoulder.

He managed a small smile. "We're all still alive, at any rate. Although I think Freddie might skin me once she has time to catalogue the damage."

As if on cue, Freddie's grim voice came through the line. "We've taken damage, Captain, but didn't lose anything as we couldn't afford to. Still have our guns and our shields. Running engines ain't going to thank us, but we can limp back in, and the FTL drive didn't take damage."

"Thank you, Freddie." As always, Silas was almost shocked at the calm in the captain's tone. "That's good enough for now, and once we get to the Stacks, Recoil'll let us have a dry dock if we need one."

"We'll need one." Freddie's voice was still grim, but touched with a hint of humour. "Tell the lad he's just made a hell of a lot of work for himself."

Silas managed another small smile.

Gracie smiled back, but there was something comforting about the hardness under her expression. "Well, lad," she said quietly. "That ain't going to do to a ship of the line what it'd have done to us if you'd been half a second slower, but they won't be expecting it. Figure by the time they come through that, they won't be in much shape to fight." Her smile widened, just a little. "So I suppose now we wait and see if Captain Ives can manage a jump without her nav equipment."

Silas closed his eyes just a moment, and he couldn't tell, exactly, if what he was feeling was excitement, or dread, or some mix of both.

But he knew damn well it didn't matter one whit.

28

Hollis

Hollis stood on the bridge, her hands clasped on the back of her chair.

She and Archibald had come to a tacit agreement—she'd stop trying to pretend not to be injured, and make whatever concessions necessary to stay upright without further injuring herself, and he'd stop trying to insist that every damn thing she could do on the bridge she could do via holoscreen from the med bay.

It was true, in a technical sense. The ship easily had the technological capabilities to broadcast her face and voice onto the screens on the bridge. In a technical sense, to be perfectly honest, she no longer had any authority on the ship.

But Foster was right. Every person on this crew who'd agreed to go after Mad Dog had done it because of her. Every one of her sailors had put their lives in her hands. And if she was taking them to their deaths, she'd do it upright from the bridge of her ship, not lying on a cot in the goddamned sickbay.

The *Sweet Jenny* was running ahead of them, heading away from the naval ships, and despite everything, Hollis could feel a tight knot of relief in her chest.

At least, whatever happened, they'd be away from the fleet. At least that she hadn't gotten wrong.

"Stay on them," she said brusquely to the navigator, without turning to look at the woman. "If they head back towards the Level, get around to cut them off."

Foster had ceded the bridge to her, and she was grateful for it. There was something grounding about being able to give orders again, being able to take control of the situation.

It wasn't that she didn't trust Foster. Even after only two voyages, she trusted Foster more than she'd ever have imagined when she first met them, with their cool, collected expression and respectful tone.

But she was leading this ship and crew to their deaths, and all aboard knew it.

Foster would have done it if she'd asked them. But she couldn't bring herself to ask. This was on her head. All of it was on her head, and she fully intended to be the one to take responsibility for it.

Besides—she managed a small, humourless smile.

It was unlikely that any of them would live long enough to face charges of insubordination back on the Level.

She tapped a line through to the gunners. "Prepare to fire on the *Sweet Jenny* the moment we're in range," she said. "I doubt she knows what damage we've taken. She may be gambling on the possibility that we've been injured badly enough that we won't have the firepower to take her out."

It was unlikely. But at this point, she would cling to any shred of hope she could find.

"We're gaining on her, Captain," the navigator said, her own voice tight with strain.

"Gunners on the alert, all shields up," Hollis snapped through the general line. "Prepare for a broadside."

She'd seen the *Sweet Jenny* run before. If the *Verity* was gaining on her, it was because Mad Dog wanted them to.

Then, abruptly, the pirate ship flickered, and was gone.

"Captain, they've jumped. Permission to follow them before—"

"No!" Hollis snapped out the word at the same time Foster did, both of them leaping forward involuntarily.

The woman froze, her hand hovering over the control as Foster reached her, yanking out power to the nav equipment. Hollis let them deal with it, doubled over in agony herself and gasping. By the time she'd straightened, the nav equipment was disabled, and Foster had turned back to her.

Their lips were pinched, strain drawing their face, but they didn't say anything, just waited until she'd recovered.

"I'm afraid they're out of reach," Foster said, voice grim. She could hear in it that they knew the same thing she did—that the *Sweet Jenny* had drawn them far enough out from the fleet to leave it even less protected than before.

She swore. "I will not let her get away that easily," she snapped.

"Captain, with respect," Foster began, the harshness in their voice telling her more than anything how close to the edge they were.

"We'll jump on dead reckoning," she said.

For a moment, there was silence in the bridge.

"Come on, sailors, you've heard of dead reckoning?" she snapped impatiently. "Every last one of you who studied in the Academy had to take an exam in it, I believe?"

"Captain," the navigator said at last, her voice shaking slightly. "Yes, Captain, we all took an exam on dead reckoning an FTL jump. But ... but they warned us only to use it in case of an utter emergency, if there was no way to get help. If you do it any less than perfectly, you lose the ship and all souls on board."

"Then we'd best do it perfectly, hadn't we?" said Hollis, sinking into a chair. She pulled up a screen in front of her and tapped through the sensors, studying the faint energy-glow that indicated where the *Sweet Jenny* had jumped.

They had fifteen minutes, maybe less, before the *Sweet Jenny's* jump path was too faint to follow.

"Captain," the navigator said. Her face was pale. "They told us in the Academy that an FTL jump on dead reckoning had a fifty percent chance of failure."

She didn't say the rest, what failure meant—ships vaporized, crews turned into frozen space debris. They all knew it perfectly well.

Hollis closed her eyes a moment. "Those statistics are based off a ship without a defined jump path to calculate off of. Mad Dog's given us that, at least. And most of the failures are attributable to human error, which means if we do the jump perfectly, they will be eliminated. Taking human error from the equation leaves us with an acceptable level of risk."

The navigator was still staring at her, face pale.

Hollis ignored her, and bent over the charts she'd pulled up.

Dead reckoning was more an art than a science, used mostly by the navigators in the earliest stages of FTL flight development. The technique had developed somewhat, but the fact that no one used it anymore except in cases of sheer survival meant that the technique was still fundamentally the same as it had been centuries ago.

The principle was, you took a reading of where you needed to be, studied the star-charts and the most recent readings of space debris, its path and trajectory, and mapped out a quick and dirty course with the use of a complicated math formula.

With the *Sweet Jenny* having done a jump in front of them, they could also use her jump-point and the amount of energy expended in the jump to judge the direction and length of the *Sweet Jenny's* path, which would help. The navigator had been correct—a jump on dead reckoning without a path to follow had just over a fifty percent success rate. With a jump path to follow, it raised their odds.

But still—failure could be attributed most times to human error. Which meant that if, as she'd told the navigator, they did the jump perfectly, their chance of success was within an acceptable range.

She closed her eyes a moment, forcing her pain-dulled brain to focus on the problem at hand.

"Officer Sullivan, Officer Wilson, please perform your own calculations as I work mine," she said into the silence. "As Officer Davis pointed out, we cannot afford human error. I would like at least three calculations done independently."

They had minutes before the jump-path would be faded enough not to be of use. But a jump path would do them no good if the calculations were off.

There were murmurs of, "Aye, Captain," and she copied the base information onto a holonote and sent it to hover in front of her two junior navigators.

"Price," she said. "Once we have a final calculation, I shall ask you and Greene both to check it independently. In the meantime, the ship is yours."

"Aye, Captain," said Foster, that same brittleness in their voice that she'd heard there since the moment she'd asked them to ask the crew for their consent.

Foster was furious with her. There was a small part of her brain still thinking clearly, still analyzing the situation, reading every tone in her first mate's voice. Foster was furious, and at some point she'd have to reckon with that, talk to them, figure out what the hell they would have had her do instead. But not right now. Because right now Foster was willing to follow her nonetheless, and behind her was a fleet of disabled naval ships stranded within running distance of Blackrock, two full days away from rescue through standard naval shipping channels, and if she couldn't find a way to take out the *Sweet Jenny*, or at least distract Mad Dog for long enough for reinforcements to arrive, they'd all die.

She groaned inwardly and turned back to her calculations.

This would be easier if every member of the bridge crew hadn't been exhausted, the hours of sleepless strain telling on even the most collected of them. Easier if she had had even a few moments of true rest since the beginning of this voyage, easier if her mind could focus calmly and clearly on the mathematical calculations that could mean the life or death of whatever remained of the three hundred and fifty crew that had been entrusted to her.

But then …

She managed a small, wry smile.

That was the entire point of dead reckoning calculations, after all. They were only to be used in an emergency. If there had been a captain in the last century who'd used dead reckoning to perform an FTL jump who hadn't been strained, exhausted, on the verge of collapse, with a skeleton crew and a broken ship, she hadn't heard of it.

No wonder the largest factor in a critical failure was human error.

But she was determined that this time, there would be no human error.

She finished her calculations and double-checked them, then leaned back in her seat and closed her eyes for a moment.

Four minutes passed already.

She was tempted to go over the calculations a third time, but she knew herself well enough to know that it would do no good, and going over her figures again after she'd already double-checked them would be more likely to lead to error than simply leaving them.

A moment later, Wilson's voice, cut sharp with strain, said, "Captain. Here are my figures."

She opened her eyes and pushed herself upright, glancing back and forth between her own figures and the ones on the holonote hovering in front of her with eyes bleary with exhaustion.

"And mine, Captain." Another note appeared, hovering in front of the first.

She looked them over quickly, then stifled a groan. "Sailors. One of the calculation results does not match the others. Please redo the calculations from the beginning, as shall I."

Seven minutes. The jump path on the screen was beginning to fade.

There was a murmur of, "Aye, Captain." Hollis squeezed her eyes shut a moment, trying to push the cobwebs from her brain, and swore quietly, then bent back over her calculations.

The second time, the three calculations came out identical.

Twelve minutes.

"Mate Price, Mate Greene," she said, sending the holonotes over to their stations. Then she pulled up the space charts, the diagrams and figures blurring and dancing before her eyes.

"I don't see any error in the numbers," said Foster at last, looking up at her. Their eyes were dark with exhaustion, but there was still that crisp competence in their tone that told her that whatever else happened, whatever else they may be feeling, she could trust their calculations. "But look where the jump will come out."

Hollis frowned, and peered down at the charts again, where a red circle illuminated a small patch of space.

She swore.

Of course. Mad Dog had them coming out in the centre of a debris field. Nothing that would be fatal to the *Verity*, but enough to knock them off-balance.

She wouldn't have thought to check, exhausted as she was. Not one in a hundred sailors would have thought to check, if they were following another ship's jump path.

But Foster had. Because they were Foster, and of course they had.

"We'll come out point zero one of a light second past where Mad Dog's route would have taken her," she said at last. "That should bring us out past the debris field, and still close enough to the jump site that we'll be able to locate the *Sweet Jenny* on our sensors."

It would be a close thing. If Mad Dog had jumped, paused, and jumped again, by the time they located the traces of the second jump, it was entirely possible that the signals would be weak enough to strand them with no way to get back and no trace to follow for their calculations.

She'd simply have to trust that she'd read Mad Dog correctly, and that the woman wanted to shoot her down, rather than simply leave her stranded.

She may be wrong, and if she was, she could be condemning everyone on board as well as the fleet she'd left behind her. She desperately needed more information, more technology, more damn time.

But she was captain. There was no time, and she had to make the decision with or without sufficient information.

For a moment, she almost laughed.

The assassination attempts, the pirates' trap on Blackrock, Mad Dog—this whole expedition had been an exercise in dead reckoning, scrambling to keep her crew alive and set a course without any damn certainty that the data she was working off was correct, and with no room for the slightest error.

She lifted her head. "Greene? Have you finished checking the calculations?"

"Aye, Captain." Emmett's voice came through the comm. "I didn't find any errors."

Fourteen minutes. They still stood a chance, barely.

"Very good," she said. She turned to the navigator. "Correct the course to come out zero point zero one light seconds past the calculated jump point, and prepare to jump."

"Aye, Captain." There was stark fear in the woman's voice, but to her credit, there was no hesitation in her response. "Prepare to jump on my mark."

It was a short jump. Mad Dog had jumped just a few light-minutes, either in an attempt to lose them, or an attempt to get them just far enough away that no help could reach them.

"Jumping in three. Two. One. Jumping."

Hollis grabbed for the arms of her seat, the accumulated weakness and exhaustion of the past few days making her head spin at the jump. Around her, the quick, laboured breathing of her bridge crew told her that every person here was on edge, waiting for disaster.

But she'd checked her calculations twice, and matched them with Wilson's and Sullivan's calculations, and even if she wasn't certain of her own mental capabilities at this exact moment, she had no doubt whatsoever of Foster's and Emmett's.

The strain in the bridge crew was almost palpable, hovering in the air like a fog. Hollis closed her eyes, trying to force herself to relax, but her brain wouldn't let her, playing the result of any potential failure or misjudgement over and over and over behind her eyelids until she had to force her eyes back open, or risk going stark mad.

"Coming out of jump on my count."

Hollis jerked her head up, blinking. It couldn't have been long enough already. Could it?

"Three. Two. One. Coming out."

She felt like she might vomit as the ship shuddered, her overwrought nerves magnifying every sensation.

Then they were out, and she blinked at the chart in front of her, the fuzz of an FTL jump clearing into a scene of empty space.

She stared for a moment, not entirely believing her eyes.

Then she flinched involuntarily as the bridge erupted into ragged, exhausted cheers.

"You did it, Captain!" someone was shouting, and hands were clapping her on the shoulders, grabbing the back of her seat, and she had to bite down hard to keep from screaming …

Foster barked something in a sharp tone, and the shouting died down, and she closed her eyes and sucked in a long breath, trying to regain her equilibrium.

"Captain. We appear to have made the jump successfully." Foster's voice was still, somehow, calm. "I'm engaging the sensors to locate the *Sweet Jenny*."

"Thank you, Mate Price," she managed, opening her eyes at last with a grimace. She tried momentarily to push herself to her feet before giving up and turning in her seat. "Well done, sailors. You performed exceptionally." She wanted to say more, but she could hardly promise them a promotion or an award at the end of this. Even if they survived, she was almost certain to be relieved of her command.

And suddenly, the thought hit her in the stomach with the force of a blow.

She'd be relieved of her command. But not just her. She'd take down Foster and Emmett with her, and Archibald as well. Her crew, whose heroic actions had been far beyond what could have been expected of them in the call of duty, would find those same actions hanging around their necks like shackles, dragging them down from any chance of promotion—the crew that had served under the disgraced Captain Ives.

She'd destroyed her crew. Even if they survived this encounter with Mad Dog, she'd ruined them. Her first and second mate, her ship's officers—every sailor aboard would bear the taint of having sailed under her.

Foster had told her. Foster had warned her, but she'd been so concerned with saving the fleet that she hadn't stopped to think about her crew—ridiculously loyal, willing to walk into the very jaws of death at her command.

She'd been willing to do it to herself, but then, she had nothing to lose. From the moment the commodore had ordered her relieved of command, she'd understood that her career was over. And she hadn't even stopped to think as she used the flames of her disgrace to torch the futures of the rest of her crew. She hadn't stopped to so much as consider what they'd pay for it.

"Captain? Are you alright?"

She blinked up into Foster's concerned face.

They were angry. She'd known that. She could deal with that.

It was the affection, the genuine concern under the anger, that cut her open.

She cleared her throat. "Yes, Mate Price, I'm sorry. I'm fine." She tapped the comm line. "Mate Greene. Order the gunners to prepare to fire on command."

She may have destroyed her crew, ruined her officers' futures. But for now, she needed to focus on saving their lives, if it was still possible.

"Aye, Captain," came Emmett's familiar voice through the line, still cut with strain. "Right away, Captain."

She paused a moment, gathering herself, then turned to Wilson. "Set our sensors to locate the *Sweet Jenny*, if you please," she said briskly. "I doubt they'll be expecting us to come from this direction."

There were some appreciative chuckles at that, and a moment later Wilson said, "Captain. I've located her. Looks like she's just noticed us."

Hollis glanced down at the screen.

Her junior navigator was right—the *Sweet Jenny* was just now turning to come after them.

Which meant, for the first time since the beginning of this nightmarish journey, they stood a chance.

She felt a slow smile spreading on her face, perhaps the first since the pirate's ambush in the space around Blackrock.

They might just beat Mad Dog at her game yet.

"Davis, chart us a course," she said, turning to her navigator. "Bring us in close on her port side, and we'll—"

"Captain."

She paused, something about the tone in Emmett's voice through the comm stopping her words in her throat.

"Yes, Mate Greene?" she said at last, praying her voice was steady.

Nothing could have gone wrong. So much had gone wrong on this goddamned voyage, nothing else could have possibly …

"I'm … afraid it's not good news, Captain." He was speaking to her through her private line, she realized numbly. "The guns are non-functional, as are the shields. Thank God we didn't come out in the middle of the debris field, or we'd have been torn to shreds."

For a moment, she simply stared straight ahead of her, her weary mind trying to make sense of the words her second mate was saying.

"What the devil do you mean?" she asked at last, the words coming out almost automatically. "How are the guns and the shields non-functional? We inspected them after the pirate attack."

The others on the bridge were looking at her, but she was almost too numb to care.

"I know, Captain." The grimness in his voice told her he'd already considered this. "There's no reason why they should be offline. But they are." He paused. "I've been going through everything, trying to figure out how the hell it happened, and there's no reason. Except that one of the sailors told me he saw someone headed up to the gun tower right before the jump. A woman, and I suspect I know who it was. I suspect our friend who tried to kill you, and escaped during the battle, was behind this."

For a long, long moment, Hollis said nothing.

There was no way out.

The *Sweet Jenny* had already noticed them, turned to come after them, and the *Sweet Jenny* was a much faster ship than they were. They were trapped here, with no reinforcements, no way to run, no way to jump to safety—even if they were to follow their previous jump track, in the time it would take her to perform the calculations for a cold jump, the *Sweet Jenny* could easily disable the *Verity*. And if she did jump, she'd be leading the pirate captain directly back to the stranded fleet.

The *Sweet Jenny* would take the *Verity* to pieces at her leisure, and without guns or shields, there was nothing at all Hollis could do to stop her.

She could feel the anger bubbling under the surface of her mind, feel the heart-stopping fury of it, that after everything—after the pirates and Mad Dog and an FTL jump on nothing but dead reckoning, after she'd sacrificed her entire crew for this—it was someone from the Level who'd finally doomed them.

But over the anger, over the fury, over the helpless, impotent rage, there was a cold, sick despair.

She closed her eyes.

"Captain?" It was Foster. She could tell by their voice that they'd either overheard, or had opened a line to Emmett and been briefed separately. "What are your orders?"

She drew in a long breath, then another. It was more difficult than it rightly should have been—her lungs didn't seem to want to expand, and there was an odd, heavy ache in her chest.

"Mate Price," she said at last. Her words came out dull and heavy. "Please open a line through to the *Sweet Jenny*. I intend to offer our surrender, if Mad Dog will accept it."

For a moment, Foster was silent. "And if she won't?" they asked at last.

Of course Mad Dog wouldn't accept her surrender. Hollis had heard enough of the stories. Mad Dog was merciless. At best, she'd get the pirate captain to laugh in her face for her troubles.

But she had to try. She had to at least try, because her crew had followed her here. She'd give up her dignity, her position—her life, if it would make the slightest difference—to save them. And if she couldn't save them, she had to know that at least she'd tried.

Hollis turned to her first mate and managed a bleak smile. "Then I suppose we show the pirates that we can die bravely."

29

"Well. Our friend Ives earned her rankings in the Academy, right enough, in case there was still any doubt. Been a good while since I've seen a jump on dead reckoning like that one."

Silas jerked his head up at Gracie's mild voice. His nerves were enough on edge that even her quiet voice made him start.

She caught his eye and gestured with a jerk of her chin to the screen in front of her.

He glanced over at it. It took him a moment to see what she'd seen, then he swore.

The *Verity* had jumped, right enough, but she'd come out a few hundred kilometres past the debris field he and Ari and Gracie had been trying to lead her into.

That would have been an impressive jump even with nav equipment—not everyone would have thought to check where a jump path would come out, especially if they were in hot pursuit. Knowing they'd done it by dead reckoning …

He shook his head, impressed despite himself.

Gracie's mouth twitched in a grim smile. "Almost seems a shame to shoot her down, don't it?" She turned to Ari. "Alright, lass, bring us in. Best take the *Verity* down now, before her captain has time to think too hard about the fact she's stranded out here without anyone coming to save her. Set us a course, then you and Sil can get on the guns."

Ari nodded without speaking. Her face was grim, and her fingers moved across the controls with an easy competence.

Silas leaned forward, ready to push to his feet and head for the gunner's tower the moment Gracie gave the orders, but his eyes were glued to the screen in front of him.

The *Verity* had clearly seen them, judging by the way the ship had moved, orienting itself to be in position to deliver a broadside the moment the *Sweet Jenny* came into range. Ari had noticed as well, because she made no attempt at subtlety in her approach, simply running the *Sweet Jenny* in as quick as she'd go.

Gracie turned from the screen, catching Silas's eye. "Alright, lad," she began, her voice quiet.

Then a sound crackled over the ship's comm, an incoming transmission from the *Verity*.

Gracie raised her eyebrows and hit the button to accept the transmission.

"This is the captain of the *Verity*, paging the *Sweet Jenny*." Hollis's voice was sharp and crisp, but there was a ragged undertone of exhaustion to it that made Silas wince in sympathy, despite himself.

"This is the captain of the *Sweet Jenny*," Gracie responded, a touch of grim humour in her tone. "And what is it you'd like to say, Captain Ives?"

There was a moment's pause. Then Hollis's voice, still crisp and clear, even with the sharp undertone of despair. "Captain Mad Dog.

I wish to negotiate the surrender of myself and my crew."

For a moment, Silas stared at the ship's comm, not entirely certain he'd heard correctly.

This was Hollis Ives. This was the woman who'd sent a skiff practically into the maw of a black hole to rescue the sailors off a dying vessel, the woman who'd performed an FTL jump on dead reckoning to come after the *Sweet Jenny* with no backup and millions of kilometres from help.

There was a slight frown on Gracie's face, as if she, too, was trying to judge the meaning behind Hollis's words.

"Don't rightly see that a surrender is on offer," she said at last, leaning forward. "Don't figure you'd have accepted a surrender of the innocent souls on Blackrock who you were determined to bomb into smooth glass, would you have?" Her tone was still grimly amused, but there was a steel under it that told Silas she was far from jesting.

"Captain Mad Dog." Hollis's voice through the comm was steady, but Silas could hear the hopelessness behind it. "As I said, I am willing to negotiate a surrender. We are, it appears, outgunned. You may name your terms. I only ask …" Her voice broke, just a little. She cleared her throat. "I only ask for the lives of my crew and my ship's officers."

Perhaps it was the break in her voice, after it had been steady for so long. But somehow, Silas's chest tightened with the same dread as when he'd seen Temple collapse beside him, the dread when he'd seen the grim look on Vee's face.

Because he'd heard in Hollis's voice the same thing he'd heard in his own when he'd thought someone he cared for would die for his mistakes.

He glanced at Gracie's face, and for a moment, he was almost shocked at the bitterness he saw there.

She leaned forward again.

"Wait."

Gracie turned to him, eyebrows raised questioningly.

"Wait," he said again. His heart was pounding hard enough he thought it might bruise his ribs. "Captain." He closed his eyes a moment. "We don't have to take down the *Verity*. You heard her. She'll accept any terms, if the crew lives."

He could feel Gracie's eyes on him, the intensity of her gaze hot enough to burn.

He pushed on. "Hollis Ives is the danger. Hollis Ives is the one whose death will weaken the Admiral. So kill her. Take the ship, put the crew on the life vessels and leave them here for the navy to rescue. They'll not be able to stop us getting Temple back to the Stacks for treatment, not like that, and with Hollis dead and the *Verity* in your hands or lost, her reputation will be as ruined as it would have if we'd shot her down."

"And tell me, lad, why would I do that?" Gracie's voice had taken on that soft, thoughtful tone that Silas knew meant danger. "Why would I save the crew of a ship as tried to bomb Blackrock, kill every pirate crew they could find, stopped me from taking my rightful vengeance, came after us meaning to shoot us down as my own navigator lies dying in the med bay? Tell me that, Sil."

Silas met her eyes, his jaw clenched tight. "Because I'm yours, Gracie. Body and soul. You want to use me to take down the navy, and I'm smart enough to know it's because you think I'll be useful. So here I am. I stole for you, helped you plant the codes that would have taken down an entire fleet. I always admired Hollis Ives, but you give me a pistol, and I'll be the one to shoot her through the head. I want to take the navy down, and I'm with you until the end

—I'm yours until we do it, or we die trying. But—" He paused a moment, forcing himself not to drop her gaze, even though he wanted to. "But I want to keep my soul, Captain. After all this, I want to keep my soul."

She watched him for a long, long moment.

She didn't need to agree. He knew that well enough—he'd tied himself to her with bonds of treason and lies and murder, and the only thing waiting for him on the Level was the executioner's noose.

But at long last, she nodded. "Very well, Sil," she said, her eyes still fixed on his. "Very well. I'll relay those terms to your Captain Ives. I'll need her first mate to die as well, since from the sounds of it, they're acting captain. But if she don't agree—if for one second she hesitates to accept my terms—you'll get up in the gunner's room with Jumper, and you'll shoot the *Verity* into space dust your ownself."

He nodded brusquely.

She watched him for a moment longer.

At last, she turned away, tapping open the line. "Captain of the *Verity*," she said. "Don't usually accept surrenders when it comes to naval ships. But I have a lad here who once shipped with the navy, crew member of mine. And he asked me to offer you terms." She paused, and when she spoke again, her voice was cold iron, a menace to it that made her unmistakable—Captain Mad Dog, the scourge of the Level navy for two decades. "You'll turn yourself in, you and your first mate. You'll bring a skiff to my ship, the two of you alone. Your second mate will evacuate your crew into the life vessels, and will turn over the *Verity* to me. And then my naval lad here will shoot you and your first mate dead on my deck. Those are my terms, Captain Hollis Ives of the *Verity*."

For a moment, there was no response.

Silas closed his eyes, feeling his pulse in his fingertips.

If she refused, if she chose to fight—

Well, Gracie was right. If, after all her brave talk, she wasn't willing to die for the crew she'd led here, she'd deserve whatever justice Gracie deemed fit to dole out.

Then the line crackled again with a returning transmission.

"Captain Mad Dog. I accept your terms. I'll instruct Mate Greene to begin evacuations. Please stand by for my skiff—I'll open a vid-feed so you can see that we're abiding by your conditions."

The line clicked off, and Silas wasn't certain if the rush of emotion at Hollis's words was relief, or dread.

But he'd done it.

Hollis had shown him he didn't have to lose his soul in pursuit of his objective.

And in return, he'd kill her, and save her crew, and possibly her soul as well as his own.

30

Hollis

For a moment after the line went dead, there was utter silence on the deck.

Hollis couldn't bring herself to look at Foster.

There had been one desperate moment, when Mad Dog had given her ultimatum, where she had. Where she'd glanced over at Foster standing beside her, and seen the look on their face before they'd managed to hide it, the quiet devastation.

And for just that moment, she'd been tempted to refuse. To try to renegotiate, even having heard in Mad Dog's voice that this momentary offer of mercy would be the captain's last.

Then Foster had looked up and caught her eye. Their lips had pinched, face gone once again bland but for the fury crackling in their eyes, and they'd shaken their head in a short, sharp motion that she could read as easily as she could read her own face in the mirror.

Foster recognized, as well as she did, the desperate, unthinkable chance the *Verity* was being given. The fact that their life would be forfeit along with hers was only a minor detail.

So she'd accepted. She'd accepted her own death, and she'd accepted Foster's, and she'd watch this pirate who'd once been in the navy, whoever he was, who'd somehow negotiated this offer, shoot her first mate in front of her.

Her first mate, who was only in this position because of Hollis's own goddamned stubbornness.

"Captain." It was Emmett, who'd joined them on the bridge.

She wasn't sure she could bear looking at him either, but she turned anyway.

His normally pale face was white with a mixture of shock and anger. "Captain, you can't mean to go ahead with this. I think I can speak for the crew when I say, we won't let a pirate shoot you dead without a fight. I say—"

She held up a hand to stop him. "Mate Greene," she said in a low voice. "This is a ship of the line, not a damned democratic parliament. Prepare the crew for evacuation, if you please."

"Captain—" It was the navigator this time.

Hollis spun to face her bridge crew, hissing in a sharp breath at the pain of the uncalculated movement. "That is enough!" she snapped, her voice stretched with the pain. "I have given you a goddamn order, and I expect you to obey! I will not brook insubordination, not here on the bridge of my own damn ship!"

It wasn't her ship, not anymore. She was already a traitor in the eyes of the navy, and so was Foster, for following her orders. So were the rest of them.

But Emmett's life could still, possibly, be saved. The lives of her bridge crew, her ship's officers, her sailors, could still possibly be saved.

The navigator's mouth snapped shut, but Hollis could see the horror in the woman's face—in the faces of everyone on the bridge.

She closed her eyes and drew in a long breath.

Damn this, damn all of it.

At last, she opened her eyes and turned to Emmett. "Mate Greene," she said, her voice regaining a semblance of its usual calm. "You will be in charge of the evacuation. You and the ship's officers will ensure that everything goes smoothly. There will be no heroics, no rescue attempts. This offer is a mercy on Mad Dog's part, and we will not jeopardize that. Do you understand me?"

He stared at her for a long moment, his eyes going between her and Foster. His face was still pale and tight with strain, a muscle working in the corner of his jaw.

"As appointed Acting Captain, I echo the Captain's orders," said Foster in a low voice from beside her. "Do your duty, Greene."

"Aye, Captain," said Emmett at last, turning away.

Hollis could feel her shoulders droop with relief.

She must have swayed on her feet, because Foster caught her elbow, inconspicuously guiding her hand to the table so she could lean against it. "I'll get the vid feed fixed, Captain," they murmured, turning away.

She closed her eyes and focused on pushing back the pain as, in the back of her mind, she heard Foster's quiet orders to the bridge crew.

A moment later, they were beside her again. "I have the vid feed set, Captain, and Greene is organizing the crew to evacuate."

She could hear, faintly, through the door to the bridge, the barked orders, the sound of running footsteps—the barely controlled panic of an evacuation.

But they'd have their emergency broadcast capabilities, and the life vessels would keep them alive, if not entirely comfortable, for upwards of two weeks, even at full capacity. They'd live through this, at least, even if she'd destroyed their reputations and careers.

And that was more than she'd allowed herself to imagine.

She straightened. "Very well, Mate Price," she said. "Shall we go?"

"Aye, Captain."

She drew in a deep breath and turned to the bridge crew, clearing her throat. "Thank you, all of you," she said, forcing her voice not to tremble. "You have each gone far above the call of your duty, and I'm honoured to have served with you."

She turned away before she could read the responses on their faces, and stepped out through the door, forcing her traitorous legs to hold her up by willpower alone. She could sense Foster beside her, but she kept her pace steady, her face ahead.

She paused as she stepped out onto the captain's deck. From below, she could hear the hushed voices of the crew, see the way they'd slowed their preparations to look up at her.

She hesitated for a moment, then she turned to them and saluted, holding the gesture for much longer than necessary.

There was the murmur of voices below her, carrying something that sounded uncomfortably like adulation.

She'd thought, once, as a young sailor, that something like this—the regard of her crew, the hushed whispers, the admiration bordering on worship—would be everything she'd dreamed of.

Now that she was presented with it, it twisted in her stomach and burned her throat like vomit.

But she owed them this. She'd brought them here, and she owed them this, at least.

At last, she turned away, and Foster had to catch her elbow again as she staggered.

"The lift, I think, Price," she said, a hint of wryness creeping into her tone.

Foster nodded silently, and turned with her towards the lift.

She could feel their stiffness through their hand on her elbow, sense it in their posture like the chill off a block of ice.

The two of them rode the lift down in silence. Foster didn't move their hand from her arm, and she didn't pull away—it would have been pointless, and she'd rather not lose what dignity she had left by falling on her face as she tried to walk to the skiff.

The lift came to a halt, and she and Foster stepped out, side by side, and made their slow way down the corridor to the skiff. The crew who'd prepared it stood at their approach, saluting silently, and Hollis returned the gesture.

She could feel their eyes on her back as she and Foster stepped into the small skiff.

She fell into one of the seats, her legs almost ready to give out under her. Foster, thank God, stood between her and her watching crew, as always, there to hide her moment of weakness. When she was settled, they turned and tapped the controls that would close the door to the skiff.

The pneumatic hiss of the door closing was loud in the silence.

Then it had closed, sealing them in, and they were alone.

"Mad Dog sent through the coordinates, and they've been set into the controls," Foster said, crossing over to her and strapping themself in. "We don't need to worry about piloting her."

Hollis nodded shortly.

She could hear, through the walls of the skiff, the clang of the airlock sliding open, feel the acceleration as the skiff started forward.

Then they were free, and the sudden, utter silence was almost disconcerting.

Foster sat beside her, and when she risked a glance at them, they were staring straight ahead, their expression fixed, tight lines of anger around their eyes.

She closed her eyes and drew in a breath. "Mate Price," she began at last. "I … apologize."

Foster snorted, not looking at her.

She cleared her throat and soldiered on. "You … were correct. I was not thinking when I took the actions I did. I should not have been … so reckless with your reputation. With your life. Had I the option of keeping you out of this—"

This time, Foster did turn, and there was something under the fury in their face, a sort of raw hopelessness, that took her aback. They stared at her a moment, incredulity playing across their features. "You think that's what I'm angry about?" they said at last. "You think I'm angry because you somehow took me down with you?" They shook their head and turned away, dropping their face into their hands wearily.

Hollis watched them, blinking back her shock. "I'm … sorry," she said at last, stupidly.

They didn't raise their head, and suddenly she was hit with a jolt of anger herself. "Mate Price," she snapped. "If you are angry with me, that is certainly your prerogative. But for God's sake, if you expect me to apologize, at least tell me what you're angry at me for! What the hell would you have had me do? What in God's name did you want me to do? I failed, and even if I were to live through this, that's something I would never entirely forgive myself for. But what did you want me to do?" To her utter humiliation, there were tears trying to well up in her eyes, tears of exhaustion and frustration and defeat.

She'd known she'd lose her life.

But she'd condemned Foster, as well, and the thought was a knife-wound through her chest, and even though she knew they had every right to blame her for it, there was some small, childish part of her that wanted to cry—not that she'd lost her life, but that she'd lost the closest person she'd had to a friend.

Foster closed their eyes for a moment, pulling in a long breath. "That's exactly the problem," they said at last, still not looking up. There was a bitter humour in their voice. "There was nothing else you possibly could have done. Any other captain, if they'd been injured as badly as you were, would have taken a medical leave. Any other captain, if there had been an assassination attempt on their life, would have been more concerned about their own security than protecting the navy's morale. And another captain, if they'd been relieved of their command and still, somehow, managed to save the entire naval fleet from disaster, would have left running a suicide mission after Captain Mad Dog to someone else. But not you. No. You're such a goddamn hero that you can't help yourself. Of course you'd do it." They shook their head. "And when everything went wrong, of course you'd believe the best course of action, the only course of action, would be to give your life up like the noble hero you are, and let Mad Dog shoot you down like a dog."

Hollis stared at them, unable to formulate a response. Her mind was still spinning through the words, trying to make sense of them.

"I ..." she began at last, then trailed off, unsure what to say.

Foster raised their head from their hands at last and met her gaze, a small, bitter smile on their lips. "I don't mind that you took me down with you, Captain," they said quietly. "I knew, from the moment you decided to take on Mad Dog rather than let her have the *Agate*, that one day I'd die following your orders. But you're the best damn captain I've served under. The most bull-headed, maybe, but the bravest, and the most principled. You've given your damn life to the navy, and this is how they reward you—left to be shot dead by a pirate, your name dragged through the mud, your reputation ruined. And your crew, too. They deserve accolades for what they've done, I've never seen a crew volunteer for a mission like this one, knowing what it would entail. But you'd never think to demand it, not for yourself, and not for them. You'll take this and you'll be grateful for it, and your crew will go back to the Level disgraced, and you don't even see how you—how we all—deserved so damn much more." They blew out a breath. "I don't blame you for my death. How can I? I followed you here. But if you have any sense of decency at all, you'll ask Mad Dog to shoot me first, because I don't damn well want to watch you die. That's all I ask."

She watched them for a long time.

She could see the trace of stubbornness in their face that they normally hid so well—the stubbornness that had saved her life and the life of the crew of the *Agate* back in the black hole, that had induced Foster to defy the commodore's orders and help her save the fleet. That had rallied the crew when she insisted they go after Mad Dog to lead the *Sweet Jenny* away from the injured ships.

"Perhaps you're right," she said at last, softly. "I was willing enough to sacrifice my own life, and I had that right. I had no right to sacrifice all of yours. I failed my crew, and I've failed you. And for that, I'm sorry. It's not enough, I know, I can't make up for it. But I'm sorry."

They looked up and met her eye. "Captain—" they began, then they broke off, shaking their head. For the first time she could remember, she heard their voice catch.

She found she was smiling, just a little. "You accuse me of being a hero. But I don't believe I've ever served with anyone quite as heroic as yourself, Price."

They glanced over at her, startled. Then they huffed a short, quiet laugh. "Quite the pair we make, then, Captain. Fools, the both of us."

She nodded ruefully.

The two of them were quiet again, but the silence now had a camaraderie to it that had been missing before.

Hollis found she was studying her first mate from the corner of her eye, unconsciously, trying to memorize their face.

She'd do what they'd asked. She'd request that they be shot first, and she'd watch them die. It was the least she could do. But selfishly, she wanted to remember them like this. She wanted to fix this picture in her mind—Foster, their body slumped with weariness, chin in their hands, their expression somewhere beyond exhaustion. Their posture was more informal than she'd ever seen it, as if here, at the end, they'd decided there was no point in keeping up appearances, and there was something oddly comforting in that. This was how she wanted to remember them—not a bloody body sprawled on the deck, or a vicious ghost. What she knew would be the last sight she'd have of them, before she was shot herself.

She looked up at the soft deceleration, something that would have been barely noticeable on a vessel any larger than the tiny skiff. Foster had looked up as well, their posture turning proper once more. "Captain," they said, turning to her, their voice once again calm and businesslike. "Are you going to need help off the skiff?"

She managed a small smile. "If you'll be so good as to help me to my feet, I think I can manage. I doubt we'll have far to walk, we can thank Our Lady of Mercy for that."

Foster gave her a small smile in return. "I still can't decide whether to sing your praises or curse your name, Captain Ives."

The skiff lurched, metal scraping on metal as it attached to the airlock, then there was the familiar jolt of the airlock sealing.

Foster unstrapped and stood, holding out their hand. "Captain?" they said, and when she looked up at them, she could see, under the grimness in their expression, that same mixture of concern and affection she'd seen earlier.

She took a deep breath and gave them another small smile. They helped her to her feet, and she leaned on them for a moment, finding her balance. The pain had faded to a dull ache now, something she hardly had the attention to spare for.

That, at least, she wouldn't have to worry about for long.

She let go of Foster's arm, and they glanced at her, eyebrows raised.

She nodded, and Foster stepped forward, tapping the control to open the skiff door.

Hollis turned to face the opening as the door slid silently back, her jaw set.

The first thing she saw was the walls of the reinforced airlock—the same airlock, a stray thought told her, that she'd sent her crew to die in weeks previous, in exchange for taking out the *Sweet Jenny's* stabilizers.

And gathered there, just past the airlock entrance, three figures.

The pirate captain, Mad Dog, stood in the centre. She was a woman a little past middle age, her black hair going to grey, lines of age and wear traced across her weathered skin and gathered around her eyes. Her clothing was neat, but nondescript, the only thing marking her as captain the way she stood and the obvious respect the others held her in. But there was something cold and perceptive in her gaze, an unspoken danger in her posture, that would have been impossible to mistake.

A younger woman, tall and pale, with blonde hair and startlingly blue eyes, stood beside her, a grin on her face and a pistol held steady in her hand, pointed at Hollis's head. She wore a naval uniform, ill-fitting and spattered with blood, but everything from the easy way she held the pistol to the relaxed casualness of her posture told Hollis that she was pirate through and through.

And beside her was the man who, Hollis guessed, had been the one who'd negotiated this bargain.

He was around the young woman's height, his tan skin and brown hair a sharp contrast to her pallor, and he too, was dressed in a naval uniform, although his jacket was missing and his shirt soaked through with drying blood. Blood was spattered across his face as well, and matted in his dark hair, giving him a dangerous, desperate look. But his posture was naval-straight, and he met her questioning gaze with narrowed eyes and a grim expression.

"Captain Hollis Ives," said Mad Dog. That mild, amused voice was so familiar, from the broadcasts to the *Verity* and from the nightmares Hollis had woken from in a cold sweat in the weeks since their first encounter, that Hollis almost started at it.

Mad Dog's glance roved over her and Foster, her eyebrows raised. "And this must be First Mate Price," she said, turning to Foster.

From the corner of her eye, Hollis could see the tension in Foster's stance, but they nodded without speaking.

Mad Dog smiled a little. "Very good." She paused. "Sil here told me you'd accept the terms. I admit, I wasn't convinced. But you're as proper a naval captain as he said you'd be—sacrifice your crew for the greater good, sacrifice yourself and your first mate for your crew. Everything the navy could have asked of you." There was something mocking in her tone that made Hollis want to retort.

She bit down on her tongue.

She was here for one reason only. She was here to die, and by doing so, save her crew. A pirate captain's taunts were hardly something worth taking note of, under the circumstances.

Mad Dog tapped the comm on her wrist. "Jumper?" she said into it, her tone casual, but clearly meant to be overheard. "Keep an eye on the vid feeds. Don't want the *Verity's* second mate to get any ideas about going back on his bargain."

The response came in a series of taps that the pirate captain seemed to understand, because she turned back to Hollis with a smile. "Your second mate seems to have followed your orders," she said. She shrugged. "I'd prefer to keep the *Verity* intact, of course. Seems a pity to waste all that good tech before we shoot her down. But if your second mate has any thoughts about going back on our bargain, I'll shoot her down crew and all." Her smile widened, just a little. "You're a brave woman, Captain Ives, and a clever one. Seen enough of you to know that. But the only reason your crew ain't floating out in space is the lad Sil here. So best thank him." She was still smiling, but there was something cold and dangerous in the expression now. "Because if it weren't for him putting his neck on the line for you, you'd see no mercy from me, Captain of the *Verity*."

Hollis held her head high and didn't respond. Her heart pounded rapid and unsteady in her chest, and the pain of her injury was seeping across her consciousness again.

She hoped, for her dignity's sake, that they'd shoot her before she was forced to steady herself on something or risk her legs going out from under her.

"Alright, Sil," said Mad Dog at last, turning to the man beside her. She pulled out her energy pistol and handed it to him butt first. "No point in wasting the captain's time."

Sil took the pistol from her and stepped forward, and Hollis let herself meet his eyes.

"Captain," he said, tipping his head to her respectfully. There was a grim note in his voice, and Hollis realized, suddenly, that whatever this man had done, whatever had led him onto Mad Dog's crew—he didn't relish this. He'd take no pleasure in killing her.

She closed her eyes for just a moment.

Whatever his story, whatever his motives, he'd saved her crew. She'd condemned them through her hubris, and this man, who'd betrayed the navy and every oath he'd sworn in its service, had somehow saved them nonetheless.

She opened her eyes and met his gaze. "Thank you," she said softly.

He dipped his head in acknowledgement.

She cleared her throat. "If I could ask one favour—I'd like to die last."

The wording would make her sound a coward, but she hardly cared. Sil seemed to understand, though, because he nodded again, turning to Foster with his eyebrows raised in question.

Foster gave a brief nod.

Sil checked the pistol, and for a moment, Hollis thought she might be sick.

Her own death she could face. But not this. Not watching her first mate die in front of her, because of her.

But she had to. This was what she'd condemned herself to, and she was sailor enough to face it.

"I'll make it quick as I can," he said in a low voice.

The blonde-haired woman stepped up beside him, sparker ignited in her hand, and Sil levelled the pistol at Foster's head.

Hollis forced herself to look, forced herself not to turn away.

She'd witness this. She owed Foster that much, at least.

Then there was a flurry of taps through the open comm line.

Hollis's head jerked up, and she caught the sudden flash of anger on Mad Dog's face.

The woman took a step forward, laying her hand on Sil's arm. "Hold, lad," she said, voice sharp.

Sil frowned at her, but stepped back.

The pirate captain turned to Hollis. "This your doing, Captain Ives?" she asked, and there was a note of danger under the mildness in her tone. She pulled up a note over her wrist comm, large enough that Hollis could easily make it out.

She sucked in a quick breath, and heard a matching gasp, bitten off, from Foster.

She could see, on the screen, the tableau as she'd seen it on the *Verity's* controls—the *Verity*, and just close enough not to be under threat of the *Verity's* non-existent guns, the *Sweet Jenny*. There were specks around the *Verity* that must be the life vessels.

And to one side, the shimmer on the screen of a ship coming out of an FTL jump.

For half a second, Hollis's heart stuttered with a mixture of relief and panic—had the navy got word somehow, sent a rescue mission? And if they had, was it still possible for the *Sweet Jenny* to take down the fragile life vessels surrounding the *Verity* before the ship was in range?

Then she saw a second shimmer, and a third, and she noticed the vis-tags on the ships.

Something sick and heavy settled in the pit of her stomach as her brain made sense of what she was seeing.

The ships' vis-tags were foreign. Not Level ships at all, then.

These ships were from the Rosette System. The one, if rumours were correct, the Admiral had been trying to convince Parliament to declare war on.

"Couldn't have jumped in this close without a signal." The hard anger under Mad Dog's voice would have sent a chill up Hollis's spine at any other time. Now, she hardly had the attention to spare.

She glanced at Foster, and saw in their face that they'd come to the same conclusion she had.

"Captain Mad Dog." She was distantly pleased to note that her voice didn't shake. "This was not my doing, nor my ship's officers'." She paused a moment. "There is someone on my ship who attempted to assassinate me at the beginning of our voyage. In the course of our pursuit of the *Sweet Jenny*, they managed to sabotage our guns and shields. I did not understand what they were after, but it seems …" She trailed off, gesturing with her chin to the screen.

Mad Dog studied her a moment, eyes narrowed, then turned back to the screen.

"Paging the ships *Verity* and *Sweet Jenny*." The voice over the general line was unfamiliar, the words clipped with a sharp accent. "You are to stand down immediately and prepare to be boarded."

When Hollis glanced back at the screen, she could understand the arrogance in the speaker's voice.

Five more ships had come out of FTL.

There was nowhere to run.

Mad Dog's jaw was clenched tight, and for a moment, Hollis thought she'd order Sil to shoot her and Foster and be done with it.

Hollis herself was so numb that she wasn't sure she'd have been able to muster the energy to care.

This was what it had been, then, after all—the attempt to kill her, back on the Level. The attempt to hamstring the Admiral's ability to recruit officers from the Stacks, at a time when additional officers would be badly needed. It all fit together too neatly. The anti-war protests in front of the government buildings, the sudden urging for an attack on Blackrock—a perfect distraction for the naval ships.

And now this.

If the enemy fleet took the *Verity*, that could give them the disguise they needed to get their ships in close enough to the Level, flying under her vis-tags, that they could launch a surprise attack. And the *Verity* was the perfect target—split off from the fleet, isolated, with no one looking for her. Likely enough the commodore had already given her up as lost, a sacrifice made for the survival of the fleet.

She felt sick to her stomach.

Mad Dog was still watching her, eyes narrowed, but at last she seemed to come to a decision. She turned sharply. "Sil, keep an eye on our guests. One wrong move and you shoot them both down, understand?"

"Aye, Captain." Sil's voice was as grim as Mad Dog's.

The pirate captain tapped her comm line. "Toothpick, Jumper, stand down from the guns." There was a grimness to her tone that told Hollis she'd measured the situation and come to the same conclusion Hollis had—there was no way out of this for any of them.

She turned to the woman holding the sparker. "Ari, let the skiff loose, clear out the airlock. Looks like we're going to be boarded."

31

Silas

Silas kept the pistol steady on Hollis and her first mate. His heart was pounding hard and fast, and he couldn't tell if it was because of the sudden horror of what they'd just seen, or a desperate relief that he'd not have to pull the trigger and watch Hollis and her first mate die by his hand.

Behind him, Gracie had stepped over to Ari, and the two women were conversing in low tones. He couldn't make out their words, but he hardly had to. He'd seen the same thing they'd seen—the enemy ships surrounding them, blocking off the jump-paths. Far too many to fight.

The *Verity's* first mate was watching him, the horror on their face echoing his. Hollis was staring straight ahead, her face pale, and there was an expression there that told him most of her concentration was focused on staying on her feet. Whatever the hell had happened to her in the battle at Blackrock, she looked all but dead standing.

"Sil," said Gracie at last, raising her voice to carry. "Move our guests out of the airlock."

Ari stepped past him to the airlock controls, and the grimness in her expression told him everything he needed to know.

Even Gracie didn't have a way out of this.

Silas gestured with his pistol. The *Verity's* first mate met his eyes, their expression challenging, and made a brief gesture towards their captain. "If I may?" they asked, voice icy.

Silas nodded, and they stepped over to catch Hollis's elbow as she swayed on her feet.

"Thank you, Price." Hollis's voice was barely a whisper.

There was a ragged exhaustion in Price's posture as well, but there was something about the protective way they stood beside Hollis that made Silas's chest tighten.

He could remember, as a ship's officer, feeling that same unconscious, unearned loyalty to his captain—the instinctive knowledge that he'd die for them without question. Although, he supposed, if what he'd seen was true, Hollis had earned her officers' loyalty.

He glanced reflexively at Gracie from the corner of his eye.

She was standing on the deck, talking quietly into her comm. He could see the strain on her face, the readiness in her posture, but her tone was calm and measured.

He'd risked his life for Gracie's, just as much as he might have for his captain on a ship of the line. But the difference was, that had been his choice. Even after she'd saved his life in the solar flare, she'd not expected him to save her life in return. She'd never demanded his loyalty, or his life.

And when he'd given it anyways—he'd no longer been able to hide behind his unquestioning duty. It had been his own choices that had led him here.

Maybe that's what he'd been running from this whole time.

But it wasn't something he could run from forever.

When he'd left the navy, he'd given up the excuse of just following orders. Every choice, from that moment on, had been on his own head. And he was sailor enough, he supposed, to face that.

"Come on," he said quietly, gesturing with his pistol.

Hollis and Price stepped aside to where he gestured them. There was a *click* from the airlock as the outer door sealed and the naval skiff detached from the *Sweet Jenny*.

It was only a few minutes later that a broadcast from the Rosette flagship informed them to prepare to be boarded.

Toothpick, Freddie, and Jumper had joined Gracie in the airlock, and Ari came to stand beside him, her own pistol drawn.

There was the scrape of metal on metal of a skiff hooking on to the outside of the airlock. Gracie nodded to Freddie. "Open the airlock door," she said, her voice quiet.

Freddie hit the controls, and the door slid open, revealing the inside of a large, well-appointed skiff.

A man stepped out, dressed in the dark blue and burnt-orange uniform of the Rosette navy, a dozen armed sailors in his wake. They raised their guns at the group of them gathered on the deck of the *Sweet Jenny*, but it was hardly more than a formality.

"Captain Mad Dog," the officer said, bowing to Gracie. "Your reputation precedes you." He glanced around. "I hear you have the captain of the *Verity* on board your ship."

Gracie nodded with a wry smile. "Aye, that I do. Captain Ives and I were in the middle of a chat when you arrived."

"So I heard." The man smiled as well, a sharp, predatory smile, and turned to Hollis. "Captain Ives. I'm Officer Allard, second mate of the flagship *Chasseuse*. Your second mate, Greene, explained the situation. Under the circumstances, it seems I'm compelled to request a surrender from both of your mates as well as yourself—not the usual, perhaps, but then this seems to be far from a usual set of circumstances." He paused. "Greene has been taken prisoner, and upon his and your surrender, will be treated as befits an officer taken in battle. He'll be held aboard the *Verity* for the time being. But he has indicated that he will wait on your direction before he offers his own surrender." The man's smile widened. "It appears you've engendered an admirable loyalty in your crew, Captain Ives."

Silas glanced at Hollis. Her jaw was set, but she gave a brief nod. "I'll offer you my surrender, then," she said quietly. "And I shall instruct Greene to do the same."

"And you, Acting Captain Price?" The man asked, turning to Price.

"I'll follow my Captain," said the first mate, their voice calm.

"Very good," Allard said. He turned back to Hollis. "Your surrender is accepted. Now, if you would, I'll bring you back to my ship, where you will be held as befits an enemy officer until we have the leisure to bring you back to our system. And for the rest of you —"

He turned back to Gracie. "I'm afraid, Captain Mad Dog, that I cannot make you the same offer. Our rules of war only extend to naval sailors. So I'll ask the rest of you to go back to the brig, and I'll send my sailors to lock you up."

Gracie watched him, a small smile on her face. "Figure if you know my reputation, Mate Allard, you'll know it ain't my style to go down without a fight. But I'll accept it, on two conditions." She paused. "I have an injured sailor in the med bay. Don't rightly figure as he or my medic can move down to the brig without him dying. So my first condition is that you let him and Vee alone. Guard the door if you need to, but they stay in the med bay."

Allard was watching her, a mixture of offence and amusement on his face, but at last he nodded. "That's acceptable. And your other condition?"

Gracie's smile went sharp. "My other condition is, you take all the naval scum with you when you go." She gestured to Silas and Ari. "Don't want those two on my ship any longer'n they have to be. Petty officers from the *Verity*, them, and I don't trust them not to try to take their revenge on my crew."

Silas clamped his jaw shut on a startled sound.

The man watched Gracie for a moment, then turned to Silas and Ari, frowning. "Is that true, lad? It looks to me like you were ready to shoot your captain."

"That was my fault, I'm afraid." Gracie's voice still carried that familiar trace of humour. "Told the lad and the lass that they'd shoot their captain, or I'd not honour the surrender."

The man raised his eyebrows at Silas.

Silas hesitated, then jerked his head in a quick nod.

Gracie had something up her sleeve after all, then.

"Captain?" The man turned to Hollis.

Hollis's eyes flicked over Silas and Ari for a brief moment, then found Gracie's.

Then, to Silas's shock, she, too, nodded. "The pirate's telling the truth," she said coldly. "These two were following my orders. And as their captain, I request that they be given the same consideration as the rest of my officers."

He didn't look at Gracie again, but Silas had shipped with the woman long enough to see from the corner of his eye the way her posture relaxed, ever so slightly, in relief.

"That's settled, then," said Gracie, her voice still mild. "I'll hand in my weapons, and we'll go to the brig with your people."

The man gestured, and the front row of sailors stepped forward smartly, the back row keeping their pistols trained on the pirates.

Gracie handed them her cutlass, hilt first, and her second energy pistol, and Freddie and Toothpick and Jumper did the same with their weapons.

"Commodore Matisse would like to speak with Mad Dog," said Allard, waving his hand. "Take the others away."

Two sailors stayed behind, their weapons trained on Gracie, while the others herded the rest of the Sweet Jenny's crew out of the airlock.

"Now," Allard said, gesturing to the skiff. "If you'll follow me?"

Every muscle in Silas's body was tight, but when he glanced at Gracie, she gave him the tiniest nod.

They were relieved of their weapons as well, although with more courtesy than the *Sweet Jenny's* crew had been shown.

Silas ducked his head respectfully, and followed after Captain Ives and Mate Price into the skiff. He didn't have to look at Ari to know she was as tense as he was.

Silas, Ari, Hollis, and Price were led to one side of the skiff, Gracie to the other. Silas didn't try to catch her eye again.

He wouldn't give away her game, whatever it was.

Hollis kept her gaze fixed straight ahead, but Silas could feel Price's calculating gaze on him and Ari.

He narrowed his eyes and ignored them, following Hollis's example.

It seemed like an eternity before they reached the *Chasseuse*. At last, though, the airlock door hissed open, and they were prodded through.

A man stood to meet them just outside the airlock door, and Silas guessed instantly that this was Commodore Matisse.

He bowed to Hollis. "Captain Ives. A pleasure to have you aboard my ship." He gestured down the corridor behind him. "I'll send one of my midship officers to take the four of you to your quarters. Your second mate will remain on the *Verity* for now, but as he has offered his surrender upon your orders, he will not be mistreated."

He turned to Gracie, and bowed again. "Captain Mad Dog. It's a pleasure to make your acquaintance. I'm afraid I can't offer you the same accommodations as I do these naval officers, but I hope we'll be able to come to some agreement."

And it wasn't until Silas had turned away to follow Hollis and Mate Price, and caught the look on Gracie's face, that he finally realized.

This was no scheme on Mad Dog's part to take down the ships that had captured them.

She'd simply been doing the same thing for him and Ari as she had for Vee and Temple—trying to keep them safe, to the best of her ability.

He and Ari had been dressed in naval uniforms, and she'd used that to save them. But she had no plan beyond that. No plan to save the *Sweet Jenny*, and none to save her own life.

He glanced quickly at Ari, panic clutching at his chest.

She was walking beside him, but her hands were clenched into fists in the sleeves of his old naval jacket, her face as pale as he'd ever seen it.

She knew, too.

She met his eye, and for just a moment he saw there the same spark of desperate panic and hopeless determination that he felt.

He gave her a short nod, and turned to face front again, every muscle in his body aching with tension.

They'd find a way to get out. Maybe that hadn't been what Gracie intended, but he no longer cared.

He and Ari would escape, and they'd save Gracie and the *Sweet Jenny*, if it killed them.

32

Gracie

Gracie watched Sil and Ari follow Hollis Ives and her first mate down the corridor. Her chest was tight with a mixture of relief and dread, but she managed to keep her expression mild.

There was something about danger that did this to her, anyways. Something about the sharp irrefutability of what she knew was coming, the mixture of fear and the thrill of anticipation that facing death always brought.

She'd saved Sil and Ari, at least. She hadn't been certain, when she'd told the lie, that Ives would back her up. But the naval captain seemed, at least, to have recognized what Sil had risked to save the crew of the *Verity*.

This time, she did allow a small smile to reach her lips.

She'd have killed Hollis, given the opportunity, and she'd have done it without a twinge of conscience. Perhaps Sil was right— perhaps the sailors before the mast, disproportionately made up of desperate people from the Stacks and resource planets, or from the lower strata of Level society, didn't deserve vengeance for what they'd done out of desperation. But people like Hollis Ives—people who knew exactly what they were doing, who'd calculated the risks and benefits and decided to give their lives to the navy knowing full well what it was—they didn't deserve mercy or pity.

But she could see why Judith had put her influence behind Ives. And Gracie couldn't help but admire the Stacks woman's baldfaced courage, whatever else she might condemn her for.

"Captain Mad Dog."

She turned back to Commodore Matisse.

He was a tall man, dressed in the uniform of the Rosette Navy, with light skin and light hair and an imposing posture, and the air of someone who knew his own importance.

He smiled at her, but she could read the threat behind the smile.

She kept her expression mild, despite the way her heart pounded quick and heavy in her chest, and nodded in acknowledgement. "Commodore."

He studied her for a moment, expression going thoughtful. "Mad Dog," he said again. "I'm certain you're aware of our military laws of engagement? I'm constrained by them to treat enemy combatants with respect and dignity." His smile broadened, just a little. "But, as I'm certain you are also aware, that does not extend to pirates."

She didn't bother to answer. He'd say what he wanted to say without help from her.

"You know," he said at last. "Even in my home system we've heard stories of you. An exceptionally brilliant and brutal captain, I've been told. There's a reason we factored you into our calculations. Our agents back in your system went so far as to send someone to ambush one of your crew in the hopes of making you angry enough to plan an engagement against the naval mission to Blackrock, and we slipped you information on the Level's plans so you'd have time to prepare. You were key to our plans, truth be told—we knew you'd be able to put up a stiff enough fight against the naval fleet that you'd keep them occupied. But even we had no idea how truly vicious you could be. Our agents were almost convinced you were going to ally with the navy, when you sent your crew up to the Level. They would have killed them if they could, which I now realize would have been a pity, but I've been briefed by my intelligence officer who infiltrated the *Verity* and took down her guns. I know why you sent them there. You were going to cause another Starfire." He shook his head. "It's a shame, really, that my officer wasn't able to take down Captain Ives before she put a stop to it—that would have been truly spectacular, and so much more than we could have hoped." He smiled again, a shark's smile. "But even so, there's a way you can still be useful. There are rumours that you know more about Admiral Usher than you let on."

She raised her eyebrows in polite question, the faint smile still pulling at her lips. "That's an interesting rumour," she murmured. "Don't suppose them as told it to you gave you a good reason why, if I knew enough to take the Admiral down, I'd not have already done it?"

He shook his head, expression amused. "Don't worry, Captain. Your hatred for the Admiral is legendary. That's why I'm willing to offer you the bargain I am. I need something on the Admiral, something compromising. I have my sources, of course, but I know you know more than you say." He leaned in, lowering his voice. "So here's my bargain, Mad Dog. Give me something I can use to take her down. You and I both know that wars are fought in the court of public opinion, as much as in the sectors of space. Give me something I can feed to my agents, and I'll use it to destroy Admiral Usher so thoroughly that her name will be a curse for decades to come, before I instruct them to kill her outright. Do that, and I'll treat you with the same courtesy I will your naval counterpart."

Gracie watched him for a moment.

In her mind's eye, she could still see the scene from decades ago, in the courtroom, Judith's face, pale and set.

Her voice seemed to come through a haze, the words oddly clear, but distant. "I swear before God and before the officers in this courtroom that the testimony I give is true."

"Judith Usher. You were the prisoner's lover, correct?"

Jenny didn't look at her, but Gracie could read the stiffness in her shoulders. "Yes."

"And during your time with her, have you ever heard the prisoner express sentiments that could be considered treasonous?"

There was a short hesitation.

For just a moment, Gracie's stomach tightened in desperate hope.

And then Jenny said, her voice low, but clear, "Yes. I have."

The words fell like a blow. Like a cutlass-slash through the stomach, slicing through her vital organs in a breathtaking horror that was too sharp and bright for pain.

Gracie tried to remember how to breathe.

She'd die for this. She'd die, on the strength of her lover's word.

But in the sick, disorienting horror of the betrayal, of the world as she knew it crumbling away around her, she could hardly bring herself to care.

Gracie closed her eyes, her breath catching at the remembered despair.

"Anything compromising, anything that we could use to make the Level question her loyalty. That's all I'd need, Mad Dog."

Unlike in that courtroom so many years ago, the evidence she had against Jenny was real, and damning, and Jenny had handed it to her without question—the ship she'd taken to Blackrock could be traced, surely, no matter how careful she'd been, and the time she'd been away would have been noticed. The moment the Naval High Command suspected that Judith had spoken with Gracie—she'd be finished. She'd die, the way she'd condemned Gracie to die.

Jenny, laughing up at her, eyes sparkling, the cool shadows shaping her face contrasting with the bright spark of her gaze, the brilliance of her white-gold hair, the quiet, calculating intelligence of her—distant and beautiful and perfect, and yet somehow, still, Gracie's.

God's eyes, she loved this woman. She loved her until it hurt, loved her like a lit flame in her chest, burning and bright and almost unbearable. She'd do anything —anything at all—for Jenny Usher. It was a truth she knew in her bones. She'd burn the world and walk through the flames.

Jenny leaned in, still laughing, and Gracie leaned forward to meet her, and her lips on Gracie's were a spark and a flame.

She'd die for this woman. She'd damn herself for this woman. Because if she lost Jenny—she'd lose herself.

She opened her eyes and smiled at the man in front of her.

He could take Judith down. With her help, he could destroy the woman, she had no doubt of it. It wouldn't be her that did it, but did it really matter, as long as Judith was crushed? Destroyed, the way she'd destroyed Gracie?

Judith's face, weeks before on Blackrock—the streaks of grey in her hair, the weariness in her expression. The way she'd tipped her head back, not fighting Gracie's hand around her throat.

Not trying to save herself, even though they'd both known Gracie could kill her.

"I'm sorry," she said quietly. "I don't figure as your sources were all that good. Don't rightly know what I could tell you to help out."

His eyes narrowed, and again she saw the sharp threat behind his gaze. "You know what this means, Captain," he said at last. "I'm afraid I can't take your word for that. But I have people who are trained to extract information."

She raised her eyebrows. "Torture, then. Well. Didn't figure you were any better than the Levellers, and I guess I was right."

His smile now was cold. "I am very sorry that this will be necessary, but you must see, you've given me no choice. Now." He bowed to her again, stiffly. "I shall instruct my sailors to take you to your new lodging."

He turned on his heel and strode off as two sailors, weapons drawn, stepped forward.

"Come with us, Mad Dog," one of them snapped.

Gracie did as she was told, the small, wry half-smile still lingering at the corners of her mouth.

33

Judith

Judith stared down at the printout reports, sent in by Commodore Webb.

There was an icy numbness coating her mind, and some vague part of her was grateful for it.

Mad Dog Gracie Madox, ruthless, vicious, merciless—the woman she'd once loved—had almost destroyed an entire fleet.

Had almost caused a second Starfire.

She closed her eyes, forcing back the choking horror of the realization.

She couldn't deny there was a poetic irony to it. Gracie had been banished from the Level, sentenced to death, for her supposed role in a tragedy she'd had nothing to do with. And now, if she'd succeeded, she'd have caused a repeat of the very tragedy that had condemned her. But this time it would have taken down, not Gracie, but Judith, and with her, the ability of the Admiralty to do what was necessary to keep the Level safe.

She knew well enough that over the years she had, in essence, become the Admiralty. If she was taken down—and she had no doubt a disaster the magnitude of the one Gracie had planned would have done just that—the navy would be thrown into shambles. Oh, they'd pick up the pieces eventually, after the backstabbing and the infighting had died down. And it was possible that the person who'd step into her place would be competent, although it was equally likely they wouldn't be. Politics in the Naval High Command, as with any political post, had at least as much to do with your family name and influence as it did with talent, or even competence. Even so, Judith wasn't conceited enough to assume that she was irreplaceable. But now? With war so close she could taste it in the air?

She could still hear the low rasp of Gracie's voice, soft against her ear: *"One day, Jenny—one day I'll kill you for it. But first, I'll see you ruined. I'll see everything you care for and everything you fought for and everything you earned by betraying me crumble before your eyes. I'll take you down, Jenny, if I have to destroy the Level to do it."*

And with this, she would have. She would have destroyed the Level, and Judith with it, in a horrifying tableau of death—sailors and ship debris spread out across space in a debris field so vast and haunted that decades later ships would go out of their way to avoid sailing through it. If it hadn't been for the prescience of the *Consolation's* captain, she'd have succeeded.

The thought of it sent a chill of ice through Judith's bones.

She could have stopped it. Perhaps that was the worst of it. She'd had everything she needed, every breadcrumb, every clue, and she'd let them run through her fingers. If she hadn't been distracted, if she hadn't let her memories of Gracie dull her instincts, she could have stopped it herself.

And she hadn't.

She still wasn't certain if it had been distraction, or if, in a deep subconscious part of her, she'd felt as if she'd owed it to Grace.

She drew in another long breath, then, with an effort, pushed herself to her feet.

She felt old, and so very tired.

The numbness had spread, as if the news had been like a shipboard surgeon's scalpel, wounding and freezing at the same time, so you could watch yourself be cut open without feeling it.

The *Verity* had gone after the *Sweet Jenny*.

That, after everything else, should hardly have been a pang on her conscience, but the thought of it made her ill.

She could picture Hollis Ives as she'd been days ago, standing in front of Judith's desk, pale and weak and barely able to keep her feet, but stubbornly refusing to either offer excuses for herself, or any concession whatsoever to her injuries.

She'd faced Mad Dog once and survived. She might think she'd survived on her wits, and Judith had no doubt whatsoever that a lesser captain would have been turned to space-dust. But she'd survived, ultimately, because she'd impressed Mad Dog enough that the woman had let her live. Judith had no illusions as to how far Gracie's mercy would go if the Stacks woman went up against her a second time.

Hollis Ives was the captain she'd needed to bring the Naval High Command around to accepting officers from the Stacks and resource planets. But somehow, in the course of working with the woman, Hollis had become more than that.

Now she was almost certainly dead. And Gracie had killed her, to revenge herself on Judith.

She tapped the comm line on her desk. "Vice-Admiral Wright?" she said when he answered, although she could scarcely recognize her voice. "I'd like you in here, please."

By the time he arrived, she'd prepared the note. He stepped inside her office, and she sent the orders over to him with a flick of her fingers.

He glanced over the note quickly, then up at her. "Admiral?"

She gave a tight nod. "Send out the orders, please. I want three fleets of ships—everything the navy has. I want them to sail out as soon as possible—have them at Blackrock in three days at the outside. I don't want time for word to get out. I want to take down Blackrock so completely that there's no chance of pirates or anyone else setting up a settlement there in the next three centuries."

"But that will leave the Level practically unguarded. The war—"

"Will be easier to win if we're not fighting it on two fronts," she snapped. "This won't take out the pirates completely, but it will take them months to regroup after something like this. I want my navy freed up to focus on the war when it comes. I want Blackrock destroyed, and I want the *Sweet Jenny* taken down—I don't care what it takes. And if the word I've received is correct, it's almost certain that the *Verity's* been taken by Mad Dog. If you see her, don't let her approach. Shoot on sight. "

He watched her for a moment, then bowed his head respectfully. "Aye, Admiral Usher."

When he was gone, she sank down into her chair.

Slowly, she dropped her head in her hands.

She could still see Grace behind her closed eyelids, still see the way she'd watched Judith in that courtroom.

Judith hadn't known. That, at least, was the truth—she hadn't known Grace was innocent. Every word of her testimony had been the truth. She hadn't known that testimony would be the final cog clicking into place that would doom Grace, and Judith, and Hollis, and all of them.

But there was no taking it back now.

After this moment of weakness that had almost led to disaster, she'd been forced to look at herself, at her priorities.

And after everything they'd both done, she knew now, with an iron certainty: if it was a question between Gracie and the wellbeing of the navy, she'd do it again. Even knowing now what she hadn't then, she'd do it. She'd condemn her lover, innocent or no, to save the Level.

She'd be damned for it, if she wasn't already. She knew that somewhere there was a future of endless torment waiting for her for what she'd done, for what she'd be willing to do again.

But she'd do it regardless.

Thank you for reading!

I hope you enjoyed the book! Book three, Enemy Colours, will be coming soon.

You might also enjoy the following, also by R.M. Olson:

The Ungovernable series (beginning with Zero Day Threat):

A mouthy ex-smuggler pilot, a grumpy demolitions expert, a tech genius and a hacker. They're pulling a job on the most dangerous weapons dealer in the System. They're stealing tech that could change the course of history. And every one of them has something to hide.
What could possibly go wrong?
"Spectacular and thrilling! Olson's debut novel is filled with compelling characters and endless excitement." -SD Simper, author of the Fallen Gods series

The Singularity Series (beginning with Redshift):

A scientist searching for the cure to an uncurable disease, a canny elder stateswoman in game of politics that could spell the beginning of a new era or an end to humanity as we know it, and a cheerful assassin on the run.
Add in an emotional support murder-octopus and first contact with an unknown alien entity and, and it's an open question if the Joias System will survive this.

You can find the paperbacks on all major retailers.